HONEYMOON STAGE

HONEYMOON STAGE

a *nOveL

MARGAUX ELIOT

Little a

This is a work of fiction. Names, characters, organizations, places, events, and incidents are either products of the author's imagination or are used fictitiously. Otherwise, any resemblance to actual persons, living or dead, is purely coincidental.

Published by Little A, New York

www.apub.com

EU product safety contact:
Amazon Media EU S. à r.l.
38, avenue John F. Kennedy, L-1855 Luxembourg
amazonpublishing-gpsr@amazon.com

ISBN-13: 9781662533129 (hardcover)
ISBN-13: 9781662533105 (paperback)
ISBN-13: 9781662533112 (digital)

Cover design by Erin Fitzsimmons
Cover image: © Luke Liable / Stocksy; © Orlova_Anna, © retro studio, © Vector Image Plus, © Phakorn Kasikij / Shutterstock; © nemke, © moodboard / Getty

Printed in the United States of America
First edition

For the Avengers: AJB, KG, and SS

And I hope she'll be a fool—that's the best thing a girl can be in this world, a beautiful little fool.

—F. Scott Fitzgerald, *The Great Gatsby*

Because we thought we knew them, they were "just like us."

—Andy Cohen, *For Real: The Story of Reality TV*

October 2007

The camera pans and here I am. I'm in jean shorts and a white T-shirt, a far cry from bridal chic, slightly out of place amid the fanfare of this afternoon's rehearsal. Production is expressing serious concern that the processional song might end in the middle of a chorus, but I can't help feeling like we all know what to do by now. We're on hour three of this. I'm antsy.

Then I see Gabe grinning across the lawn, dimples slicing through both cheeks, and I'm swept into the fantasy despite myself.

Ready, he mouths. And so am I. I am *so* ready. I'm ready to say *I do*. I'm ready for this circus of a wedding to be over and to actually be married. I'm ready for the TV special to air and my subsequent embarrassment to hopefully fade into mere memory. I'm ready to wake up next to Gabe knowing we've committed to each other, and then sprawl out on the couch in our pajamas and finally finish that eight-thousand-piece jigsaw puzzle of da Vinci's *Last Supper*. That part is going to be wonderful.

Thinking about that part helps me look at this ostentatious stone mansion, and the impractical California lawn on which our wedding party has gamely assembled, with hope for the future. The venue's main house looks air-dropped in from Rhode Island or Connecticut: capped turrets, perky dormer windows, a wide front drive ideal for valet parking, and a garden that makes no sense in this climate. It isn't ugly, just soulless, as if Palisades Pines wants all who visit to forget that we're in Santa Monica and the Pacific Ocean is just out of view. This is not the spot I would have chosen to marry the love of my life. Gabe's not especially drawn to the country-club life, either. We're standing here, surrounded by golf courses and gold-painted chairs, because of the production company and the reciprocity deal they struck, where our TV special will showcase this venue, and in return, we're able to use this facility and film free of charge. Well, at least without handing over actual money. What Palisades Pines loses in rental fees, they should more than make up for in unpaid advertising and cultural clout.

The director gives the go-ahead, and Gabe's seven-year-old niece expertly tosses imaginary petals from an invisible basket, giving little plié curtsies and hamming for the empty rows of chairs.

Take that spotlight, kid. It's yours.

The two seasons I spent working as a production assistant on *Honeymoon Stage* have robbed me of the ability to lose myself in the magic. Reality TV icons Jason Dean and Maggie McKee, the then-newlywed subjects of our groundbreaking television series, have shown me that if something looks too good to be true, it *is* most likely too good to be true. It's not that I think dreams can't come true; it simply means that everyone has to pay for them one way or another.

The price for the dream Gabe and I share is this exclusive tie-in television special: a *Honeymoon Stage* wedding, featuring cameos from the original cast of the show.

At least the cast members that are still alive.

Gabe straightens his shoulders, gives a small wave to my mom. He's doing that thing with his mouth that he does when he's focused—writing a new guitar riff or doing mental math. His brow furrows, and his tongue slips to the side, and this is one of the things that I love about Gabe. The way he'll focus. How much he cares.

As bride and groom, Gabe and I are theoretically the stars here, but we're just a sideshow. Maggie McKee and Jason Dean are the real draw—after all, this once was their wedding venue too. They haven't been seen on-screen together since the abrupt finale of their megahit show, which ended two and a half years ago. Gabe and I signed NDAs and contracts last month. We signed paperwork regarding residuals and time slots and the sorts of ads the network could run. We have given up our wedding to the masticating maw of Reality television in exchange for the goodwill and exposure that will fuel our professional dreams. I'd marry this man anyplace, anytime—we alone own the dream of our lives together. But the chance to mend broken ambitions and propel ourselves each into the careers we've been fighting for? That's only ever been on offer because of Maggie and Jason's involvement.

Tomorrow Maggie McKee will wear a cornflower blue bridesmaid's dress and stand up beside me. She's in this wedding not because we are dear friends and I have asked her to be part of my big day but because I am trying to right a wrong. Not to Maggie—I owe Maggie McKee nothing. But she was part of my misstep, and so I need her here to fix it. She hasn't shown up yet—technically her contract is only for tomorrow—so my brother's girlfriend fills in for her now. I think, not for the first time, that I'd prefer this relative stranger he will probably dump next week to be my bridesmaid over Maggie.

Maggie and I haven't spoken in four years. It's a slap in the face to both of us to have her step-touch over scattered flower petals, carrying a petite version of my ranunculus and roses.

Right now, I'm holding a paper plate laced with the ribbons from my bridal shower gifts—a trash bouquet that, to me, feels exceptionally silly but matters quite a bit to my mother.

"Cassidy!"

It's my turn. In tennis shoes, I traipse the lawn that I will walk in heels tomorrow, timing each step to a hired string quartet. My stepfather has been chatting with one of the producers, but he skedaddles back to take my arm. We proceed. I bug my eyes out for the camera crew when we get up front to the rest of the bridal party, and my friend Jen gives me a literal slap on the wrist. She has a bleach pen in her pocket and dabs it on the hem of my T-shirt where I've spilled Diet Coke.

"One more time!" Here comes Lauren, our producer. Once, all I wanted was to be another Lauren—to have her poise and self-assurance, her ability to see through the bullshit. Even if Lauren wasn't always happy, at least she was the one conducting.

What's the line in that song? *I'd rather be a hammer than a nail.*

Today, her hair is dyed black as licorice. She's already in her yellow flower-print cocktail dress, wearing a full face of makeup. On the original *Honeymoon Stage*, she would have never—time spent on glam for any crew member was both time wasted and a reason for the rest of the team to take them less seriously. The line between a woman trying too hard and sloppy unprofessionalism is subjective, ephemeral, and subject to drastic career consequence when crossed.

We run the sequence five more times. A boom is in the shot. Someone has to use the bathroom. An airplane passes overhead. Finally, Lauren says, "Okay, we've got it."

"You're good?" I ask Gabe.

"Absolutely." He puts an arm around my shoulder. "You?"

"Yeah," I say.

"It's not too late to bail," says Gabe. "You and me, Vegas by sundown."

"Don't tempt me."

Even without the legal ramifications of breaking our contract with the network, we both know Vegas is not an option. My mother would be disappointed. His mother would cry. We can't now deny his niece the chance to be on television. Gabe's career needs the publicity of this *Honeymoon Stage* wedding-special tie-in, and I need the reference Lauren promised in return for my cooperation. I still have student loans to pay off. We want to buy a house. If we back out now, the reciprocity deals will all be voided, and we'll be stuck with the bill for this whole affair.

⚜

Tomorrow will be a performance, so tonight is the actual party. The rehearsal dinner is at a small Italian spot with a back garden that seems straight out of Tuscany, all distressed pillars and starbursting lavender and weeds sneaking between patio stones—the sort of place I would want to have our actual wedding were it not for the constraints of the crew. Jen and Celia get the toasts going immediately after dinner, telling stories about when Gabe and I first met.

"We were like, really? *The* Gabriel Leighton?" Celia's teeth are stained red with cabernet, and I get the sense her celebration began long before our courtyard cocktails. Jen nudges, but it's not enough to stop her. "Like, oh my god, here he is in our shitty apartment, sitting on our ugly couch." I'm glad tonight's not being filmed, though I see Lauren's eyes dart back and forth with interest. Always looking for story, her crowbar ready to pry you apart.

"It was a great apartment." Jen steps in. "And Cass is a catch."

"Aww, thanks," I say. Gabe and I are seated at an adjacent table, dessert plates mostly empty in front of us. I take his last bite of chocolate mousse.

Gabe kisses me while I'm swallowing. "I was the one who had to do the wooing." He raises his glass, charming as always in that understated way he has when talking to a crowd.

"Write a song about it!" His friends, too, are drunk in the back. Gabe is shiny eyed and loose. He presses his knee into mine.

"Though I haven't always made the best decisions," he says to the room in an understatement I do not correct, "you all know I love this woman completely."

He hasn't raised his voice, but even those friends in the back can surely hear. Before Gabe, I was anti-PDA. I didn't want anyone to serenade me or declare their affection in grand gestures. But Gabe is a grand-gestures kind of guy, and in loving him, I've mostly come around to them. He rubs his thumb over my wrist. When I lean my forehead down, he follows, and for a moment we're alone behind our clasped hands.

"Hi."

"Hello."

I feel an almost unbearable surge of excitement and luck.

Maybe working on *Honeymoon Stage* hasn't ruined me for romance. Maybe I *can* have my three-tiered wedding cake and eat it too. My happily ever after seems just around the corner.

For once, tomorrow will go off without a hitch.

1.

August 2002

I got the *Honeymoon Stage* job offer while I was microwaving a Lean Pocket and talking to Celia about one of her customers, who always claimed she'd left the foam off his cappuccino—*Is he flirting,* she wanted to know, *or just a jerk?* We often had trouble telling the difference. At the time, we were a year and a half out from our college graduations, and naive to the ways of the world.

I had moved to California three months earlier, against my mother's advice. She thought I *already had a job in television* and *should stick close to home, just in case*. In case of what, she didn't elaborate. I could practically hear the air quotes around *television*, the tutting that I hadn't chosen a more practical career. My stepdad, Ron, agreed with her, as he always did. He basically existed to agree with my mother, which, after what my dad had put her through, she probably deserved.

I'd been working as a booking assistant for a cable news channel in Manhattan, which was close to the job I wanted in the way that JFK-airport sushi is technically the same meal as omakase in Tokyo. The pay was terrible, and I often crashed at my ex-boyfriend's place because it was easy and right off the B train. I knew I'd have to pay my dues, but I didn't feel like this gig was getting me anywhere other than Josh's stained futon.

Like many others who had grown up on *Tiger Beat* and *Baywatch*, I had always had Hollywood dreams. Specifically, I wanted work in sitcoms. I wanted out of this chaotic city high-rise swarmed by tourists, to be nestled inside the relative safety of a studio lot. I wanted a tight script with a laugh track. Steady work for twenty-two episodes and change. By that August afternoon in my Silver Lake kitchen, talking soy milk with Celia, I'd come to the realization that this dream job would be difficult to find. Still, I wasn't ready to give up just yet.

Celia might have been my best friend from college, but television was the best friend I'd had between fourth and eighth grade. My mother was a single mom who always worked a full-time job, and I'd been the quintessential latchkey kid, keeping myself company with after-school specials—some sitcom mom cooking dinner in the background while I did math homework and waited for my own mom to finish her shift. My older brother played hockey and mastered AP biology. I took daily doses of *Saved by the Bell.*

There was comfort in the structure of network television—its predictable beats, the way even the most distressing B story would be mostly forgotten by the start of the next episode. I liked how the characters responded to situations in the way you would expect them to. In retrospect, I probably should have had a good talk therapist, but my mother was parenting alone—that is, until she met Ron.

TV had always been my safe space, though it didn't escape me how unstable my career prospects were at the time of my *Honeymoon Stage* offer. My roommates were at least making strides in the directions they wanted to go. Celia, the conventionally hot one of our trio, had a gig at a coffee shop that sustained her between cattle call auditions, and Jen, more demure, though no less of a go-getter, worked in accounting for a sports agency. I'd been doing informational interviews while moonlighting as a dog walker, slowly blowing through my meager savings and ignoring the growing possibility that I might have to move back east.

I hadn't considered a job in Reality television. At the time, Reality TV meant mostly talent competitions or game shows—often gross ones in exotic locales. There was a popular show about a group of random people living in a house together, talking about society's problems, but I didn't think that was for me.

"Your phone." Celia gestured. I didn't recognize the number, and I froze, awash with hope. Could this finally be my chance? I let the call go to voicemail, but I played it right away and then called back immediately.

Yes, I was available. Yes, I was interested. No, I hadn't worked for the network before, but of course I grew up watching it. A courier would come by this afternoon with paperwork and some clips that would get me up to speed? Yes, okay, of course. I'd sign whatever they wanted. I was theirs to command—while, of course, also being my own totally interesting adult person with life experience and taste that would strengthen the show.

As it turned out, Maggie McKee was the reason I got the job. She was my Aunt Dede's friend's daughter and the one person I knew working in Hollywood. I had known Maggie as a child, gone to school with her in Ohio the year after my dad left, when my mom had dragged us back to her hometown to "get our bearings." Maggie sat next to me in art class. She was a dancer. Even then, she had the shiniest hair. After my mom spent a year in night nursing school and we'd had a few sessions of family therapy, my mother took us back to Philadelphia, where I entered fifth grade. Maggie entered the national anthem–singing circuit. She became a useful trivia bit throughout my adolescence. People love a celebrity connection—the one time they sat next to an actor at an airport or when they shared a college dorm with some politician's sister. Maggie was my connection to something bigger, and people always asked me if she was the same in real life as she was on TV.

I didn't know. Probably? We hadn't exactly been friends when we were nine. Likely she didn't even remember me. We didn't stay in touch. When it aired, I'd barely watched the kids' variety show she was on. *The Tiger Crew* cut a bit too close to the vulnerable, effusive part of myself that, even at thirteen, I was trying to avoid. So I really didn't know her once she became Maggie McKee up on some marquee. Aunt Dede, too, lost regular access. But Maggie was my tether to the stars, proof that, although my life seemed ordinary, I'd once played Pretty Pretty Princess with someone important.

Aunt Dede still knew Maggie's mother, so she dropped my name when I moved out to Los Angeles. When *Honeymoon Stage* suddenly needed a replacement production assistant halfway through filming Season One, my inexperience was nothing against Maggie's mother's recommendation.

Maggie's team sent me the tapes in a package camouflaged as "Civil War History," a label meant to deter anyone actually interested in watching two B-list celebrities navigate their first year of marriage.

Celia went to work, and that afternoon I turned on the stringout footage. I sat there in my sweatpants, one corner of my screen smudged with what must have been my thumbprint, our spider plant dying, our windows in need of a wash. And suddenly there was the sign that read "Palisades Pines." The looming house, the white gazebo. Then came Maggie McKee in a custom wedding dress, feeding Jason Dean a slice of cake. Her long-sleeved, low-necked lace. Her intricate updo. The tiniest trace of the girl I half remembered, if I squinted. Jason looked suave in his tux, broad and handsome as he tucked a piece of hair behind her ear. He had a thick neck, chiseled cheekbones, and a strong chin—the kind of guy who would have had his looks to coast on, even if he hadn't been a font of athletic talent. A close-up of Maggie's bouquet, a tight pink swirl of orchids and Juliet roses that probably cost more than my rent. A shot of Jason adjusting his jacket. Essentially, it wasn't all that different from the photo spread they'd sold to *People* magazine, a curated collection of moments I'd later realize was, like the show, going to help Maggie and Jason pay off this wedding. It was extravagant so that it could be sold, and they sold it so that they could afford the extravagance. Watching this intimate cut, I felt like a guest—or at least one of the cater-waiters. There was Maggie staring into space, fiddling with a ribbon. She checked her teeth for lipstick with a finger, turned to a bridesmaid to confirm she was all right. She rested her arm lightly atop her father's. Jason pressed his lips together when he saw her walk through the door.

Then they were sitting on a couch, in jeans and T-shirts, surrounded by half-emptied moving boxes. Maggie looked very young and thin, and almost orange from her tan, which was something I thought they might want to fix in postproduction. She had those big brown doe eyes and a nose so pert and straight she might have been a cartoon princess. Big boobs, supposedly natural. Jason gave her a little kiss on the top of the head, and she giggled. It wasn't exactly compelling television. I thought it unlikely that this would be my big break.

The production assistant before me had supposedly buckled under the demands of the role—she had a fiancé and hobbies and a real life she didn't want to miss out on. This would not be a problem for me—an ambitious young woman with no significant other, few local friends, and no money for leisure. The line producer had described the job as like being on location for a nature documentary, sitting silently in the Sahara, watching for movement. Occasionally running off to print out MapQuest directions. Repositioning a sofa. Refilling a bowl of chips. Getting Dan the director a ginger ale. Hours of nothing interesting, punctuated by high drama.

Ultimately, I would not get to watch two lions fighting for dominance or a gazelle taking its first steps or the sun rising over the grassland. I would watch semifamous people in their acts of daily living. I would watch the male of the species unkink the hose, while the female flipped through catalogs. I would watch them take phone calls, nodding along, jotting something on the pad by the receiver. I would watch them walk through airports and office suites and hotels and their living room. Watching them on the couch that day, I feared there was no way the show would last beyond this season, after which I'd have to find a different gig.

And then I got to a scene on that tape with Maggie trying and failing to close a kitchen drawer. It was clearly off its track, but instead of reaching back and popping it in place, Maggie just repeatedly slammed it, little sighs of exasperation floofing her bangs as she blinked mournfully, wondering what could be wrong.

"Gosh darn it!" In that moment I saw it. I understood. Maggie McKee was not just another teenage pop star. She was Lucy Ricardo meets Marilyn Monroe. She was unknowingly watering a plastic houseplant. She walked head-on into a glass door. And then there'd come Jason, to crouch down to where she'd collapsed on the kitchen floor in clueless frustration, to kiss her on the top of the head and roll his eyes and call her ridiculous as he slid the drawer back in its slot.

"Oh," I said aloud. This kind of TV wasn't printing off a three-act script and having somebody read through it—this kind of TV was looking at a person's life and deciding what it would mean. Reality producers weren't just running the prewritten play—they got to change the rules of the game. Nothing could happen that they didn't decide had happened, even to celebrities like Jason Dean and Maggie McKee. They had the final cut.

This was exactly what I hadn't known I wanted: the power to tell the story, to decide how it would end. To be the puppeteer ensuring that everyone stayed who and where they were supposed to be. I was addicted from that very first drawer slam.

With *Honeymoon Stage*, we were going to watch Maggie McKee make a fool of herself and then smile endearingly as her husband cleaned up her mess. Maggie was the stereotypical TV housewife, despite her inability to cook or clean or iron, despite the fact that she'd worked all through her childhood and opened for Take 5 at Madison Square Garden. She was in need of a man to shake his head and say *Oh, Maggie* every time she did something dumb, while viewers sat at home and laughed. She might not be the best singer or the best dancer, but she was pretty and blond and not very bright, and people were going to want to watch her.

That afternoon, I signed my name on the network's papers as a guarantee I'd keep my mouth shut, but of course the first thing I did when my roommates got home was show them the tape. I was twenty-three and had no sense of consequence or self-preservation.

"Should you be sharing this?" Jen asked me. She was always the brakes. Even back then she seemed about to turn thirty.

"Technically no." I felt a little sheepish, but the cultural currency was just too good. And I'd known Jen and Celia for years; they were as trustworthy as it got. I pressed play and watched my friends watch the screen. I wanted to gauge their reactions and glean from them some ideas for how to make myself indispensable once I got on set. I'd be the one on staff who had the pulse of the youth population.

"I don't really understand what there could be for you to do here," said Celia. "No offense, but it looks like someone's just using a camcorder."

"Yeah, but a camcorder on Maggie McKee and Jason Dean," said Jen. "They probably need someone to remove their pink jelly beans or someone to, like, set their fan at the right angle whenever they change seats."

"People like the pink jelly beans," said Celia.

"Irrelevant," I said. "I'm going in as a production assistant, not Maggie and Jason's assistant."

"Aren't they the product?"

On-screen, Jason mowed the lawn. Maggie sliced through swaths of bubble wrap, wedding china emerging in a bloodless cesarean.

"Weird that they don't have people doing this for them," Celia said, nibbling on the edge of the same potato chip she'd been eating for the past five minutes.

"That's the point, I think," said Jen. "Celebrities—they're just like us."

"With money." We licked salt from our fingers.

The thing was, Maggie was just very, very dumb. Mispronouncing words, malapropistic, but also apparently utterly unprepared for everyday human life. Had she been like this as a kid? Was this what happened when you performed all through your childhood? My friends and I stared at the stringout footage, a rough assembly of the moments that a story editor had flagged to make it onto the show, not yet cleaned up in editing. Maggie didn't understand an ATM. She put the pasta in the pot before boiling the water. She bought a $200 air freshener. Jason would roll his eyes at her, even occasionally break the fourth wall to raise a brow at the camera, like could we believe this? They'd fall into the same toxic conversational patterns:

"Are you annoyed?"

"No."

"Are you sure?"

"Well, now I am."

"So guys will watch this and think, 'Yeah, he gets to sleep with Maggie McKee, but also he has to put up with her.'" Jen squinted at the screen.

"And girls will think, 'Yeah, she gets to be Maggie McKee, but also she has to manage with five working brain cells.'"

"It's smart," Jen said. "In a gross, calculating way."

Celia stood up, cracking her shoulders. "I don't know, I'd still rather be her. Dumb people don't know how dumb they are, right? That's kind of what makes them dumb?"

Was the show gross and calculating? I couldn't be sure. It was certainly going to be entertaining. Society loved little more than to lift a woman up to watch her fall. Take a young woman—or better, a girl—and cram her into a character and surround her with sycophants and, likely, a lot of older men, and then act all surprised when she shoplifted or developed a drug habit. This was the American way, and in 2002 we were all still feeling fairly patriotic.

Maggie McKee met Jason Dean just before the debut of her first album. *Found You* was a bizarre candy jar of ways her label thought she might distance herself from her child-star reputation, despite her still being a child. The executives wanted her to be sexy, but relatable: someone who'd wash her fancy car in a string bikini and then go clean her own pool. What high school senior wasn't writhing around in pleather pants to some culturally insensitive Indian drumming? What seventeen-year-old wasn't rubbing shoulders with movie stars and models and famous pro athletes who, despite an eight-year age difference, took them on publicly extravagant dates?

Her record label trotted her out on shopping mall tours and to management soirees. In her low-rise jeans and bedazzled crop tops, she'd walk the red carpet for teen-movie premieres and pose for photos at nightclubs she wasn't legally old enough to enter. She showed her face at all the major radio stations—a few days in Los Angeles, then Nashville, then New York. This was how she met Jason. It was the first season of his new megawatt contract, and the team had him making the rounds. Broadcasters loved him: because he was built more like a Greek god than an MLB pitcher; because he jokingly talked trash with club reporters; because when he was well, he could throw 98 mph. He and Maggie ended up as back-to-back interviews on a morning show in Atlanta, and as soon as they met, it was, as both would tell it, "fireworks."

"He was older, yeah, but I'd been working since I was a kid," she says in the daytime-TV interview that inspired the network to cast them for *Honeymoon Stage*. "We just understood each other right away."

They sit next to each other on a blue velvet couch, legs not quite touching, in a way that seems more intimate than the usual famous man's arm over the famous woman's shoulder.

"The funny thing about it is she wasn't a baseball fan at all," Jason laughs. "The studio guys were asking all these questions, and when it was over, she stopped me and said, 'What do you do again?'"

"Well, then I sang in the studio, and you were the one who was curious." Maggie smiles. "I was promoting my first single, and he looks all surprised and goes 'I like that song!'"

She soon became a staple on the ballpark bleachers. He'd sometimes join her on tour. At the time, I was finishing my senior year of high school.

2.

Since *Honeymoon Stage* was not scripted television, there was no union guaranteeing the staff's base rates, no health insurance, no residuals. The network had little to lose on the project, and because of this, they'd somewhat washed their hands of their day-to-day involvement.

"Which is good," said Lauren, the associate producer who welcomed me in on my first day. "Because we can basically do what we want." Her leather mules seemed expensive, but it was pretty clear her red hair color had come out of a box. Although only five foot three, Lauren held herself like a supermodel. She was the competent kind of pretty: perky nose, ambiguous ethnic heritage (which I would later learn was half-white, half-Vietnamese). I wanted to be her immediately.

I'd arrived at the house after forty-five minutes of bumper-to-bumper traffic with only AM radio, the busted audio buttons on my brother's old Volvo sedan one of the reasons I'd inherited it. Lauren had apparently been watching for me—she'd probably been the one to buzz me through the gate—and before I'd even fully parked, she was ushering me inside. I double-checked my watch, confirming I wasn't late.

Shutting the car door reminded me of saying goodbye to my mother outside the dorm on my first day of college, equally intoxicating and scary. Hopefully there'd be a Jen or a Celia somewhere inside. I wasn't betting on Lauren to share lipstick or start braiding my hair.

She brought me briskly through the rotunda-ed entryway, and I followed her around an ornate curved staircase, across marble-tiled floors and past blank cream-colored walls. The whole place smelled like an expensive candle, the kind with a nondescript name like Golden Breeze or Juniper Sunlight. It did not seem like someone's home. Other than the couch I'd seen in the stringout, the downstairs rooms were devoid of furniture. None of the overhead lights were on, and the midmorning haze combined with that emptiness made what might otherwise have been a typical Calabasas mansion into something ghostly and strange. The light strips under the cabinets buzzed.

"So here we are," said Lauren, leading me to the butler's pantry. I jumped back to avoid being hit with the swinging doors. "Here" was a room roughly the size of my whole galley kitchen, outfitted as Video Village—monitors running visual feed from all the cameras placed throughout the house, plus what I assumed must be the manned ones, those particular screens blank. A few laptops and some thick pairs of headphones. A sound-mixing board and a guy in the corner with a Big Gulp.

He looked up. "New PA?" He was a nerdy-looking guy, gangly with a prominent nose, probably in his early forties. He had on basketball shorts and a T-shirt, which made me feel ridiculous in my own borrowed Oxford shirt and Mary Jane pumps.

"Dan's our director," Lauren told me.

"I'm Cassidy Baum." I held out an awkward hand. Dan mugged for Lauren, but then shook it.

"Dan Iaconetti." His grip was firm.

"Where's everybody else?" I asked. Dan took a noisy slurp.

Lauren had been tossing equipment in a heavy-duty black bag—what looked like a charging cable, another headset. She added a sleeve of Zebra Cakes. "Those are exclusively for Devon. Don't let anyone else have them." Devon was not someone I knew, but that didn't matter. It seemed that Lauren was sending me somewhere, that I was about to undertake my first official mission. The recording studio, maybe, where Maggie was at work on a new album. An exclusive Beverly Hills boutique. "They're filming at a gas station on Las Virgenes. Take a left past the gates, and it's the one by the trailhead. Come back after, and I'll show you around."

I shouldered the bag and was almost out the swinging doors before I forced myself to turn. "After . . . I drop this off?" Already the strap bit into my arm.

Lauren blinked at me. "And then whatever else they need."

Noted. Be wary of clarifying questions. In New York, my superior had given instructions so clear my own breath couldn't fog them over. Double-check this spreadsheet. Xerox this man's ID. Get the coffees. I'd been forever getting coffees. Already, it felt like *Honeymoon Stage* was letting me in on the action.

I let the doors swing shut on Video Village and retraced the steps we'd taken through the mostly empty house, my bag of AV goodies thumping along beside me. The bag was too big for my trunk—I didn't want to break any equipment or, god forbid, crush those snack cakes by cramming it down—so I maneuvered it into the back seat of my car, where it sat on top of some boxes I'd been meaning to deliver to Jen's storage unit and blocked most of my back windshield.

Maggie and Jason had shelled out for their own private gate in this gated community, and a driveway that twisted the length of a long city block to hide their front yard from the street. It still shocked me how many places in LA were entirely hidden, how many ways there were to disappear from a city that always had eyes on you. Just around the corner was a bustling expressway, but at the right angle, coming down from the McKee–Dean drive, you could imagine you were the only person on earth.

I inched my way backward, an exercise in blind faith. I was bubbling with excitement, though aware my giddy energy could easily push me over the top of the bottle. This opportunity could turn into a trap, waiting to shunt me back east to my mother and that ex-boyfriend I did not especially pine for but had never been able to quit.

I was at the end of the driveway, through the gate, and backing into the street. No matter that a less punchy PA would have known to turn her car around in the circular drive—I was successfully embarking on my real life, done with walking people's dogs and regrettable booty calls and postcollege anxiety. Here came Cassidy Baum. Delivering important snack-food items and whatever else was in that massive bag blocking my rear windshield from view. Backing into oncoming traffic with an ear-splitting crunch.

"Shit." I whispered it under my breath, so soft that even I could barely hear myself. Maybe I could just sit there and pretend it hadn't happened. I did sit there, hands on the wheel, knuckles growing ever whiter, hoping whomever I'd hit would go away. Instead, a man came over and tapped on my driver's side window. Seat belt still buckled, I cranked it down.

This wasn't my first car accident, but it was the first in which I was obviously at fault. The irony of the apologies I'd made in high school when some minivan rear-ended me—seventeen-year-old Cassidy jumping out of the car in the rain and acting so contrite that an uninvolved woman sidled up and whispered that she'd seen the whole thing and I should shut my mouth or I'd have trouble with insurance—was not lost on me. I sat there trying not to look at the guy leaning down toward my car.

"Are you okay?" The first thing I saw was his hands. They were large and lean, big palms, long, slender fingers. A bicep tattoo peeked through the sleeve of his T-shirt, maybe a shield of some sort, I couldn't tell. He wore an expensive-looking watch and a thumb ring that theoretically should have turned me off but instead did the opposite.

"Oh," I said finally, prying my own hands off the wheel. "Um." I swallowed and let myself look at his face. "You were coming up on me pretty fast," I said. Dress for the job you want, respond to the situation in which you wish you'd found yourself.

His mouth pursed. Of course he had a nice mouth, a nice everything. He seemed to be in his mid-twenties, with dirty-blond hair and blue eyes and the kind of face that seemed both handsome and endlessly transformable. Uncomfortably good looking, but not in that overly groomed Los Angeles way.

"*I* was coming up fast." When he spoke, his voice was gravelly, and though his expression remained serious, I thought he might be laughing. I unbuckled my seat belt and got out of the car.

"Well, I guess not that fast," I said, looking between my dented back bumper and his relatively pristine front. I'd expected much worse. He smiled at me. He had dimples. Goddammit. I fought my instinct to apologize, both for backing up without looking and for standing there all bland and frazzled in my silly little work clothes.

My job. I couldn't let some sexy stranger ruin it. If my car could still drive, I had to drive it to the ARCO. I wouldn't slack on my first official PA assignment, no matter how perfectly dimpled the cheeks of my interruption were.

"This is so flaky, but I really have to go." I looked back up the driveway, hoping Lauren wasn't flapping down to fire me. "You're not hurt or anything? Do we need to, like, exchange insurance?" Really all this guy had was a small scratch in his paint, surely something those hands would have no trouble fixing. I'd gotten lucky.

"How about numbers?" he said. Was he asking for *my* number? Like, *asking* asking? I dug around in my glove box, then handed him a takeout napkin and a pen. The ballpoint blotted at the first digit, and his tongue went to the side of his lips as he scratched out the rest.

Before I got back in my car, I pulled the passenger seat all the way forward and repositioned the boxes, shimmying the equipment bag down to free up a sliver of my windshield. Through it, I watched the man watch me as I drove away.

Why do you watch another person? Because you can't look away. Because you want something from them. Because you want them. Because something has sparked, and it's not fire season yet, but you're still wary of the flame.

⚜

At the ARCO, everyone was doing about what you'd expect of a production team parked at a service station. One big van held cables and C-stands and a portable soundboard. Maggie's BMW convertible sat by a pump. There she was in the driver's seat, flipping through a magazine, while Jason leaned on the side of the car, talking to someone out of my view. I'd thought I'd feel a rush of something when I saw Maggie in person. But she seemed less a person I'd once known than a character I'd once seen on TV. To my left, a guy shot B-roll. Someone else was playing *Snake* on his phone. At the house, Lauren had asserted herself as my immediate superior, but here I couldn't tell who I should defer to. I sat in my parking spot for a minute, considering, before diving into the action.

"Are those the lav replacements?" The guy who'd been on his phone looked up at the slam of my door. "You're the new PA." He stood up from the curb and walked over to me, pointing at himself. "Devon. Sound."

"Oh!" I let the bag thump down from the car. "These are for you."

As Devon untangled the microphone wires, Jason Dean himself walked over, all six feet two inches in the flesh, to ask if we were finally ready.

I'd grown up watching Jason on ESPN, my brother at one point fancying himself a shoo-in for Major League Baseball. Jason had been that rare thing, a pitcher who could hit, and in the prime of his career, I'd often stumbled on a Dean jersey in the sweaty pile of clothing on our upstairs landing. For a few years, he was the king of my hometown of—right outside—Philadelphia. The Phillies had traded Jason just before he got hurt in '98, and although his career-ending injury was a boon for us, my brother still mourned. I could picture Jason on the front page of the sports section, a photo of him giving a thumbs-up, the field behind him kelly green. Now he stood beside me, thinner, tanned, wearing tinted aviator sunglasses. He hiked up his shirt for the new microphone pack, revealing the same muscular torso he'd bared in the Got Milk? ad I'd ripped from a magazine in my dentist's office and hung in my childhood bedroom.

I tried not to stare. Having delivered the Zebra Cakes, I wasn't sure what to do. Should I open the cellophane and put them on a platter? Go tap the camera guy on the shoulder and ask if he needed, what, a Coke?

"Where are my manners?" Jason Dean was talking to me. I'd been given strict instruction not to initiate conversation with the talent. "I'm Jason." He held out his hand, the angle slightly awkward as Devon adjusted his tape.

"Cassidy."

"Nice to meet you, Cassidy."

I felt strangely drunk. Jason Dean had introduced himself. I stood there, wondering if Maggie was going to come over. If she remembered me from childhood, what would I say? *Thanks for the job. Do you still play with Breyer horses?* She tucked her hair behind an ear and examined her fingernails, the solitaire diamond engagement ring visible even from across the parking lot. Sitting atop the pavé wedding band, it looked like a sparkling tumor on her frail little hand.

Devon went back to the van while Jason hopped in the car next to his wife and gave her a tiny kiss on the side of her forehead before the cameras resumed rolling.

In this scene, Maggie is—surprise, surprise—getting gas. She approaches the pump like it's a horse she has to tame, eyeing it warily, her movements slow so as not to startle. Will the traumatized teen girl bond with the wild stallion, or will she need a man to step in? She does okay popping the access door and screwing off the cap, but then she stands there, looking troubled. What to do?

"Can you hurry it up?" Jason says from the passenger seat, absorbed in his BlackBerry. Maggie gives a chipper "Mm-hmm." Digs through her Louis Vuitton purse for a credit card, presses some buttons, frowns.

"Jason, it's not coming out."

"What isn't?"

"I have the thing on the thing, but there's nothing coming out."

"Did you hear the click?"

"What?"

"Did the thing on the handle click down?"

"I stuck it in, but I just . . ." Then the trademark sigh with the bangs floof, the sexy chew of her lip. What can she do? What else can we expect of her?

Jason rolls his eyes, puts his BlackBerry down by the windshield, where the camera zooms in on its sad little screen while mood music plays.

Jason, hero that he is, knows how to pump gas and demonstrates this knowledge with admirable skill. Look at those biceps! Maggie is certainly looking. She wraps her arms around his waist and nuzzles into his shoulder, and although she has wrenched our leading man from his very important business, we love her, because she is, at her core, sweet and lovable. We wouldn't want her to be perfect. God forbid she look this good and also know how to get gas.

"Thanks, babe."

"No problem, babe."

I didn't actually watch this scene film, only saw it air when everyone else did. Unsure of who to assist, I'd instead obeyed Lauren's instructions to return to the house. When I got back, the lights were on, and there was more crew milling around, which made the whole place feel even more like a set getting dressed on a studio lot. Lauren walked me through the camera setup. In agreeing to the show, Maggie and Jason had effectively agreed to live their entire lives for Big Brother. They had a permanent camera on top of the living room television, and another angled down to catch anyone standing at the kitchen island. One hung on the side of the house to get the patio and pool, another the garage. And of course there were the camera operators, shadows that shifted not with the sun but the direction of the drama.

Since shooting was an almost twenty-four-hour endeavor, we had two ENG crews that traded off—a field producer-director and their assistant producer, two camera operators, the sound mixer, a camera assistant, and me, the PA—working in a fairly continuous relay. Production admitted that there likely wouldn't be much to film between one and five a.m., so we could theoretically all be off, although in practice there was usually someone hanging around with a Red Bull and unfortunate undereye bags, fiddling with equipment or emailing the story producers. Ian's team, to whom I'd just made my delivery, would take off today around two p.m.

My crew, Dan's team, was assembling at the house, awaiting the return of our stars. Nominally, Dan was in charge of us, but anyone could see the real buck stopped with Lauren. She'd gone to school in Boston (yes, Harvard), and was maybe ten years older than me, with the general vibe that unless you were announcing her winning lottery ticket you were always wasting her time. Vinnie, our sound mixer, was basically her polar opposite: a bear hug of a guy with time for everyone. Eli and Rahul operated the cameras, and during my tenure, they were assisted by a series of gangly white men who either found a better gig or pissed Lauren off enough to get walked off the property.

Everyone was there that first day when I got back from the ARCO, checking camera feeds and going over Maggie's upcoming travel schedule.

"Cassidy." Lauren always said my name like it was a clipped call to attention. "The housecleaners put away Maggie's bags. We need them back in the entryway."

I nodded, having learned my lesson about follow-up questions. Put bags back in entryway. How hard could that be?

What kind of bags? Where were they? The foyer closets had more unpacked moving boxes shoved into them, but nothing that seemed like a bag Lauren needed set. Upstairs, then.

I crept up the spiral staircase, without having had the tour of the house Lauren had promised me, unsure of what constituted Maggie and Jason's personal space. Luckily, a camera was setting up in the den. Adrian, camera assistant du jour, stood in as Rahul adjusted for natural light. I knocked on the open door.

"Ummm, hi. I'm Cassidy?"

They both looked up at me and waved, introduced themselves by name, and went back to their own jobs.

"Lauren says to get Maggie's bags. Any idea where those might be? It's just—I don't know if I'm allowed in their bedroom."

"Oh, you can go in. She won't notice," Adrian said. He was the younger and clearly less senior of the two, so I wasn't sure how seriously I should take him. "Officially the bedroom is off limits, but it's not like they know if you're popping in or out. Lauren probably means the suitcases."

"That's not, like, a violation of privacy or contract or anything?"

Adrian blinked at me. "They're celebrities putting their lives on TV. What even is privacy?"

This was clearly not the time for an ethical debate, but I chewed my cheek for a second, considering.

"I don't think Maggie McKee would even notice if you disappeared that suitcase entirely," said Rahul. "She'd just find another of her dozens. The other day Eli took some of her hand cream home for his wife after she messed with his shot. You're good just walking in her room."

"We got your back," said Adrian in a tone that failed to assure me. Still, I thanked them and slunk over to what seemed to be the primary bedroom.

While the rest of the house was a blank canvas for the show and its producers, Maggie and Jason's bedroom felt lived in. Sweatshirts lay jumbled on the divan, and a parade of pill bottles lined the bathroom counter. Both nightstands held piles of books, though nothing I immediately recognized. The suitcase I assumed I was seeking sat just inside the room, and despite Rahul and Adrian's claims, I couldn't bring myself to trespass any further.

The bag itself was well made and expensive to be sure, but not the ostentatious designer advertisement I'd expected. It was cream leather, which was relatively simple, and monogrammed with a swirling *MMD*. Maggie McKee Dean. I didn't realize she had legally changed her name.

Or had she? This was before all the answers to the world lay just a finger tap away inside your purse or back pocket. Without perusing *Us Weekly*, I couldn't have told you Maggie's star sign or her favorite color, though that information was available to me for the low cost of $3.99.

I did know that Maggie McKee had begun her career in entertainment with tap and ballet lessons as a five-year-old in Youngstown, Ohio. Even when I'd known her as a kid, she'd had that charisma. Maggie was always a star.

By fourteen—long after she'd left Ohio behind—Maggie was more than pretty. She'd sashayed past that awkward stage of braces and zits with a Lolita twinkle in her big brown eyes, which were by that point broadcast weekly on the songs and sketches of *The Tiger Crew*. She'd made it to TV via her national anthem circuit—singing "O say can you see" for minor-league hockey teams and local rodeos and NASCAR. You had to pay your dues, I guessed, and then pay them even more while you did choreography and sang harmonies in sparkly top hats for a billion-dollar network, and then by recording bubblegum pop in your underwear. To me, the cost seemed high, but that was one of the many reasons why I was Cassidy "Get Me a Coffee" Baum, and she was Maggie McKee. I didn't have monogrammed luggage.

What I did have was luggage you could actually wheel through an airport, or, in this instance, down a carpeted hallway. I hefted Maggie's suitcase down the wide spiral stairs, wondering how much it would have tarnished the artistic vision of its designer had they chosen to add wheels. It seemed that if one was going to spend ungodly money on a cream leather suitcase, someone else would be the one to carry it.

I was both awkward and overdressed. Despite the instruction to wear comfortable clothes, I'd chosen that dress shirt and a kitten heel, my desire to appear competent in direct opposition to my actual competence. Sliding the suitcase down the tiled entry floor, I felt a blister forming on my left big toe.

"We need those flowers in water." Here was Lauren again, clipboard in hand, gesturing toward a giant bouquet in a cardboard box by the front door. I nodded.

The card, from a fancy florist in Beverly Hills, was pale-pink, scented card stock, with *Maggie* written in perfect felt-tipped calligraphy. I found a pair of scissors in the mostly empty kitchen drawers and snipped the peony stems, then began to look through cupboards for a vase. Paper plates, crystal tumblers, several packs of meal-replacement shakes in mocha and strawberry vanilla. They'd amassed an impressive collection of the sort of kitchen items you could only have with ample space and which now sat collecting dust: a panini press, a pasta maker still in its cellophane.

I felt embarrassed to be searching their things. This was a space they'd made available to the production crew, and surely they assumed we'd get to know it, but it was still Maggie and Jason's home. These were still their muscle relaxers, their joke coasters. A birth announcement for someone named Taryn hung on the fridge next to a magnet for a dentist in Santa Clarita.

What it felt like, I realized, was my dad's place in Virginia. I'd only been there a few times, as a teenager, when he'd reached out wanting to connect. Before he'd decided again that he wanted to disconnect. It was that same sense of trespassing on other people's space, even though I'd been invited. My dad had told me to help myself to whatever was in the fridge, but I was scared to take anything, and eventually convinced myself that if I hadn't finished his orange juice, maybe he would have kept me around. If I hadn't asked where I could find the towels. As it was, at the end of my third visit, he dropped me back in Pennsylvania and said, *See you in the summer*, then called my mom a few hours after that to say that he was out. It was too much for him: the parenting, maintaining the relationship. He'd tried, but this still wasn't going to work.

I reminded myself this was a television set. I belonged here. This wasn't my dad's house—this was my job, and I was going to make sure that I was good at it.

I found a vase in the small cabinet over the refrigerator and hoisted myself onto the counter to reach it. After arranging the flowers, I figured I'd earned the peek I stole at the card. *Welcome home,* it said, and where I'd expected to see *love, Jason*, it read *Until next time . . .*

In a different context, on a different day, I might have wondered more about this. I might have asked at least Rahul, if not Lauren, who these flowers were from. I might have considered the knowing looks between Lauren and Dan, the brief flashes of tension between Maggie and Jason. I might have run, as they say, for the hills. But there the hills were, dusty sage, outside my window. The flowers were pretty. I'd set them up well.

Until next time, I thought. And I went about my day.

The episode we filmed that day is well known, mostly because Jason carried Maggie piggyback up the main stairs, the bedroom door closed, and then we were meant to assume that they had sex. Production couldn't afford to license any popular songs, so they ran something that sounded enough like Boyz II Men to suggest the reference but not so close as to cause problems with legal. This doofy unknown track would become a cult favorite, the kind that you can never quite tell if people love to make fun of or unequivocally love. The lyrics go something like "Tonight / I'm going to slip inside / Your body and soul." The episode credits roll when the instrumental break kicks in, and the camera remains on that door. We hear a giggle, a playful thump.

If you rewind a bit, you'll see Maggie come in, dragging her suitcase. She calls out for Jason, who stubs his toe on her bag. They bicker. She pouts. She pulls her hair into a ponytail, then drops it, then pulls it back again. He says something about how he's also working—should he be expected to drop everything the second she walks in the door? Maggie rolls her eyes at this. She goes into the kitchen to put her purse on the island.

"Are these for me?" Her nose is deep in the flowers, inhaling. "You got these for me?"

Jason neither confirms nor denies.

"I missed you, baby," he says, coming up behind her. Her face is in the flowers, and his face is in her hair, and they sway a bit before he kisses her neck, and she laughs, and they agree to go upstairs.

It wasn't until I left work that first evening that I remembered my car. A more thorough examination determined it was dented but working; in no way worth the trouble it would take me to get it repaired, or the resulting increase in my premium. I'd shoved the napkin with the other driver's phone number into my pocket, and at home I ironed it out with my palm. He'd been attractive. He wasn't pissed about his car. Maybe I should have let myself flirt with him a little. Maybe he'd want to meet for drinks.

I stopped myself. I was in LA for the right reasons. I had my eyes on the prize. My focus was work. This encounter would be an anecdote I used at conferences and dinners once I'd crested the summit of Reality television production and was asked about my early trails. *Oh yes,* I'd say, *on my first day as a PA, I played bumper cars with no actual consequence.*

I'd hit this guy's car and somehow gotten off scot-free. The power of the producer was already rubbing off on me. I taped the napkin to my mirror, a reminder that with the right frame of mind, I could turn all situations to my favor—a memento of the day I got my start.

October 2007

The rehearsal-party room devolves into the sort of chaos I know we won't see tomorrow: Gabe's uncles sloppily cheers-ing their pints, and my friends unbothered by their fading makeup or the occasional snort in their laughter. People are at their best when they think no one is watching them. Not necessarily their cleverest or their most altruistic, but their most loveably human. I'm glad my guests haven't been transformed by cameras. Tomorrow is for the viewers, but tonight is still for us.

Lauren's talking to my brother, which is cringeworthy but not yet dangerous. Andrew fiddles with his shirt collar, drink empty. He looks surprised and shakes his head. I wouldn't put it past Lauren to go digging for my childhood trauma. I remind myself to keep keeping an eye.

Celia brings a round of shots to a table of our friends. Someone has found a way to broadcast the baseball game, and my cousins jostle each other to listen to the end of the eighth inning. Whispers wing through the room, the shared disbelief that tomorrow they might actually get to meet *the* Jason Dean. Of course he'll be here—strategically seated as far from Maggie as possible and ushered out of any room that she walks into, per her contract. Who knows how up he'll be for autographs, but my Uncle John will damn well try.

There's a line for the VIP bathrooms, and I'm not precious about going into the main part of the restaurant to use the general ones. My lipstick's faded where Gabe kissed me, a happy blush across my lower lip. I don't reapply. Instead, I turn my head one way, then the other. Tomorrow I'll have a professional painting on my makeup. Tonight, I still look like me.

The weather's perfect, so I skip snaking past tables to return to the party room and instead go out around the back. I float through the parking lot. I make it to the patio, the Tuscan garden where we had spritzes and little skewers of mozzarella before moving inside for our sit-down dinner. One of my heels gets caught between the stones, and I sit on a weathered bench to wipe off the dirt. Then I hear Gabe's voice.

"I know I should have just come clean with her." He sounds upset, tone low and urgent. "But seriously, you can't tell anyone."

I freeze. *Her. Anyone.* Me. If I crane my neck, I see Gabe's back in his rehearsal-dinner suit coat, his hair freshly cut for tomorrow. Who is he talking to? I do and do not want to know. A woman's voice murmurs back to him, her body hidden behind what I'd once thought to be a charming display of rosemary and cypress but am now ready to go at with a hacksaw.

My stomach drops. My stupid garden bench is sinking, a high heel in mud.

A memory comes unbidden: Maggie McKee, cocking her head at me, half smiling, gloss sticky on her lips. *How well do you really know him, Cassidy?*

"It'd be a disaster," Gabe says now.

A disaster? I'm too stunned to cry, too frozen even to breathe. The woman quietly tries to assuage him, but I can hear Gabe's irritation in the way that his shoe taps against the stone.

I can't believe this is actually happening. This is everything I've dreaded. After everything we've been through, Gabe is lying to me.

I have to stand up and confront them—my almost-husband and whoever he's confided in. This man to whom I'm supposed to publicly declare my eternal devotion. This man I still can't fully trust.

"It's not going to—" Gabe starts, but he's cut off by the sound of Celia stomping through the garden from the street-side entrance. He stiffens and says, "Never mind." I watch him disappear in the direction of the party room, his mysterious conversation partner a rustle of shrubbery moving toward the opposite side of the parking lot. I'm going to be sick.

"There you are!" Celia shimmies around a bush. "Cold feet already?" She's the level of drunk at which I can't tell if she's joking or genuinely asking me. I am very cold, despite the mildness of the weather. When I try to respond, all I can do is swallow.

"Oh, Cassy Cass." Celia sits down next to me, lets me lean on her shoulder. "It's totally normal, you goof. I'd be surprised if you weren't worried about all those cameras tomorrow." One of her rings gets caught stroking my hair.

But I'm not worried about filming tomorrow, not anymore.

I'm worried about marrying Gabe.

What will I say when the officiant asks tomorrow if anyone knows of a reason why we two should not be wed? What will Gabe say? I'd thought our secrets were shared secrets, that anything unsaid between us was only for our mutual protection. I'd thought we had moved on. I had believed him.

Or have I been ignoring the obvious all along? Have I just buried my suspicions about Gabe, deciding it's easier to live on the surface of our life together? It's easier to believe that Maggie McKee was the one who lied.

What to do? My instincts kick in, the possibilities splaying out in front of me like fast pitches in production meetings: Go find Gabe now and confront him. (Dramatic! Cringeworthy! Toss-your-drink-in-someone's-face TV!) Call off the whole thing. (Boring, and financially disastrous.) Keep a cool head, slow down, wait until tomorrow. (This is what Lauren would tell me to do. This is what I always do. Slow down. Watch carefully. Let someone else make the move.)

I should have known today was too good to be true. I should have known this was coming.

We sit for a while, Celia contentedly loaded and me silently running through worst-case scenarios. I've always been a worrier, but when things started going downhill on *Honeymoon Stage*—that first descent, before I realized how low we'd all actually go—I saw disaster everywhere. Not just the accident itself—the swelling, the stumble, the scratch of fingernails on skin—but my complicity. I could have paid closer attention, could have done *something*. Because I didn't, I'm now forever trying to stitch up gashes before they leave scars.

3.

September 2002

In one episode of the show, Jason is sitting on the couch in the sunken living room when a squelching slap against the glass patio door interrupts his television viewing. After a close-up of his furrowed brow, the camera zooms in on the smudge on the glass, a fairly innocuous mark, even through the eye of an expensive TV camera. Because Jason is aware that he is on television—and more importantly that Maggie is quickly becoming our primary catalyst for action—he does what any enterprising cast member would do and gets up to investigate this mystery. He does not necessarily want to get up from whatever sport is on TV. What the viewer does not see on-screen is Lauren or Dan or maybe even me asking him what that sound was. What they do not see is Lauren or Dan or maybe even me popping out onto the patio, discovering its source, and firmly suggesting that Jason get out there. A bird has flown into the window at such an angle that it now lies twitching on the terra-cotta tile. The camera captures its futile flutters, but this will be screened out in edits. For all our metaphors about nature documentaries, we are not that kind of show. What the audience will see is Jason standing over the bird, frowning, sighing, scooping it up with rubber kitchen gloves. The camera follows him as he removes it from the property and, as he does, zooms out to reveal more birds just around the corner, a trail of dazed birds circling the house, a trail that Jason doesn't see.

I quickly learned that the most exciting aspects of *Honeymoon Stage* came in postproduction, when the hours of nothing were tossed out, the wheat rescued from the chaff. In later years producers would shoot Reality television specifically for story, but as pioneers of the genre, we had no clear trail. Maggie's and Jason's teams would tell us where they needed to be that day for their other gigs and whether or not cameras were permitted on location. Then we'd follow them around. Much of my job entailed printing out releases and chasing down the regular people who happened onto a shoot, cajoling them into signing away their anonymity or else plastering the shooting area with legal-approved fliers informing the general public that walking into this space meant giving us their consent to be filmed. I also set up lots of crates, then took them down at the end of the shoot.

When our supervisors were out of earshot, I'd crack jokes with Rahul, who was quickly becoming my favorite of the cameramen, or listen to absurd Hollywood gossip from Sally Ann, who did Maggie's makeup and had dated a paparazzo and thus claimed to know all the hip Beverly Hills spots. Vinnie liked to show me wallet-sized photos of his kids, and would offer me fatherly advice about biding my time and rolling with punches until they promoted me. The crew on set felt like a family, one that I was gradually becoming a part of. I liked being indispensable, even if it was only because no one else remembered which shirt Maggie had been wearing when we'd filmed the day before, or how to fix the DVD player. I liked preempting Dan's requests by already knowing he'd want the lights set up just so. We weren't about to win an Emmy, but I was contributing. Every day was a new challenge, and even though some afternoons could be boring, life on set was never dull.

I was also the resident gofer, which meant I got to take myself on field trips. My second week on set I drove to the KFC in Thousand Oaks and picked up lunch for the whole crew. By the time I arrived back at the Calabasas house, all the food was room temperature, and my car had absorbed what I knew would be a semipermanent fug. Adrian—if my memory serves correctly and he had not, in fact, already been replaced with another camera assistant—helped me distribute the meals.

"Oh, that one's mine." Maggie came up behind me.

We hadn't interacted much at that point. Lauren had told me to keep away from the talent. Maybe she thought I'd pump Maggie for a juicy story I could sell to *Star* magazine or force Jason to sign my bra. *Just ease into it,* she'd said, like I was taking my first hit of weed. Because of this, I still wasn't sure if Maggie remembered me.

Maggie was on tiptoe, leaning over my shoulder toward a two-piece meal. She smelled like shampoo. It seemed impossible that she would have freely chosen Kentucky Fried Chicken over whatever carb-free, taste-free, sugar-free concoction she had stocked from her dietitian. Then again, I hadn't taken the order, and I didn't see why she would lie to me.

At the time, everyone was on some fad diet. You couldn't be young in Southern California and not at least be doing Weight Watchers or Atkins. Eli was a vegan. Sally Ann was gluten- and sugar- and fat- and nut-free. Even I wanted to have my body achieve its maximum potential. I'd come of age in the '90s, when between the hours of eight a.m. and dinner, I watched as my mother regularly ingested only a glass of white wine, half a SlimFast, and two hard-boiled eggs. That afternoon I, for myself, had inexplicably ordered only a medium fries.

"Don't look so surprised," Maggie said to me.

She and Jason waited until the crew had finished eating to sit down to their own cold chicken and saturated fat. Maggie instructed the cameras to close in on the takeout bag, flimsy with grease. Eli rolled his eyes when Dan okayed her impromptu direction. While Vinnie set up the sound, I stood around the corner, close enough to hear what Maggie and Jason had gone out of their way to keep private.

"You don't have to be eating," Jason said to Maggie softly. "We can scrap the idea. It's so weird to have people watch you eating."

"No, it's fine," Maggie replied. "It's easier to just give them what they want."

I wasn't sure if "them" was the crew, or our audience, or Maggie's team trying to rebrand her as "an everygirl." Rahul and Eli got behind their cameras, and Vinnie gave the okay. Maggie ate her chicken as if it was not several hours old and was a meal she consumed regularly. Jason called her gross for dousing everything in ranch.

"What even is ranch? And why is it called that?" Maggie asked, licking the sauce from a finger.

Jason rolled his eyes. "It's a salad dressing, babe. So, like, mayonnaise and spices."

"Yeah, but why do they call it ranch? Because of horses? They like carrots, right?"

"I don't think horses are dipping their carrots in ranch dressing." Jason made eyes at the camera, his signature deadpan can-you-believe.

"You should have some." Maggie wiggled her paper plate toward him.

"I'm not gonna eat that stuff."

A twinkle in her eye as she nodded in mock seriousness and said, "Because you're an athlete."

"Nah, just common sense, once you've dipped that dirty little finger in it."

Maggie's mouth was full. She sputtered, smacking him on the forearm. "*Jay*-son."

They had this same interaction—his playful dig and her faux offense—at least twice a day, and I had already noticed it was most likely to occur in direct view of a camera. They finished their food in a comfortable silence, and then Maggie excused herself to the bathroom while Jason cleared the table.

Contractually, the cameras couldn't follow the cast into bathrooms or bedrooms, with the exception of, say, a segment discussing interior design. There was nothing to stop the crew from camping out and filming the closed door while the sound engineer strove to pick up whatever retching or bumping or crying was happening inside—nothing, that is, but common decency. Lauren would roll her eyes when Maggie begged privacy.

"People have seen her full ass cheeks on the magazine rack at the airport. I don't know what she thinks she's hiding," Lauren said to me on more than one occasion. This seemed unfair. There was a difference between posing and being caught in an unwanted candid.

Long before any microphones were wired and my contract was signed, Maggie's team had set the boundaries for what she was comfortable divulging. Although one of the goals of the show, from their angle, was to portray teen sex symbol Maggie McKee as a regular girl and thereby grow her female audience, she didn't want to be too regular. The show would still be her real life, they'd argued, just not every aspect of it. She had an image to build as America's sweetheart, and to capture her with zit cream would ruin it. "How is it reality to be up first thing in the morning with perfectly blown-out hair and three coats of mascara?" Lauren grumbled.

"Cut her a break," Dan would say. "She's laying bare her few functioning brain cells. We don't also need to see her take a shit."

On a Reality show with regular talent, production didn't care if the cast was uncomfortable. The goal was to make them uncomfortable: Discomfort made for good TV. Nothing played better than a riled-up cast member threatening to quit and stalking off into a previously undisclosed corner of set to be coddled by producers while he—it was almost always a he—swore he was finished with all of them. Here, we were balancing more carefully. Maggie and Jason were both producers and product, and alienating or upsetting them risked disrupting the entire ecosystem. Still, we had a job to do, and Maggie hiding out in one of the off-limits spaces made it harder for us to do it.

"Cassidy, go find out how long she'll be." I had not grown any more comfortable with Lauren in the time I'd spent assisting her. I'd been hired to do the grunt work, and she knew that instructing me in a gentler tone didn't change the fundamentals of plunging a toilet. If a production crew was, as so many executives waxed on about, a family, then Lauren was the older sister who refused to let me borrow her blouse. I worshipped her. She terrified me.

"Like, ask Maggie if . . . ?" I looked at Rahul, shouldering his camera, with a panicked plea for help. He shrugged.

"Cassidy." Lauren snapped her fingers three times quickly.

"Yeah, okay." And off I went to bother Maggie McKee.

She sat cross-legged on a bed in one of the guest rooms, thumbing through a magazine and drinking a green juice. Where it had come from, I couldn't say. Her team of stylists and management and scheduling people constantly bustled through the house, responsible for both making Maggie McKee and maintaining her. I tapped on the door, and she cheerfully told me to come in. When I did, she looked up and said she needed her nails done.

My mouth fell open, and I did some dumb little move with my jaw.

"Not by you. I know who you are." Maggie smiled at me. "I'm just mentioning."

"Lauren wants to know when you'll be back down to film?" I didn't love the uptick at the end of my own sentence.

"Lauren, Lauren, Lauren," Maggie said, not unkindly. She slid a straw wrapper into her margin to mark her place, and when she closed the magazine, I saw it was not a fashion spread but *TIME*. "I just needed a minute."

To expel your cold KFC? I wondered but did not say aloud. Maggie stretched, her T-shirt rising to reveal a sliver of flat stomach. "I do know who you are," she continued. At this I paused, standing very still as she slid off the bed and into her slippers. "You're Dede's niece."

"Oh yeah," I said, as if I was just remembering we had a connection and Dede wasn't the sole cause of my current employment.

"I remember you from, what, kindergarten?" Maggie said as we walked. It was third grade, but I didn't correct her. "You lived with her for a while during that family thing. Your brother was so cute. I was a baby, but he was, like, my first older crush."

I personally hadn't found Andrew cute as an eleven-year-old, but it wasn't entirely implausible that she had.

"He's in medical school now," I said. "In Chicago."

"And still cute?"

I shrugged. "I'm the wrong person to ask, I think." By now we were down the spiral staircase and reentering the arena.

"Bring a picture tomorrow. Important questions must be answered." At that, Maggie slipped into the living room, where Jason stood fiddling with the remote control. She came up behind him and wrapped her arms around his waist.

Lauren caught my eye, one brow raised. I had done well.

That night I thought a lot about how seriously to take Maggie's dictate. I had pictures of my brother from various family gatherings, nights out in the city, an old holiday card. I could easily pop up with my laptop and show her adult Andrew, and we could reminisce about that year in Ohio, and I'd feel less like her hired help and more like her pal. But if I did, I could just as easily be met with a blank stare, like the one she'd given when Lauren asked about getting an interview with Maggie's old songwriter.

"We could do a segment on how you two work together. Get him out to the house, show a day-in-the-life." Lauren had been spitballing, hardly committed, but Maggie's reaction stopped her short.

"No." Maggie's voice was hard, her expression icy with disdain. This was a mistake on her part. She'd shown Lauren a vulnerability. This songwriter was clearly a sore spot. I could see Lauren filing the response away, though she didn't immediately press Maggie further. I didn't blame her. Maggie's was a cruel knifelike cold, worse than anything I remembered from middle school, when I'd been stabbed in the back by many a fellow tween girl.

One of my few childhood memories of Maggie was when I'd had on a T-shirt that said GIRLS CAN BE ANYTHING and, upon reading it, Maggie told me that they couldn't. It stuck with me, the way she'd smirked, her hair mouse-brown then, and in pigtails. I had cried that day because I wanted to be a firefighter—god only knows why—and Maggie swore that it wasn't going to happen.

I was afraid that she would make me cry again now, that she would tell me something about myself and this job that I knew to be true but was set on denying. She'd take the little model world that I was building and smash it to pieces.

Maggie McKee and I were not friends, and we weren't ever going to be friends. I wouldn't bring my laptop, or a photo. Maggie wasn't to be counted on, no matter what face she'd put on with me that day. Instead, I would focus on Lauren. If anyone was going to help me advance at *Honeymoon Stage*, it would be Lauren, with her henna hair and sensible footwear. Lauren, with her headset, whispering down the spooked horses, sowing the seeds, running the farm.

Around the same time that we shot the first season, Maggie was working on her second album, and one morning we all went with her to the recording studio. It wasn't that we, as a crew, were usually discouraged from joining her, but rather that we were not as enthusiastically encouraged by her manager and publicist in the way we were encouraged to follow her out to the mall.

"It doesn't showcase the marriage," her manager said, implying that somehow her shopping habits did.

This time, however, the network was filming a special on the making of the album, which we would capture in a bizarre ouroboros of camerawork. Our team would continue to act as crew for *Honeymoon Stage*, and Ian's team would be the documentarians. I packed into a van carrying lighting equipment with the other PA, Lauren, and Maggie's makeup artist, Sally Ann.

As a general rule, Sally Ann acted for the *Honeymoon Stage* cameras the way Maggie McKee did onstage: glittery, half naked, always mugging with a massive Dentyne smile. She was a Maggie lite—not quite as blond, not quite as busty, her eyes smaller and her freckles harder to hide. She was around my age, maybe a year or two younger, and I got the sense she wanted more for herself than to be a makeup artist for the stars. LA was full of this type of girl—biding her time while she looked for her big break. We weren't friends, and we weren't really colleagues. She definitely made more money than I did.

"So exciting!" Sally Ann squeezed my knee, and I faked a smile.

Rahul had told me that Sally Ann came from a small town in Kentucky, where she sent money back home to support a kid she said was her sister, though he had his doubts. Rahul wasn't generally a gossip—unlike Sally Ann—so I was mostly inclined to believe him. Whatever the story, I'd personally seen the inside of Sally Ann's locket, a silver heart on a chain she always wore, with her on one side and a toddler on the other.

"Can you believe it?" she said, as if we weren't simply traveling from one place of Maggie's work to another.

It was my first time in a recording studio, and I was struck by how dark it was. Black sofas and black soundboards and a huge sheet of glass through which we watched Maggie warm up her voice. She had on a T-shirt, Uggs, and this purple infinity scarf that looked to me like she'd made it herself but probably cost $500. Rahul and Eli filmed the cameras filming Maggie, and I was surprised by how good she sounded.

"Why doesn't she sing like this on her other album?" I asked Sally Ann, who'd remained next to me, ready to pop around the glass to powder Maggie's nose. The girl-next-door look did not abide oily skin. Sally Ann shrugged.

Maggie did a few takes of her new song, her producer pausing her every so often to give notes that only she could hear through her headset. Then she changed into a leopard-print shirt and had Sally Ann gloss her up. There wasn't anywhere designed for primping, so I held up both a mirror and one of our set lights.

"Not too much," said Maggie. Sally Ann blotted with a tissue that she then tossed on the floor.

"I'll get these lashes on you, and then we'll be ready."

Maggie sat on the couch, legs crossed at the ankles. Ian asked her questions, and his cameraperson framed her as a talking head.

"It's definitely more of an adult sound," Maggie said of the new album. "Growing as I grow, you know." There was a Maggie that read *TIME* magazine in her slippers, and a Maggie that leaned into not knowing what a sponge was for, and yet another Maggie that writhed onstage in knee-high boots. This Maggie was a different iteration. She spoke softly, with a demure sweetness that belied the entire project of herself as a pop star. *Who, little old me?* she seemed to be asking us. "Ian, can we pause?"

He nodded, and we all took a break, which in this case meant we all stood around in the tight studio space waiting for our break to be over. Sally Ann brought Maggie a cough drop and a large bottle of water. "Okay, sweetie, is that better?"

Maggie nodded. She was just starting up again when we heard tapping on the door. Jason entered without apologizing for the interruption.

"You look amazing," he told Maggie, who smiled the first genuine smile I'd seen all morning. "I was just coming from the gym, and I thought I'd stop by." The back of his T-shirt was wet from the shower, as if he'd rushed to get here. "Take your lunch break now?" Although he posed it as a question, he didn't actually seem to be asking. His hand was already extended to help her up off the couch.

"Baby, we're still working." Maggie used her interview voice, which made me wonder who she was trying to be for her husband. The cameras were no longer rolling.

"Baby." Something passed between them then, a conversation that the rest of us weren't privy to. Jason's eyes got slightly harder; Maggie's smile got tight. If ever I'd believed in telepathy, it would have been in that moment as we all stood and watched them wait each other out.

"Ian?" Maggie asked finally.

He nodded. "Give us fifteen."

Jason softened, his affability returned. For the next fifteen minutes, I watched him watch Maggie, waiting to see if he would show that sharpened edge. I imagined there might be some lingering jealousy on Jason's part—his career doing what he loved had ended, while Maggie's seemed newly begun. This was the center of her professional world, and he had to be thinking about how he'd never stand up on the mound again, the crowd around him cheering, the game in his control. He'd never do those sweaty postgame interviews, his team all piling on after a nail-biting win. But he looked at Maggie with undiluted pride, nodding as she talked about her process. Either he was a much better actor than I'd realized, or else he truly did love her.

It seemed to me that love was easier for the rich and famous. Sure, people complained about the downsides of fame, but at the end of the day, if you had money, all the rest of it was simpler. You could stay because you wanted to stay, not because you had to. When my dad walked out on us, my mother had two young children and an English degree. She hadn't worked since before Andrew was born. I didn't believe in the kind of love that launched a thousand Hallmark cards. But I did believe that money made leaps of faith more possible.

Maggie started talking about the logistics of the vocals she'd put down, animated and effusive as she explained her inspirations. The way Jason smiled as she lit up was sexier than any photo shoot. Jason had always been handsome, but this was the first time he had kind of turned me on.

Rahul saw it too. He got a perfectly framed shot of Jason's face as he watched his wife.

4.

In an early episode, Maggie is at a boutique, and she browses racks of clothes and lifts up pieces of jewelry. She says "I love this," and "I like this!" and "Oh, this is so wonderful!" The audience does not know the name of this particular boutique, a fact that seems, from a modern perspective, like a huge missed opportunity. Maggie purchases some things and does not purchase others. When she gets home, she shows Jason her spoils, and he makes a big to-do about how much money she has spent on the miniskirt and sweaters, as husbands—har dee har—are wont to do. Over the course of the series, there is never any mention of how money is coming into the McKee–Dean accounts. Maggie certainly works a lot. She's always on the road; she's filming commercials and playing small-to-medium-size venues. She's putting out her own line of gel pens, booking a guest spot on a sitcom. But when she's at home? Boy can she spend money. Here she comes out the door of the boutique, laden with shopping bags, a single paparazzo snapping her from behind a hedge. Across the parking lot, a man stands with his hands shoved in his pockets, his face blurred.

"Who is this guy?" Dan held up his laptop, showing the team a paused frame of footage labeled August 18. "We have releases for those people over there, but nobody thought to give this dude paperwork?"

Dan's management style was a direct contrast to Lauren's. Where she made you feel stupid by telling you outright you were stupid, he did so by asking affable questions in a low-key way that underlined how reasonable he was being in the face of your incompetence. *Oh, so you meant to leave those numbers off the spreadsheet. Did you realize that camera lens had cracked?* In this specific situation, mine was not the incompetence in question. It couldn't have been—on August 18, I'd not yet heard of *Honeymoon Stage*. I had probably been walking some celebrity chef's dogs.

"That was what's her name's job," said Rahul, capping a lens.

"Okay, well now it's Cassidy's job." Dan slurped his Big Gulp and turned to me. "Drop whatever you're doing right now and get this guy released."

What I was doing right then was compiling a list of spin classes in gyms big enough to accommodate our filming needs, and I was happy to abandon the mostly mindless task in service of some interesting detective work. On a larger shoot, a production assistant in post might have been sent on this goose chase while I continued with my fieldwork. But we were renegades, mavericks, making TV with a skeleton crew. I closed my spreadsheet and logged into my email to take a closer look at the still shot of this stranger who, most likely, I would never track down. Of the millions of people living in Southern California, not to mention tourists shopping in Beverly Hills, it seemed unlikely I'd find "this guy" with no identifying details save a quick still of his face.

"Oh!" I said. "It's this guy!" I was as excited at the prospect of remembering this particular man as I was to have an immediate solution to Dan's problem.

Dan frowned. "You know who that is?"

"Cassidy's got X-Men powers." Rahul held out a fist for me to bump.

"This guy hit me with his car once." There was no reason to go into any further detail. Much of my job included driving expensive things from place to place, and I didn't want anyone to question my ability to do so. Besides, that was literally what had happened, if not the full picture.

"Kismet," said Dan. "You go and get him."

"If you can't get the signature, hold that car crash over him, yeah?" Lauren said to me as I was leaving. "That kind of leverage is how we get results."

I had to drive home for the napkin with his number, and Celia was surprised when I unlocked the door.

"Shit! I thought you'd come to rob me." She was eating a yogurt and wearing her fuzzy turquoise bathrobe, *E! News* on the TV. "What are you doing? They didn't fire you already, did they?"

I rolled my eyes. "Important investigative work. I've been promoted from 'make lists' to 'find person to sign document.'"

Celia laughed. She could always be counted on to take people's jokes in the kindest possible light.

"Well good for you." She licked her spoon. "You don't by any chance still have that pair of brown heels that I could borrow for my audition this afternoon, do you?"

"My Steve Maddens?" I said. "You can wear them."

The napkin was taped to my mirror. Celia and I spent a minute debating if the second digit was a seven or a one, but the phone number was otherwise legible. My target picked up on the third ring.

"Hello?" Sometimes a sound or a smell would transport me immediately to the moment in my life I'd most vividly encountered it. I could never smell tar without the visceral sense of being stuck in the back seat of my mother's car, my brother flicking Starburst wrappers at me in an attempt to make the inching highway traffic even more miserable. When the mystery man answered the phone that afternoon, his scratchy voice popped me right back to the bottom of the driveway.

I remembered his hands. I remembered he was handsome and tall, and I was lucky he'd been nice to me after I backed directly into his car.

"Hi," I said. "I'm the one who hit your car a few weeks ago?" I remembered too late that I was deflecting all blame. "In Calabasas?"

"Ah," he said. "Yes. The other day. When I was going pretty fast."

"That's actually not why I'm calling," I said.

"Oh, it's not?" This guy was definitely flirting. Across the room, Celia wiggled her eyebrows in response to my change in posture.

"This might sound weird, but were you at the Grove like a month ago?"

He laughed. "It does sound weird, and I really couldn't tell you. It's possible. It's definitely possible." I heard a metallic crashing on his side of the call and a muffled "Hold on a second" directed at someone nearby.

"I think you were," I said. "I'm not stalking you, I promise. I work for a TV show, and I'm pretty sure you're in one of our shots. I need you to sign a release."

"What's the show?"

"What?"

"What show do you work on?"

Technically I was supposed to keep that quiet unless he signed an NDA. *Honeymoon Stage* was all hush hush until the network aired their promos, and though I found this a dumb rule, it would be even dumber of me to flat out break it.

"A network Reality show."

"Oh." His voice was flat. Did he think I was bullshitting?

"I promise I'm not extorting you to get you to pay for my bumper. I'm extorting you for other reasons."

"Oh yeah?" I had him laughing again, which was good.

"I have this job, see, and it pays my rent. So in a way you'd be, I dunno, entirely responsible for my career and well-being."

"Gabe! Come on!" The voice came from his end of the call, and he muttered to someone in response.

"Sorry about that," he said. "Where were we?"

"My career. The release. So how about it, Gabe?" I was taking a chance on the name, taking a chance on this whole thing, really. I wasn't playing things the way Lauren had instructed, but I had the sense trying to guilt this guy was going to get me nowhere. Plus I was admittedly eager to see him again. All the Reality romance had made me crave some of my own. Celia abandoned any pretense of minding her business and leaned forward at the edge of the couch, fist under her chin.

"When you put it that way," he said, "I have no choice but to consider." Music played from wherever he was, a few quick guitar riffs. "Why don't you bring by this paperwork, and I'll see what I can do. This afternoon?" I agreed, and he gave me an address in a part of West Hollywood I'd never been to. As soon as I hung up, it occurred to me that a coffee shop or park seemed safer than what might be some back alley. But I'd agreed, so I was headed there at three.

My reward for finding Gabe was a forty-five-minute drive back to Calabasas, and the shunting of my gym spreadsheet to one of the interns. These faceless peons worked in the production office in Glendale and had all the disadvantages of my own PA job without the perk of getting paid. They couldn't necessarily be trusted to do a good job, but there wasn't much risk in this particular endeavor.

X-Man, Rahul mouthed from behind his camera when I slipped back on set.

"What did I miss?"

"Not much. She's been on the phone. He's talking about repainting the railings on their upstairs balcony. The usual shit."

"Fun."

"Cassidy!" Lauren walked up behind me. "Go to Sherwin-Williams and grab all the sample cards in any shade of navy. Or any dark kind of blue."

"Right now?" She rolled her eyes at me. "I'm meeting this guy in West Hollywood. To sign the thing for Dan." I wasn't unaware of stoking a fire here—Dan had seniority, and Lauren didn't appreciate the reminder.

"Okay, go to the Home Depot in West Hollywood then."

"Is there one?"

"Figure it out."

I popped in to update Dan on my progress, then went back out to my car. I was really putting miles on the old girl, or at least putting in time. In LA, I could spend the same amount of time going three blocks that I might going thirty miles without traffic.

Earlier that day, before Dan burst out of Video Village with his laptop and a quest, back when I was supposed to be spreadsheeting and flipping through the phone book, I had been watching Jason and Maggie. It was too cold for the pool, but she'd asked what the point of having it was if they weren't going to use it, so they'd gone out together to sit on the lounge chairs. She had her feet in his lap. They'd been quiet for a moment, waiting, I supposed, for inspiration. No one followed them out—Dan must have decided that the mounted camera could get what we needed—and so for that moment they had the illusion of being alone. After eight weeks of filming, they knew that they were never alone, but just because you know a magician is showing you tricks doesn't mean you can't, for a moment, declare that you believe in magic.

I might have been wrong. They might have been thinking about how that camera was watching them. They might have seen me watching them through the dining room windows. But if they were, they did a better job of hiding it than usual, a better job of playing themselves straight. Jason massaged Maggie's foot. She tilted her head in his direction.

I'd felt an ache, watching their ease with one another. When I thought of the show as their shot at the spotlight, it was easy to write off their relationship as staged for the cameras. But up close, when they weren't doing their sitcom-marriage bit, they truly seemed to like each other. He was always seeking her out, looking across the room to get her approval. She was always touching him.

I'd had exactly one real, long-term relationship—the cute and kind and not-quite-right-for-me guy that I had crashed with in New York. Watching the way Maggie and Jason sat together by the pool, the way they knew each other's bodies, anticipated each other's next moves, I felt a slice of regret that it hadn't worked out.

I might have been dreaming of my own foot massage under a cabana, but my reality was TV bureaucracy. The closest hardware store to the address Gabe had given me was in Thai Town, and I wasn't going to be able to get in, grab all the different swatches of blue paint, and get out in time to meet him in West Hollywood by three. Instead, I went straight to our meeting spot. It was a squat converted warehouse with a row of mailboxes in the lobby and limited street parking. In a moment of panic, I thought he'd brought me to an abandoned office and now was going to rape and/or murder me, and all Celia would be able to tell my mom about where I had gone was that the guy's name had been Gabe. But that seemed so counter to the errand I was on that I decided it couldn't be possible. I circled the block; there was nowhere to park.

By the time I realized I was going to have to suck it up and walk half a mile, I was already ten minutes late. I just had to get in and get out, grab a quick signature. I double-parked out front, blocking a fire hydrant.

The building had a buzzer, but someone had propped open the main door with the broken heel of a stiletto. This did not bode well for my possible murder, and I clutched the manila folder with Gabe's unsigned release like a key chain of mace I could deploy. What was Dan thinking sending me alone to solicit a strange man? Didn't he know I was young and impressionable and clearly very weak? He'd seen me struggle to carry all that AV equipment. I left the shoe in the door—figuring there was just as much danger within as without, so it was best to keep the easy exit open—and went to look at the mailboxes. A few were labeled with last names, but others read things like "The Pencil Pack" or "Oboe"—businesses, if strangely named ones, the fact of which reassured me. I was trying to figure out if there was a letter missing in "Ball on," or if it was maybe a porn company, when an inner door opened.

"You're here." Gabe was just as tempting as I remembered. Rangy but still muscular, with lips that on a girl you'd swear had been enhanced with filler. Thick brows over hooded blue eyes. Dimples in both cheeks when he smiled. He had on a gray T-shirt advertising a little-known punk band's world tour, and his hair was just a tiny bit too long. *Get in and get out,* I reminded myself.

"Yeah," I said. "Sorry I didn't buzz. There's a . . ." I gestured toward the broken high heel.

"Huh. Cannot explain that." Gabe's mouth twitched, but he didn't outright laugh. When he shrugged, I was drawn again to his hands, adorned in the same jewelry he'd had on when I first met him: the fancy watch, the thumb ring. He broadcast a nervous energy, fingertips tapping in a pattern against his thumb, and I sensed that, were we sitting down, his leg would be espresso-jittering.

"Anyway, I have the paper here," I said, trying not to let on how much he intrigued me. "Also, I'm sorry about your car."

He gave me a look that was longer and more assessing than the way you would look at someone you weren't at least a little bit interested in.

"Water under the bridge," he said. "Consider it forgotten entirely." He smiled. "I hope you didn't have too rough a drive."

"Whatever." I shrugged. "I'm on the clock for it." Something was fluttering fast between us, the wing of an insect. In the quiet I could almost hear the infinitesimal buzz.

"You wanna come in?" Gabe nodded toward the door behind us.

My body hummed like I'd just come off running a marathon, an endorphin high that made me lightheaded. I didn't know his last name, and I was totally sober, sticky from my carousel of car rides, wearing an old pair of ratty underwear, yet I couldn't quite rule out the possibility that we were about to hook up. I was indeed on the clock. But those hands. Those dimples. He smiled again, and I knew he could tell at least some of what I was thinking.

"There's other people back there," he assured me. "The band hasn't left."

"There's a band?"

"Well yeah," he said. "My band."

"You have a band?"

"Come on in."

This was not, in fact, a conventional office building but a studio space. The band—a guy putting away a bass guitar, another lounging near a drum set—greeted me in a way that made me think I was not the first young thing Gabe had brought back behind the scenes.

"Oh no," I said, correcting their unspoken assumption. Even more embarrassing than my own intense attraction was its public recognition. "I just have this paper for him to sign, and then I'm going to go."

"Don't let us bother you," said the drum guy, although I wasn't sure to me or to Gabe. It was three in the afternoon, but in the windowless studio, it might have been midnight. Where Maggie's recording space felt like a glamorous cave, this was more like the basement of a fraternity house. Cleaner than a frat, I would give it that, but with the same bare-bones vibe of dude and purpose. Presumably they'd been at their task since before I had called Gabe that morning. A few expensive-looking guitars lay spread out across the floor.

"I just need you to sign," I said. The three of them looked at each other.

"What's this for?" asked Bass.

"A release. So we don't have to blur out his face on TV." Surely people in entertainment were familiar with this concept. I had explained it to Gabe over the phone.

"It's for real." Bass raised his eyebrows. "She's actually got paperwork for you."

"I knew it," said Drums. "I knew it, dude. She didn't realize. You owe me twenty bucks."

"Okay," I said. "I'm missing something. What's going on?"

Gabe chewed on the side of his cheek, that restless energy increasing exponentially. Drums turned to me. "You have to imagine him like two feet shorter with blond tips and a smushed-up face."

It seemed that Gabe was someone I was supposed to know, either someone I'd gone to school with or somebody famous. Had he been friends with my brother? Did he do college a capella? I tried to see the picture Drums painted, but I'd never been much good at visualizations. "Okay," I said finally. "I'm sorry for not knowing what you're talking about, but can we cut to the chase?"

"I did a TV show when I was younger," Gabe muttered. "I thought that was why you wanted to get together. It's no big deal."

Except he said this in the way that people do when it is, in fact, a big deal.

"What's the show?"

"*The Tiger Crew*." He gave a little shrug, as if he was sorry I'd caught him.

"Wait," I said. "Wait. With Maggie—"

"With Maggie McKee!" Bass said, gleeful.

"But she's on my show. The one I'm working on." It slipped out before I could stop myself, my professionalism no match for the combination of confusion and sexual tension I was currently experiencing. "I ran into you coming down her driveway."

"That's sort of why I thought you knew."

"He thought you knew because he thought you were coming to—" Drums started. He was interrupted by a combination of a police siren going off outside and an elbow from Gabe.

"Oh shit," I said. Gabe started to say something, but I shook him off. "No, it's not you. I just remembered my car."

"I don't usually just assume people know who I am," Gabe was saying. He'd trailed me down the hall to the elevator. "But you knew my name, so I figured you, I dunno, were a fan. I thought the release was a red herring because we'd, you know. That you were using it to . . . get together."

"A red herring? We're in a mystery now?" I couldn't help teasing him. It was rare to find someone so objectively hot who didn't try to hide his insecurities. "I knew your name because I heard your friends say it when we were on the phone."

"Well, now I feel dumb."

"Were you guys, like, betting on me?"

"No!" Gabe had the decency to look appalled. "No, I didn't—oh, you're kidding."

"Did you make money? If you did, we should split it."

It was a joke, but I did think it seemed fair, especially since I wasn't sure if production would pay a parking ticket I got on their errand. I'd seen Lauren dole out cash for incidentals, yet this seemed less an incidental than a stupid move on my part. Which reminded me—the paperwork.

"Here's the release." I pulled the folder out from under my arm. "It's real. You can check."

We'd reached the ground floor, and he walked with me down the hall to the main entrance. "Those guys are assholes. I'm an asshole. Obviously, I feel like an idiot."

I turned to look right at him. He seemed nervous. I felt a strange urge to take his face in my hands. His earnest face, so eager to correct my bad impression. Had he not towered over me, I might have. Instead, I looked directly into his eyes as I said, "It's no big deal."

Of course he'd been on TV. Those eyes were too blue not to be.

I had watched some of *The Tiger Crew*, but I still couldn't place him. The show had aired right when I got home from elementary school: kids in neon vests and sparkly bowler hats singing about math homework, baking brownies and going roller-skating and doing sketches about passing notes in class.

"I did—" He started, stopped, shook his head. Decided to suck it up and tell me. "After the other day, I did want you to call."

I didn't have a witty retort to throw back at him; instead, I'm pretty sure I blushed.

"But now you get why I can't sign," he continued.

"Wait, what?" I was thrown by the agility with which we moved from pleasure to business. Looking into his eyes had slowed me down to half speed, and now I struggled to catch up.

"Yeah, I'm not going to let you put a clip of me gawking at Maggie onto her TV show. It's a terrible look."

How should I play this? I sensed much more to Gabe than his physical restlessness, his sincerity, or even his good looks, a below-the-surface self that intrigued me. I liked this guy. I wanted to deliver for Dan. I needed his signature.

There was no way for me to ask if Gabe was jealous of Maggie and not have it come off mean-spirited. I still couldn't place him, not short or smushed-faced or at all, and assuring him that nobody on our crew had recognized him either was clearly not going to win me any points. Instead I said, "Were you friends with her?"

Gabe sighed. He faced some inner turmoil, a shadow passing as he considered what to say.

"I had," he told me, "the universe's biggest crush."

I waited. "And do you still?" This was bold on my end. He'd come somewhat clean about our chemistry, but I hadn't.

Gabe looked at me. His lip twitched. I found myself anxious for his answer.

"Nah," he said. "It was forever ago. But to have worked together and been, you know, on equal footing, and then the next time I pop up on TV it's her own show and I'm the creep watching her leave the shopping mall—"

"So you do remember being there."

"—that might be even more embarrassing than what just happened in the studio."

We were at the front door by now. I paused. I could use all this: the awkwardness, my growing attraction. It was all still just story, even if I unexpectedly found myself playing the lead. "What just happened in the studio?"

"I was cocky and assumed that you were angling for a date."

"And do a lot of girls . . . angle?"

"You might be surprised."

I was not surprised in the slightest. "Bad news for them, then. You're really only in the background of our shot. No big star moment. I'm not asking you to sign your life rights away."

"Can I take a look before I agree?"

"Unfortunately, no." I wasn't even going to ask Dan—he'd prefer a blurred-out face to the precedent this would set.

"Well, then I guess we're at an impasse," said Gabe. He was still watching me intently.

"Okay," I said. "Well, if these other girls are onto something, I don't want to miss it. What if you just hold on to this release, read it over, and we can revisit it the next time I see you?" My whole body was tingling, part boldness and part increasing desire to touch him. Instead of his hand, I took one of the business cards production had made for me out of my bag and offered it. Gabe grinned.

"That sounds like an excellent compromise."

I might have kissed him then, if we were actually in a TV show. I certainly wanted to kiss him. Instead, we walked outside to see a fire hydrant and an empty curb. My car was gone, the hydrant newly accessible.

"Oops." I almost started laughing. The lack of car was not especially funny, just Gabe being involved in yet another of my vehicular debacles. And it could have been worse—I could have been caught carless on my own instead of standing with a guy I did not especially want to say goodbye to.

"That's where you parked?" Gabe winced. "I should have warned you that they tow here all the time."

"That is indeed where I parked," I said. "Also I feel like your impression of my driving is now probably not a good one."

"Well, you're not giving *me* a ride." Gabe pulled out his cell phone. "I have the number for the company saved. Like I said, happens all the time."

"Girls angling, companies towing. What a life."

"You don't know the half of it."

I felt neither guilt about flirting on company time nor a pressing urge to be immediately back in Calabasas. What I did need, though, were those paint samples. The towing company was still processing my car, and the guy said it would be at least an hour before I could go pick it up.

After hanging up with the lot, I turned to Gabe. "If you want to make all this up to me, maybe we should go to Home Depot."

We found all the Sherwin-Williams navy and dark blues and some lighter ones besides.

"Imagine being the person who names all these colors," Gabe said, grabbing a swatch. "Loch Blue. Scuba Blue. Blue Nile. Adriatic Sea. How do you decide which one is Adriatic and which one is, say, Balkan?"

"Well, someone clearly couldn't," I said, holding up a pale blue that had simply been named Watery.

"This is for a balcony?" asked Gabe. He seemed much surer of himself here at the hardware store, now that we had a task to accomplish and we'd somewhat clarified our aims.

"I think a balcony railing."

"Okay," he said, turning to face me. "Important question. If you were painting your own balcony railing, which color would you choose?"

"Ah yes, a very important question," I said.

"Gets right down to the good stuff." It meant the world to me that Gabe didn't break. He blinked at me, expectant, Charlie Rose to Bill Gates.

"Well, first let me consider my nonexistent balcony," I said. "Is it a Juliet or more of a porch thing? Can it fit a hot tub?"

"Why shouldn't you have it all?" Gabe had moved closer to me on the pretense of looking at the neutrals. His arm brushed mine, and I tried to play it cool.

"I guess it doesn't really matter, given that the average person paints their railings black," I said. "Until today, I didn't even realize you could pick another color."

Gabe smelled like pine needles. I hoped I didn't smell like KFC. We meandered together toward checkout.

"Black," he said. "You have the soul of an artist."

"I had Tori Amos on repeat all through high school," I said. "The sensitive artistic type, that's me." He didn't know me well enough to know that I was kidding, and for a moment, I considered the glitter of reinvention, the potential of a relationship where I could be someone brand new. But I wasn't a performer. "I'm joking," I said, hoping he already sensed it. "But tell me about your art. Does your band make the perfect bop, or are you, like, soul searching?"

"You don't like Tori?" Gabe put on being wounded/surprised. He was avoiding my question.

"I'm sort of neutral. I don't dislike her, I just never Kool-Aid dyed my hair."

"Ah yes. Whereas I am a proud member of the Kool-Aid dye fan club," said Gabe. I laughed. I couldn't remember the last time I had so genuinely enjoyed someone I also found attractive. I wondered if working on a show about love was turning me soft.

"Soul searching, then." I answered my earlier question.

"Why shouldn't we have it all?" Gabe echoed himself. He looked up, and I realized we were in the lighting aisle, surrounded by various chandeliers. Hardware store dust in the air, the beeping of a dolly as it lifted someone to the hard-to-reach cabinetry. Bronze and gold lanterns at a hodgepodge of angles, bare bulbs and black lattice and, everywhere, white light glimmering through. I wanted him to kiss me then and there.

Gabe the musician. Well, why shouldn't I have it all?

Gabe dropped me off at my car, and had I not had to pay the towing company a large chunk of my paycheck, I might have considered this the most successful first date I'd ever been on.

When I got home that night and filled Celia in, she threw a piece of popcorn at me.

"How could you not have told me that Gabe is Gabriel Leighton? Unbelievable."

"I literally did not know his last name until you said it just now."

"Oh my god, you totally know him. He was the really dinky one, super scrawny, the nerd who was always paired with Sam C.? In the 'Where Are They Now' in *Us Weekly*, I think he said he was doing music."

"He's definitely doing music," I said. "That I know." During our time at Home Depot, I had learned that Gabe was, like me, a fairly recent transplant to Los Angeles. He was working on an album, which I assumed meant that somebody was funding him but might have meant that he was making demos.

"We have to find old clips," said Celia. "Remember how they were always like, 'Until next time, I'm so-and-so' and then did those weird little a capella harmonies? Is there a box set of *The Tiger Crew*? I wish it was easier to find things that used to be on TV."

We couldn't find any footage that night, and Gabe's internet presence just confirmed what he had told me. Born in Sacramento, three seasons on *The Tiger Crew*, and had been songwriting in Nashville for the past several years. We dug around for a minute and couldn't easily find any of his music, but we did go down a rabbit hole of Tiger Crew alumni. Most of the kids who'd joined the Crew had gone on to live fairly normal lives—there were a few, like Maggie, who'd parlayed their child stardom into reasonable careers, and one or two who'd hit true diva, but the majority of the names Celia remembered and searched were now parenting or doing real estate or running wellness camps for rich Los Angelenos. Celia kept bubbling, feeding me questions to ask Gabe.

Did they all make out with each other behind the scenes? What was the food like on the studio lot? Was it hard to transition away from child stardom? Would he do the show again if he could go back in time? Where should we do our double date?

I was not going to ask any of this. I assumed that I would see Gabe again at least once. Continuing on after that seemed unlikely. He was a celebrity. What were the chances he'd want to hang out in my crappy apartment, eating Cup Noodles? Like Romeo and Juliet, we came from different worlds. Our attraction would never hold up against the scrutiny of Hollywood cameras.

But in the back of my mind, I had the terrifying suspicion that if I let him, Gabe could be my Jason Dean.

October 2007

The restaurant's cleared out when Celia and I go back inside, only Jen and a few straggling relatives remaining.

"They've all gone off to some bar," says Jen. "As the bride, you're not invited. You're supposed to head back and rest up. Can't see the groom until you get to the altar."

"It's more romantic that way?" Celia frowns.

"Much less romantic," says Jen. "But it's tradition."

"Did Maggie McKee show up early?" My voice sounds strangled to my own ears, but my friends don't seem to notice.

"I don't think so. Still expected late tonight." Jen finds my purse, then Celia's. "But she and Jason will definitely be there tomorrow to take the pressure off you guys."

The pressure. Tomorrow. I'm supposed to put on a bridal gown and talk into a camera about how glad I am to marry my fiancé. Sentiments that, until about ten minutes ago, were totally genuine. I'm supposed to smile and laugh and be aspirational, but also down to earth. Pretty, but not too pretty. Suddenly, I'm remembering Maggie on set, reading *TIME* magazine. The way she'd looked up at me, the resignation in her smile. *How well do you really know him, Cassidy?*

I call Gabe, but his phone goes to voicemail. In the cab back to the venue, I listen to Celia babble on about one of Gabe's hot cousins, and type out a long text message I know I won't send. I flick through my phone contacts, hoping futilely to come across Maggie's number, long deleted, likely changed. Jen said she's not in town yet. Gabe could have been talking to anyone. It could be any secret he was referencing, any disaster.

But I'm convinced Maggie McKee has something to do with this. Yet again, Maggie is sticking her fingers in the pie, then coquettishly licking off the obvious evidence.

Maggie McKee. She is attraction and repulsion. She has ruined my best thing, but also brought it into being. I don't know if, from the start, she has been clawing me down with her or trying to save my life. I have to know before I'm asked at the altar if I do.

5.

October 2002

Another early episode of *Honeymoon Stage* features a clip of Maggie from *The Tiger Crew* paired with old footage of Jason on the mound. In order to establish our leading man and woman, we have to understand where they've come from. In Maggie's case, it is a stage with can lights and choreography that heavily involves the rotation of her elbows, other preteens in massively oversize sequined shirts and equally large grins. Jason's arm is also the star of his early career. In home videos of his Little League games, he's blurry in an aquamarine T-shirt, his mother overloud as she cheers behind the camcorder. Shots of him on the mound when he played for the Phillies, people lined up in Dean jerseys while holding homemade signs. Jason, on top of the world for the few years that he was starting. And then you hear our show's signature sad music—a couple of lines a guy in a studio plunked out in probably ten minutes on an electric piano—over a montage of Jason's injury: that first time he stopped the game and walked off clutching his elbow, images from rehab with his arm stuck in ice, the comeback game when he threw seven scoreless innings. And then the famous footage from a game three weeks later when his curveball went into the stands. He squeezes his eyes shut, loosens up, and tries another. He winces. The ball barely leaves his hand before the whole stadium knows from the look on his face that he's done. They don't make him face the press until a few weeks later when he announces his early retirement.

"What will you do, now that baseball is over?" Jason sits alone behind the table with the microphone, and it's clear he doesn't know.

I kept talking with Gabe after our trip to Home Depot, at first under the guise of checking in on the release I knew he wasn't going to sign, and then with no pretensions at all, simply because I liked talking to him. Gabe had been the one to reach out the morning after our tow truck date with a tepid Hi. sent to the work email address I had on my business card. I was online, checking in with Lauren before heading out to Calabasas, but of course I had to pause getting ready for work to analyze his brevity with Celia and Jen.

"He wouldn't have reached out if he didn't want to talk to you," Celia said, voice raised over the shower. "He probably doesn't realize how weird it is to send an email with just *hi* and a period."

"Is it weird?" Jen was brushing her teeth. "Or does it mean he knows grammar? Would you think it was weird if he had said it over AIM or MSN Messenger?"

Celia dropped her voice an octave to imitate Gabe. "'Hey, hottie, loved getting plywood yesterday hope your bumper hasn't fallen off from all the rough stuff I've done to your car.' No punctuation."

Jen spat into the sink. "'I'm so excited to do rough stuff to you,' comma, 'if you know what I mean,' period."

"Ew." I frowned. "You've ruined it."

I didn't respond until I was hunkered down with Dan in Video Village later that morning, email open as I messed around with spreadsheets.

Hey. Fun times with the tow truck yesterday. You changed your mind yet about my release? Then I made a little smiley face out of a parenthesis and colon, to let him know I was at least kind of kidding.

Yeah came back immediately. He must have also been at his computer. You know, I've actually decided why stop there? You can cast me as her personal assistant. Very good for my career.

I looked up at Dan, who was talking to someone via headset. I could continue this if I wanted to. I pictured Gabe, thought *What the hell*, and hit the ball back.

> You never really filled me in on said career. How can I cast you if I don't know your full range of talents?
>
> Unicycle
>
> Unicycle?
>
> Yup, that's all I've got.

I laughed out loud, which meant Dan noticed me, which meant I was sent off to xerox signs.

Ugh sorry, I'm at work. More detail please later. I gave him both my AIM screen name and my personal email.

Gabe wasn't the first guy I'd flirted with in LA, but as the weeks went on, he was the most consistent. Our conversations were unserious. We talked about his bandmates and the things that we found weird about LA. We liked the pop-up street food, bemoaned the lack of refrigerators in most rental apartments. Gabe told me his parents were in town and wanted to ride on a double-decker tour bus. I told Gabe that I missed weather. He asked if I was only happy when it rained.

> Oh I forgot you're in the Kool Aid club.

It's nice here, you should drink some.

He didn't say much about his music, and he extended no invitations to come hear him play. I did, however, complain about my own job. As promised, it had taken over my life, which meant that I was much less focused on whatever was happening between us than I surely would have been had I still supported myself by walking famous dogs. It also meant we struggled to find time to get together in person.

Things on set were nonstop, which was funny since there never seemed to be all that much happening. On the few sets I'd sat in on, crews were under time pressure to get a particular shot or finish a take. Someone was always yelling out *Five more minutes*, and there were people swooping in to touch up makeup just before the director yelled *Action*. Things were either obviously in progress or finished or else, to everyone's chagrin, still to come. On *Honeymoon Stage*, we were rolling with the punches. Nothing was ever finished, because nothing was ever planned. Dan would be in Video Village keeping an eye on all the still cameras, and if he saw something he thought looked promising, he would round us all up to go in for cross coverage. For every eight hours of shooting, the show would use about one minute of footage, which could be both a relief and a pain in the ass.

I was surprised to find how good I was at rolling with the punches. I could pivot with the best of them, sometimes preempting Lauren in knowing how to feed into a cast member's reaction or center a scene. I'd put on muscle from all the equipment I'd been carrying, and though I hadn't hit the gym in weeks, I felt good about my body. I was competent and strong. When I called in sick with food poisoning, Lauren seemed truly distressed. The crew liked me. They needed me.

I had the most fun when we were off site. Being part of the film and TV industry gave me access. I liked exploring parts of LA that were previously off limits to me—restaurants with menu items I couldn't pronounce, black cars that I couldn't afford, charity golf outings and VIP rooms at exclusive clubs. Jason and Maggie were going to Mexico for their anniversary, which would wrap up our season, and though I hadn't been officially invited, I was angling to join.

Maggie traveled a lot on her own—to give concerts and film commercials and occasionally audition for TV or film—but she didn't always bring along a crew. The show, after all, was about her and Jason. People wanted to see them together doing—or failing to do—normal married-couple things; they were less interested in her actual career. This meant that when Maggie was at home, the crew was always on top of her. We caught her doing crunches in her home gym or trying to sort laundry. Her mother would visit, and they'd gossip about somebody's boyfriend, using made-up names. Occasionally she'd practice choreography, or screen an early cut of a music video, or sit scribbling down an idea for a song, all under the eyes of the cameras. Often, she and Jason would sit together on the couch, watching baseball and bantering. In their 1970s-style sunken living room, they had a wraparound sofa that could comfortably seat up to twenty people, and they'd lie with their legs intertwined while Jason dissed some player's strategy and Maggie nodded along, pretending to care. Maybe she actually did care. They seemed to watch a lot of baseball for a couple only one of whom liked the game.

About two months into my *Honeymoon Stage* tenure, I was at the house while Maggie and Jason got ready for a charity dinner—likely something for poor animals, which this town much preferred to poor people. Jason had just gotten back from working out and was going to take a quick shower, and Maggie was already up in her room with her team. One of the running jokes of the show was that Maggie was forever getting ready while Jason yelled up the stairs that it was majorly past time for them to go. On-screen, this played as him pacing the front hall, growing progressively more frustrated. In reality, he'd watch TV, or take a call, or once he even made eggs while the car idled out front and Maggie put on her finishing touches. Maggie had her own personal hair-and-makeup people on call, and they were constantly in and out of the house. Brent, Maggie's hair guy, was a hoot. He had first come to LA to be an actor, and while he didn't have the constitution for the regular rejection, his impressions were spectacular. Sally Ann was always down to gossip, and between the two of them, they'd keep Maggie grinning through her prep. Much of what they discussed was too dirty or salacious to air. It gave me the feeling that the house was a safe space, that there was a circle of trust in which not all Maggie's relationships were merely transactional.

Six months later, I would rack my brain to remember specifics of these conversations that had not been recorded, looking for signs of what was to come. But the nature of toxicity is that it hides in plain sight—a chemical staining your lipstick a shade you'll literally die for.

That night, the fire alarm in the upstairs hallway had been giving off weird flashes of light, and I'd been dispatched to go figure out what was wrong with it. Had they not been busy, this would have been a great activity for Jason and Maggie. He'd pull the thing out of the ceiling while she fluttered below him, asking questions about eardrum damage and secondhand smoke. As it was, they had their dinner for the animals, and Lauren wasn't comfortable keeping the alarm on the fritz until they returned.

When I got up on a ladder and yanked the monitor out of its slot, it gave off three sharp yelps.

"Oh!" Maggie opened her door and peered up at me. "I'm glad somebody's fixing that."

"At least trying to," I said, pressing the reset button. Maggie had on a short red dress with a cowl-neck and a full lace back. Her hair had been curled, and her makeup perfected. The perfume she used was something fruity with vanilla, and I caught a whiff of it as she came over.

"You can probably just turn it off," she said. This struck me as a dangerous idea. "We'd all still be perfectly safe. There's one in each of the bedrooms and another at the end of the hall. Jason's memorabilia cost more than the rest of the house put together. It's very well protected."

I popped out the batteries, slotted the monitor back in, and climbed down. Maggie's bra strap showed through the lace on her shoulder, and if she were Jen or Celia I'd have said something and helped her tuck it away. Instead, I did a weird sort of shimmy with my arm to try to silently communicate. She just stood there.

"So, this thing tonight," I said. She hadn't gone back in her room, so I waited by the ladder. "It'll be fun?"

Maggie shrugged. "It'll be fine. Jason's not drinking." Jason was on the wagon three weeks out of the month and hanging slightly off the other one. I had the sense that a camera crew was good for him—we kept him in line. He wasn't—it had been explained to me numerous times by various members of his team—an alcoholic.

"Does that make it less fun?" I asked, genuinely curious.

"Not really," Maggie said. Her door hung open, and through it I'd expected to see her team, discarded dresses on the bed, abandoned lipsticks. Instead, the room was clean and empty.

"Jason's still getting dressed," I said. "And you're all ready." The look she gave me told me that she knew where I was going, that she'd been waiting for me to get there. "Why do you let them make it seem like you're up here taking forever while he waits?"

Maggie looked up at the fire alarm, the light fixture in the ceiling. "I know what they say about me," she said. "If they're going to say it anyway, it might as well be on my own terms."

I thought that I knew some of what they said about her—at least I knew how Dan bitched and how Lauren complained. Rahul thought she was a spoiled brat, and Eli wanted to sleep with her. Vinnie never said anything unkind, but that was Vinnie. It was possible he had a novel of frustrations he would never let anyone read.

A few weeks after I'd moved west, one of my ex's friends had accidentally texted me about how *fucked in the head Cassidy was* and how he was *actually much better off without her*. Clearly the guy had our numbers confused and was saying what any pal would say to his friend. Still, I had been hurt. How would I feel knowing that strangers everywhere were dissecting my waistline or my smile, debating the authenticity of my breasts or the functioning of my brain? Nobody had ever looked at a piece of my life and assumed that, by doing so, they'd put together all of me.

Just then Jason came down the hall in his undershirt and dress pants, a towel slung over his shoulder.

"What up, Cassidy? You need help carrying that ladder?" I shook my head. He turned to Maggie. "You look beautiful, babe."

This seemed like my cue to head downstairs, but Maggie was still watching me. She had so much that we children of the '80s had been taught was important: an expensive red lace dress and glimmering purple eyeshadow, a huge solitaire diamond winking at me from her left hand and a smaller set dangling from her ears. My jeans had a massive rip in the knee and another beginning at the crotch, which meant I'd spent the day walking like a robot so as not to rip them open and bare myself to the whole crew. There was some kind of grease from the ladder smeared across my inner arm. But that didn't seem to be why she was looking at me. Why was she still standing here? What could I offer her?

"Have a great night, guys," I said, closing the ladder. As I was turning the corner, I saw Jason gently rearrange that strap from Maggie's bra.

That evening, I called Gabe on my drive home. Despite three weeks of online banter, we hadn't seen each other since our date at Home Depot. Mostly this was due to my long work hours, but it was also because the thought of our potential next steps together made me nervous. The more I got to know Gabe, the more I thought we had the makings of an actual relationship. He would call me every few days, but usually I could only whisper a quick "Try me again later" from set. That night was the first time I'd called him.

"Well, hello." Gabe's voice provided the perfect antidote to six p.m. traffic.

"Hi," I said. "I'm driving home. If I hang up on you suddenly it's because I've been rear-ended."

"I'll come look for you on the 101."

"Actually," I said, "want to come look for me at my tiny and probably not-so-clean apartment in Silver Lake? And then maybe together we can go look for, say, dinner?"

I was surprised at how easy it was to ask him out. I wasn't tripping over my words or feeling nauseated or immediately regretting things. Maybe watching Jason and Maggie's genuine affection had been good for me.

When Gabe got to my place, I was getting out of the shower, but Jen and Celia were both home to let him in. It was immediately apparent that I should have had Gabe meet me at a restaurant. Jen acted normal, but Celia turned into a new version of herself. I could hear them through the wall as I got dressed.

"Oh my god, you got so tall." She had on her coffee shop voice, a higher, brighter tone than when she spoke to me and Jen.

"Lucky for me." Gabe also sounded different, an awkward politeness I hadn't heard before.

"Jen didn't watch your show, so she doesn't know. He was so little! The little sweet one." I was sure Celia would spend most of her evening regretting this whole interaction.

"Do you want something to drink?" Jen's relative normalcy made me feel less like I should abandon my makeup and rescue him. I hadn't yet had the opportunity to look pretty for Gabe.

"I'm okay, thanks."

When I got out to them, about ten minutes later, he was sitting on the edge of the couch with both my roommates flitting around him, though Jen, at least, was refilling his plastic cup of wine.

"You took a while." She raised an eyebrow.

Gabe looked up at me. It was a shock to see him again after so much digital flirtation, and he was just as magnetic as I had remembered. He had on dark-wash jeans and a button-down instead of a T-shirt, which gave me confidence that he, too, viewed this as an actual date.

He greeted me with a hug that would have been awkward even without nerves, given our difference in height, but touching him made me a live wire. My head buzzed with the sound that little metal thing made when it brushed up against the sides in the game Operation. *Wake up,* my body told me. *Pay attention.* Celia and Jen watched us leave like proud parents, waving at me from behind the curtain hanging in our kitchen window.

Neither Gabe nor I had thought about where we should go.

"I realize now maybe I should have planned ahead," I said.

"And ruined all the fun of circling the neighborhood? Never. What are you in the mood for? Tacos? Burgers?" I didn't care and told him it was nice just to be having dinner.

"My one night off for, like, the next three weeks."

We went to a Mexican place, and over steak quesadillas, I learned that Gabe was not a vegan. He thought animals were fine, but he'd be perfectly happy not to ever have pets of his own. If he *had* to have a dog, he'd be okay with it, so long as it wasn't a loud one. His ideal morning was spent hanging out at home, playing music on his guitar.

"What kind of music?" I asked. "It's weird that we've been talking for so long and I don't know what kind of music."

Gabe shrugged, getting fidgety. "Just stuff I write."

"Well, duh." I almost asked him if he was actually in a boy band that he'd neglected to mention, but, sensing his tenderness, decided to stop myself from teasing him. "We'll get there," I said. "I'll get it out of you eventually." I could feel each of my heartbeats, the strength of that *eventually* and what it implied. Gabe had been shy, but now his eyes filled with a confident intensity. I swallowed. "So, you play guitar?" I figured this question was generic enough.

"Guitar and piano." I couldn't stop watching his hands. They were on the tabletop, fingers drumming. I imagined them holding my face, thumb on my pulse point. I imagined them running the length of my body, and could feel myself flush.

"And that's how you got onto *The Tiger Crew*? By playing guitar and piano?"

Gabe laughed, breaking our tension. "I got onto *The Tiger Crew* by placing second in an Elvis Presley impersonation competition."

"I'm sorry, what? How could you not have mentioned this the second we met?" I called the server over to order another round of drinks.

"I got into Elvis through my uncle, who was always playing his records. I used to sing along and do these bits, and my uncle heard about this contest when I was ten. They put a clip of me on the local news, and my parents got a call from an agent."

"Why didn't you place first?"

"It was an adult competition. What do you want from poor preteen me?"

I knew what I wanted from twenty-five-year-old him. Our legs touched under the table.

"Anyway, I liked performing and playing music, and school was a bummer, and a variety show seemed as good a road as any. It was cool to make money. My parents weren't weird about that part. They put it away for me, and I wasn't our sole breadwinner or anything. But they had to pack up and move me and my older sister down to Florida, where the show was filming. They traded our house for a condo, and I've sort of felt like I had to prove that they made the right call ever since. Otherwise, it was a fairly cushy gig."

"For a ten-year-old."

"By then I was, like, twelve."

After the show he'd moved to Nashville, where he'd worked writing songs for other people, which was fine, but he'd have rather been performing on his own. He wasn't trying to be some sort of pop superstar; he just wanted the songs to feel real. Country music wasn't cutting it—hence the move to LA, with the band guys I'd met at their studio.

I didn't have an Elvis-contest origin story, but it would have been simple enough to tell him about my mom in Pennsylvania and my own childhood obsession with TV. I was too nervous, so instead, in exchange for details about Gabe's life, I offered him bits about *Honeymoon Stage*. Although I'd signed an NDA, it seemed innocuous to share the little stories from our set. Sally Ann often came in with sex hair. Maggie's manager had fake teeth that he could pop in and out. Jason's cousin dipped tobacco, and sometimes when he spat into a cup, little brown droplets hit the couch, which I then had to clean so that it wouldn't be gross for the show. They kept the pool at eighty-five degrees. Maggie wasn't as dumb as she seemed.

"That doesn't surprise me," said Gabe. I hadn't quite forgotten that he'd crushed on her ten years ago, rather had been successfully storing that bit of trivia in a part of my brain that would keep it from complicating whatever the two of us were developing.

"That's right, you know her."

"Knew her," he said. "It's been a while."

"I bet she'd want to say hello, if you ever stopped by." It could be nice for Maggie to see an old friend. She didn't seem to have many.

"It might be weird," Gabe said. I didn't press further. Something in me knew that asking Gabe to divulge more would change things between us, complicate our attraction in a way that I wasn't ready for. He was an itch I was both dying and terrified to scratch.

Gabe was a gentleman, and he left me at my door with a kiss. He leaned down, and I stood on my tiptoes with my hands on his shoulders.

Kissing Gabe was unlocking a secret garden door, then standing in awe at its threshold. I wanted all of him, but settled for his lips and teeth and tongue. He was a muscular kisser, deliberate and firm. I could have invited him back up to my room, but I didn't.

"I think I like you," I said, hiding my face in his chest before going inside.

"And I like you."

Much of the time on the *Honeymoon Stage* set, Maggie was at her computer or running errands or at the studio while Jason putzed around the house. In one episode, Jason decides that he wants to have a kitchen garden, never mind that neither he nor Maggie cooks. This idea was Lauren's—she'd get nervous about the risk involved in some of the things he wanted to do with ladders or forklifts, and was always steering him toward more insurance-friendly tasks. Here he is buying seeds at the hardware store. Here he is digging up sod, sweat pooling under his white undershirt, which he then removes and uses to wipe his dirty brow. It was rare to see one of Jason's projects reach completion. Their purpose, both for his own use and that of the show, was to give the feeling of purposefulness rather than actually accomplish a task. Off camera, we'd often hire a handyman to finish what he'd started.

When the digging is done and it comes time to plan this kitchen garden, Jason calls through the house to see if anyone grew up on a farm. Eli did, but he's behind the camera, so Dan tells him to pretend that he didn't. Maggie has just left for a photo shoot. Her hair-and-makeup team comes clomping down the stairs. Brent shrugs, goes to the fridge for a Red Bull.

"Maybe I can help?" says Sally Ann.

I was not invited on the vacation to Mexico. Production brought all the field producers, four of the camera guys, Vinnie for sound, and some executive's niece and her friend to be PAs. Lauren and Dan both grumbled, but there wasn't anything they could do. I thought I'd get the week off, might spend it sleeping or visiting Gabe at his studio. Instead, they asked if I would babysit the house.

I was at the house constantly, but I'd not once been alone in it. The first night that I spent tucked under the white duvet in the small upstairs guest bedroom, I thought each whoosh of the air conditioner was someone trying to break in. When the lawn sprinklers went off on their seven a.m. timer, I spilled a full cup of coffee on myself. I showered it off in the en suite guest bathroom, my chin lifted to the waterfall showerhead, soothed by the dark-gray stone. That evening my anxiety spiked. There were burglaries all over Los Angeles, and even though my neighborhood was objectively less safe than Calabasas, I never worried when I was at home, because we had nothing to burgle. No self-respecting thief would find it worthwhile to shimmy up the building's drainpipe for our secondhand cast-iron skillet or our set of mismatched chairs. At Jason and Maggie's, bounty was everywhere. Not only did the gated community and pillared porch scream money, but the Dean–McKee duo was also well known. Jason had been a member of the Phillies team that got death threats from a Mets fan back in 1995. People were nuts. You couldn't trust them to be reasonable.

By nine p.m. I'd double-checked all the locks on the doors and double-bolted the garage. My guest room had its own TV, but I felt weird staying there all day, so I was parked in Jason's usual spot in the living room, flipping through channels. Somehow the television light made the rest of the house seem even bigger, even emptier. I covered myself in the loose-knit shawl Maggie had left draped on the back of the couch and was just settling into a made-for-TV movie when I was jolted by the sound of something splatting.

"What the fuck," I said to '90s Tony Danza. The noise had come from the left side of the house, which faced the hills, which in itself made me sure that some creepo had been hiding in the mountains, waiting for Jason and Maggie to leave so he could—what? Steal Jason's baseball stuff? Maggie had told me it was valuable. "We have cameras," I said out loud. No one responded, which was probably, I reasoned, the best-case scenario.

Wrapping the shawl around my chest like armor, I made it to the back patio door. The outdoor lights were on, which meant someone had been there. Those sensors were top of the line; I had tested them myself. I was about to leap to the wall phone and dial 911 when I noticed the bird hopping drunkenly around the patio tile, the smudge on the glass. I felt immediate relief. Those birds were forever flying into the windows. I must have made a beacon of the house with all the lights.

The bird itself was less a threat than a clear warning I was losing it alone in the house, and I still had five more days to go. I considered asking Celia to come stay with me tomorrow. I considered asking Gabe.

Once I'd opened the door to the idea of having Gabe over, it became more and more appealing. I tossed and turned all night debating it. I had known him for eight weeks. We still weren't meeting all that often in person, though we'd begun to talk for longer on the phone. I'd been to his place in the Valley once, on one of my days off, when I didn't have to take care of the parts of my life I'd let backslide. We'd fooled around, but I hadn't spent the night. I'd had to be at work early the next morning. Suddenly, I had no pressing commitments.

The biggest logistical hurdle was the cameras, but I knew all of them and how to make sure they were completely turned off. No one had said I couldn't socialize while house-sitting. There were people at the house all the time, people Jason and Maggie didn't know, people production didn't recognize. It would hurt no one if I ordered some pizza and slept with Gabe in the guest bedroom to hold on to my sanity. It would be fun to have Gabe in Calabasas, to play house. Afterward, I'd wash the sheets.

Though he'd expressed disinterest in coming out to the house when the show was filming, the next morning Gabe jumped at the chance to join me while everyone was gone. I gave him the code for the entry gate, and he came up the main walk around two p.m. carrying Chinese takeout and a six-pack of beer. He noticed the camera by the front door immediately.

"Don't worry," I said. "I turned them all off." I took the beer and stuck it in the fridge, next to Jason's open Muscle Milk and Maggie's uneaten Tupperware of chef-made low-calorie dinner. Gabe did a three-sixty spin to take in the house. In a month, everyone in America would know the layout of this open-plan kitchen / living room, but right now it was just for us.

"Maggie's done well for herself, huh?" Gabe had told me his crush was long healed, but I was struggling not to pick at the scab. Maybe I wanted him to tell me I was more interesting than Maggie McKee.

"Helps to marry a pro athlete," Gabe said. He pulled me over to the sunken living room. "I'd say that they have questionable taste here, but it's excellent for this." And then we were falling onto that questionable couch, and he was kissing me.

I forgot that I was at my place of work, on a couch that, before yesterday, I'd never actually sat on, because it was behind the camera line and I was indisputably crew.

Gabe kissed my clavicle, and his perfect lips moved up my neck to nip my ear. When I'd had sex with other guys, I'd thought too much about power: why I was agreeing; what it would mean if we didn't both get off; what I could say no to and what they'd feel obliged to give. With Gabe, I was simply in the moment.

"We should go to your room," Gabe murmured into my neck.

"Yes," I said. But we were too far gone. We didn't.

There was the tattoo I had noticed the first day that I met him, some sort of coat of arms across his bicep. The long lines of his thighs, the knock of desperate teeth. It was better for having waited, for the freedom of being alone in this house. Gabe's hands had not misled me. We fit together with ease.

⚜

Afterward, we lay naked on Jason Dean and Maggie McKee's massive white couch. Gabe took a lock of my hair between his fingers, a lazy cat in the perfect patch of sun.

I figured our enthusiasm could be forgiven. We hadn't made a mess. Everyone else was either in Mexico or thrilled for their time off. I sighed, content.

It was three p.m., and we had nothing to do for the rest of the day but ensure that all the lights stayed on their timers. There was no need to get up. I'd double-checked all the cameras and turned off the breaker for the butler's pantry, just to be safe. I was giddy with sex. Reckless.

We got dressed. I poured us each a finger of whiskey from the bottle on the bar cart, then another once we'd finished that. Gabe found one of Maggie's guitars.

"You know what's funny?" I said. "Those have been sitting out ever since I've worked here, and I've never heard her play."

"She's gone pop star," Gabe said, tuning. "She probably doesn't play anymore."

"They've also got that piano in the dining room. The family room? That room past the stairs." Once my fascination with Maggie was unleashed, it was hard for me to reign myself in. I hadn't told Gabe that I, too, had known Maggie before she was famous. I burrowed my feet under the cushions. I sipped my whiskey. "I wonder if she does play other instruments."

"Stop talking about her," Gabe instructed. He had the barest tip of his tongue between his lips, off to one side, a tic I'd noticed from whenever something required his focused attention. I was about to go kiss him, but he started to play the guitar.

I was no musician, and at that point I was more than slightly tipsy, but even I could tell how talented he was. I'd half expected Gabe's guitar playing to be like that of the guys who'd bring their acoustics to show off on the quad, the same four chords and an off-pitch rendition of Guster, everyone politely pretending not to hate the whole thing. This was different. Deep down I'd always known it would be different. This was whatever emotion Gabe had bottled up inside him, all the shaky legs and jittery fingers replaced by the dance of his fingerpicking, his voice quiet and confident. He was good. He was very, very good. What had I done to myself?

I'd never thought that I'd be into a musician, particularly one who wrote their own songs. Hearing him play felt like being touched somewhere secret and vulnerable, being made to feel in a place and way that I was not used to feeling.

I was incredibly into Gabe, even with his guitar. Especially with his guitar.

He sang softly, his voice gravelly as always. The song was about opening a birdcage, which meant that it was really a song about letting someone go. I kept sipping my whiskey. He kept playing. I tried not to imagine what success would be for Gabe when he inevitably found it. Gabe making a music video; Gabe playing his guitar shirtless for some other girl he'd just slept with. He was with me right now, and that was what mattered. I closed my eyes and listened.

Later that day we looked at Jason's collection of sports memorabilia—a shrine mostly to himself—and leaned the recliners in the private basement movie theater all the way back until Gabe almost fell off his. We accidentally found a bright-pink lacy thong shoved in one of the cushions. We read the labels of the bottles in the wine cellar, and I grabbed one that I thought they wouldn't miss.

I was absolutely drunk by the time we got outside, and I assumed that Gabe was too. As the sun set, lights burst on across the patio, around the rim of the pool. The hills hovered, warm dark mounds. I shimmied out of my shirt, unhooked my bra. By the time I was unbuttoning my pants, Gabe had joined me, his chest tan and muscular, his grin delicious.

When we dove into the pool, I wasn't sure if I'd grabbed his hand or if he had taken mine. We hit the water together.

6.

The day the show first aired, I was visiting my mom in Pennsylvania.

"So . . . this is what you've been working on." My stepfather peered over his glasses.

"I don't understand it," said my mother.

"They're both hot," said Andrew, who was also home for Thanksgiving. I considered telling my brother about Maggie's childhood crush but kept my mouth shut. No need for Andrew to get cocky.

"It just seems very trivial," said my mother, wringing out a kitchen towel while clips from Jason and Maggie's wedding played across our living room TV. "What can anybody learn from this? Why would anybody want to watch this?"

"Again," said Andrew. "They're hot."

"It's looking at celebrity culture," I said. "And . . . consumption. And the way we all think about ourselves."

"The way we think about ourselves?" My mother was skeptical.

"Yeah. In relation to . . . a celebrity love story."

"Why should we think of ourselves in relation to a celebrity love story?" The theme song was playing, a generic love song off Maggie's second album. It didn't especially make my case for me.

"Mom, I'm not writing a dissertation. It's a job."

"Well, it's like the Kennedys, isn't it?" my stepdad said. "Or what was that TV show in the '70s where they followed around an average American family?"

"Those are two entirely different things, Ron," said my mother.

I said, "You're not our demographic."

Honeymoon Stage's premiere got so-so ratings, but whoever made the call to replay the first three episodes incessantly over Thanksgiving weekend deserved more than a raise. By the time our leftovers were gone from the fridge, I had gotten the email from Lauren confirming that we would be back to start shooting Season Two after the holidays. My mother told me she was happy for me, but I couldn't help feeling she was slightly disappointed. We had already discussed what I would do if the show wasn't renewed, and floated the possibility that I'd come back to Pennsylvania. With the pickup, that return to the East Coast was quite clearly not going to happen, so to make her feel better, I extended my visit from one week to six. This meant I wouldn't be back in LA until the new year. The California Christmas season was monotonous and depressing, the light displays tacky and off putting without actual winter weather to offset them, so being home among colorful foliage and brisk mornings that smelled like snow wasn't too much of a sacrifice. The show wouldn't start filming again until after the holidays, so there was nothing I needed to rush back for. The only thing that I would really miss was Gabe.

We weren't officially dating, so it seemed weird for me to broach the topic of our distance. I still couldn't fully decide if he was a semi-celebrity and I was a pack mule, if we'd had a fling that would burn itself out or if I was falling in love with him.

I'd known him three months, during which our primary mode of communication had been email. I hadn't seen him perform or really listened to his music. I hadn't met his friends. We'd only ever spent the night together at Maggie and Jason's.

"But if you think about it another way, it's like you two grew up together," said Celia over the phone. I felt like I was back in high school, lying on my twin bed, looking up at the Brat Pack poster pinned to my petal-pink walls and gossiping about boys that I imagined as entirely different people than they actually were.

"He was on TV," I said. "I didn't know him." If anything, the incongruence of our adolescent experiences made Gabe even more foreign to me. While I'd sharpened my pencil in Algebra 2, he'd been dancing on a soundstage. While I'd sat on the bench in gym class, Gabe had signed his name on photos of his face. We didn't make sense together. Yet there was the fizz in my chest.

While I had days of nothing but family board games and quick trips to the store to grab whatever my mom had forgotten, Gabe was still working in Los Angeles. He'd done Thanksgiving with the band, and though he himself had done a decent job with the turkey, apparently the other contributions were garbage. They'd stayed in town to gear up for a big meeting or to start something new at the recording studio. He was cagey about the specifics, which naturally made me more curious. I trawled LimeWire for any live recordings of him or the band. I wasn't tech savvy enough to access video files, but those were mostly from *The Tiger Crew*, so I was not especially interested. Watching a young Gabe felt creepy, which was why I'd asked Celia not to dig out her old VHS tapes of the show while she was visiting her dad. I didn't want to moon over a preteen boy. I sure as hell wouldn't have wanted Gabe to dig up old footage of me.

Listening to a bootleg recording of his solo set from 2001 felt different. Gabe was an adult man, with a growly baritone and a rootsy singer-songwriter appeal. His were simple, heartfelt lyrics with the occasional clever pun. They sounded like him, like who I knew him to be, like how he'd played on the couch when we were alone at Maggie and Jason's. Authentic. When his voice broke with emotion, I thought about his hands, his arms, the rest of him.

Live at Joe Weed's 8/6/01 became my constant companion. He had a song about his grandfather, another about a love affair he couldn't put behind him, a Patty Griffin cover.

When I spoke with Gabe on the phone, I didn't push for professional details or mention I had found his music and was playing it incessantly. I was all but doodling hearts and wedding dresses in my notebooks, but I'd never let him know. We bantered, and I joked about my mother's book club, and he vented about the rising studio rental fees. A mystery novel I was reading. A new burger place he'd found. A friend who was taking him surfing, and how much he was dreading it. My morning wandering the King of Prussia mall in search of a blue double boiler. He was headed to his parents' for Christmas, and assured me once he got there he, too, would be the king of jigsaw puzzles. I didn't ask him what his parents did or if he got along with his sister. I didn't ask him if he missed me as much as I was missing him. The August 2001 version of Gabe poured his heart out over my computer speakers every evening, but I said nothing about it. I wanted nothing to betray that I was terrified of how much I was falling for him.

During those six weeks I spent regressing in my childhood bedroom, Jason and Maggie were climbing the It List. They did a round of press to kick off *Honeymoon Stage*, and the same clip of her making kissy lips at him on *Hollywood Access* played everywhere. They were America's golden couple, the perfect alchemy of laurels and potential. He, the once-prince who would never be king; she, the star still being polished. Maggie's *Honeymoon Stage* theme song became a certified hit. Her concerts had always been solidly attended, but now they were packed. She'd done radio appearances and none had been the wiser, but now when she pulled up to a studio, she needed security to make a path for her among the swarming fans.

The other clip that made the rounds—from the *TODAY* show to *Oprah* to ESPN, thanks to Jason's clout—was the scene where Maggie was trying to make him pasta. In this episode, she lugs the pot from the cabinet and fills it under the tap. She grabs the dry boxed spaghetti. She realizes pretty quickly that, in order to fit them, she will have to break the noodles in half, so she does. The floof of the bangs. The bite of the lip. Once they're all in there, she turns on the burner.

"I hope that's not how your wife cooks you dinner," said one sports talking head to the other. "No wonder Jason Dean's dropped so much weight."

"She's going to have to go back to school for home economics," cracked a late-night host.

On *Saturday Night Live*, they had a popular male singer don a blond wig and straight up throw food all around a set kitchen, pretending surprise as marinara sauce splashed the fake fridge.

This was all excellent news for the network and, therefore, for me. Once things got rolling, the frenzy fed itself. *Us Weekly* published shots of Jason putting coins into a parking meter, Maggie grabbing a Diet Coke at Rite Aid. The more their everyday exploits made it into the tabloids, the more eyes the network got on the show. By mid-December, Maggie was hiding under blankets in the back seat of her car to avoid being trampled by her audience, and Jason had changed his cell phone number twice. Where once we might have been lucky to catch Maggie's music video on TV, it now ran nonstop. The same went for her singles on the radio. She'd traded privacy for success.

One of her escapades even made it to CNN on a bit about the perils of celebrity. Maggie and Sally Ann got run off the road by a group of paparazzi—they'd been at a nail salon, and someone inside must have tipped off the vultures. The trip back to Calabasas turned into a high-speed chase that almost sent them over a guardrail and into the canyon. The hood of the BMW in which I'd first seen Maggie was shoved in like an accordion. A reporter stood at the side of the cliff, gesturing to the dented rail.

"A salon trip almost ends in tragedy for pop star Maggie McKee and friend," the man said, somber faced in his navy logo windbreaker. In the past, Maggie had always been referred to as an up-and-coming pop star; with *Honeymoon Stage*, it seemed she'd finally come. Sally Ann apparently needed six stitches where a shard of glass had sliced her side. Maggie was photographed wearing one of those foam neck braces, ducking into a juice place. None of the paparazzi were injured.

Photos from the accident ran on the cover of *Star*, and I wondered if the same assholes who'd caused it were the ones who got paid for the images. In line at the local grocery store, I picked up a copy and flipped through.

It seemed cliché to have someone else's near-death experience wake me up to my own self-sabotage, but that was how it happened. I looked at the headlines, the pictures of the twisted metal, and imagined it had been me in the car with Maggie. What if the guardrail hadn't held? If I fell into a coma tomorrow, Gabe would never know how I actually felt about him. As scary as it was to open myself up, I had to at least try.

That night Gabe was supposed to call me, and while I waited, I thought about what I would say. I wanted something serious with him, something exclusive. I wanted him to want to fly to Philly, cost irrelevant, and declare his devotion. I wanted him to meet my family. I even wanted him to sing to me. I was in deep.

The trouble was, we hadn't discussed *us*. Every so often, Gabe would say "We should talk about—" and sensing where this led, I'd interrupt him. It was too scary. There was too much possibility that we would get hurt.

But I drank two of Ron's IPAs, and I told myself that I could do it. I would swallow my pride and confess to being afraid that Gabe was too good to be true. I'd admit to how much I'd been thinking about him, how much I wished he'd come home with me for the season, how I'd been listening to his music, how much it pained me to imagine him with anybody else.

I watched my phone, pretending to read my book as it grew later, past the time Gabe had told me he'd call. I called him, but he didn't pick up. I had another beer, regretted it. I played the opening of Gabe's bootleg concert and listened to him welcome the crowd. I checked my email, turned my ringer up. Still nothing.

The first time my dad left, he was supposed to meet me and my mom at Andrew's hockey game. He was going to come straight from work, and my brother kept glancing up from the ice at the empty seat next to me. Andrew had on all his gear, so I couldn't see his expression, but I knew what it would look like. His mouth set, lips turned in between his front teeth like he was making a fist with his face. My dad was often late, if he showed up at all. We were used to him bailing and then apologizing with some present my parents couldn't afford and we kids had never asked for. Moon shoes, a Nintendo, an Easy-Bake Oven. After he disappeared that first time, there hadn't been a present—there'd been nothing at all.

Gabe had never stood me up before. Gabe wasn't my father. He was probably just busy with his family. Maybe he'd meant nine p.m. Pacific time. Maybe he'd fallen asleep.

I brushed my teeth. I didn't have to be alone. I could go take a shot of whatever my mom and stepdad had collecting dust in their liquor cabinet, wait a few minutes for it to kick in, then call my ex, who would be visiting his own parents a neighborhood away. I'd deleted his number from my phone, but I knew it by heart. If he was sober, he could come pick me up, and if he wasn't, we could each walk fifteen minutes and meet at the park. He could save me from my feelings for Gabe. We could fall into each other.

The old Cassidy would have called him. But I was different now—both work and my romantic relationships felt real in a way that they hadn't before Gabe and *Honeymoon Stage*. Gabe hadn't picked up the phone. So what? It didn't have to change anything; I would talk to him the next day, summon the courage to confess my desires a second time. There was no need to abandon my conviction simply because Gabe got caught up talking to his sister or putting up holiday lights with his dad.

I closed my book and turned off my bedside lamp, convinced that he would call me in the morning. But he didn't.

October 2007

The brochures promised a golden morning light to honey my skin and make my dress look three times more expensive than it actually was. I was supposed to wake up confident, refreshed, ready to see and be seen: my cold cream turning my face poreless, fingernails painted powder pink, teeth whitened, and those last five pounds obliterated.

Even before I raise the bedroom blinds, I can tell that the clouds have moved in. There goes our photo shoot out in the garden. There goes our romantic beach view. A part of me is grateful for the weather. Let it rain. Let everybody's makeup smear and hair go frizzy. Cancel it all, and let me stay here in bed.

Since last night, a tent has risen on the grounds outside, and now a crew of amiable plus-ones releases plastic panels and moves accoutrements to its center in anticipation of the weather. Coffee wafts up from the kitchen, sweet and strong. Voices in one of the sitting rooms, the hiss of a steamer as it breathes onto a dress. Someone walks down the hallway humming Pachelbel's Canon. The sweet pastoral of it all hits like a hot flash, and I open a window for air.

Here comes the flower delivery, bumping down the back drive. Some assistant runs out toward the van with a massive umbrella. The day moves forward, a runaway train.

I have two missed calls from Lauren. A text from Jen.

Nothing from Gabe.

⚜

"I'm here, I'm here. I'm sorry." When I burst into the suite that's been assigned for bridal prep, my contrition is mostly performance. The old adage that the show can't start until the star is ready isn't true of Reality TV—Lauren and crew have shot getting-ready B-roll, they've tested lighting and angles, they've spitballed story and walked the grounds. All the things I used to do while we waited for Maggie McKee to be ready, the team has done today while waiting for me.

Jen and Celia sit in matching bridesmaids' robes, double-fisting champagne and black coffee. Celia betrays nothing of her hangover. She's wearing a pimple patch on her chin, which is how I know the cameras haven't been in yet.

"It's all happening!" Her squeal is entirely sincere. "You're getting married." She almost sings it, extending the vowel.

"You're getting married *on TV*." Jen sounds more the way I feel: incredulous, despite the filming we did yesterday, the evidence around us. Folded C-stands rest stacked on their cart. The makeup chair sits ready. The garment bag hangs from a stand-alone clothes rack. The crew has set up umbrellas for the lights.

"You guys haven't seen Gabe this morning, have you?" I ask.

Jen shakes her head. "But I'm sure he's where he's supposed to be. One of these people," she gestures, unsure what term to use for the crew bustling around us, "would have told us if he wasn't."

"Do you need me to give him something? Get something from him?" Celia is ready for action, intent on taking her maid of honor role seriously. She puts down her plastic champagne flute and hops off her chair.

Maybe I should tell my friends what Gabe said last night, let them do more for this wedding than just help me choose dresses and finalize place cards. Yesterday I was too shocked to say anything, but now I'm clearer headed. My friends have seen me through the many stages of my relationship with Gabe. What's one more drop of the roller coaster?

Of course I'm embarrassed to be here on my wedding day, rehashing the same doubts I had four years ago. But I swallow that embarrassment. These are my best friends. They can help me.

I'm about to speak, ready to tell them about what I overheard.

Before I can begin, a camera light blinks on, and there's a shuffling outside the door.

7.

January 2003

For Season Two, the intro credits changed from the initial mix of wedding-video, pop-star, and baseball footage to shots of Maggie and Jason together during Season One. Five seconds of them kissing or swatting or flipping their hair, and then the image would pause and zoom in, like the intro to a sitcom. Because Jason and Maggie were the only main cast, there was no "and Ann B. Davis as Alice." Just the two of them, from different angles, at different times of day. Maggie's theme song, still respectably climbing the charts, remained the same.

My first day back on set, Jason was nursing a hurt shoulder. I had thought, in my medical ignorance, that his baseball career had ended because he'd reinjured his elbow after surgery, but this was apparently not so. The elbow was okay, as much as one that was reconstructed with a tendon from his hamstring could be okay, but the resulting way he'd thrown had put stress on his shoulder, and once that tore, there was nothing to be done. That first day back, he had an ice pack wrapped on with ACE bandages, and he was crankier than I had ever seen him filming Season One.

"He was playing golf," Lauren explained. "Some guy recorded it all. Apparently Jason flipped him the bird and threatened to smash his camera. Between the network and his personal PR gal, they cleaned it all up, but I'd imagine that's money out of our budget." This season, Lauren's henna hair was bleached. It washed her out. I'd barely recognized her when I first came in.

"How's Maggie doing after her accident?" I asked. "That footage was gnarly."

"She's totally fine. Though I'd be shocked if that wasn't to blame for Jason's outburst. Sucks to think what would have happened for the show had that car crash been worse." That was Lauren, always covering her own ass.

"Is it even legal for them to be taking all these pictures?" I asked.

"Who knows." Lauren shrugged. "But it does give us juice."

"You know there's still a guy parked down by the entry gate, across the hedge, sitting in his car with a camera?"

"I did not." She sounded pleasantly surprised.

Lauren, I learned, had a new spin on the second season—rather than just watching Jason and Maggie live their regular lives, we'd find activities for them. They could get papped while going hiking, or throw a party, or drop in at a sports clinic for kids. Now that they were a known commodity, we could easily book them joint gigs. The show was no longer about a famous couple being married, but a couple being famously married. Lauren said this with a flourish that made me think she was actually writing that dissertation I'd told my mom was inane. But I figured she was right—a new angle never hurt anyone. And we weren't deliberately setting them up to fail, just setting them up to make good television. Besides, fame was quite clearly getting to both Maggie and Jason, and if we were to be the documentarians of their actual life, we couldn't avoid what it had made them become.

In the first Season Two episode, Jason and Maggie are attending a concert put on by a local school. Initially, the idea was to get Maggie back to her old elementary school, but the McKees had moved around so much she had no tether, and it was cheaper to stay closer to home.

Therefore, she and Jason have dropped by St. Mary of the Cross, a Catholic school about five miles from their gated community that has fortuitously saved its winter concert until January. It's clear that Jason doesn't want to be here. His shoulder is still bothering him, and when he puts his arm around Maggie, he winces. A little girl comes up and gives Maggie a card the class has made. Maggie gushes over how cute she is and what an honor it's been to hear them sing. After posing for pictures, Jason and Maggie pile into the hired black car. The camera follows her as she slumps in the seat.

"I am so stinking tired."

He moves to kiss her, and she brushes him off.

"Whatever." Jason stares out the window for the rest of the ride.

It wasn't just the mood on set that had shifted. I'd talked to Gabe on the phone a few more times in Pennsylvania, but he'd always seemed distracted. I had struggled to make basic conversation, never mind letting him know I wanted more from our relationship. Since my return to LA the week before, we'd only gotten together once—we met up briefly by his studio for coffee. It was out of my way, and parking had been a bear. Seeing him in person confirmed both my desire to claim him as my own and my inability to broach the topic of exclusivity. His shirt smelled freshly laundered when I hugged him, and he drank an iced latte, and I wanted to loop my leg around his. He was preoccupied with something. I kissed him on the cheek before he had to get back to the studio and I had to go to work, and I wondered if he noticed how awkward I was being. Why did caring about someone ruin all the ease of a relationship?

I thought of this now as I watched Jason and Maggie, wondering if their bickering was a crack in their relationship or a sign their love was honest and real.

"Just take the trash out." Jason sat on the couch, watching Maggie try to shove an empty milk carton into the overflowing bin.

"I can make it fit," she said. She'd been growing out her bangs and had them held back with a headband, so there was no more floofing. Maggie grunted. The lining ripped, and barbecue sauce bled onto the floor. I made a move to go and help her, but Lauren held me back.

"Babe?" Maggie huffed.

"Yeah?" Jason had one eye on his basketball game, the other on his wife.

"Hey, babe?"

"Yes?" Whereas three months ago Jason's tone would have betrayed his amusement, now he seemed purely annoyed. I mimed going to get Maggie a mop. *Absolutely not,* Lauren mouthed.

"I'm not really sure what to do here?" Maggie seemed like she might cry. She had just gotten in from the airport after two days on a photo shoot in New York. We all knew there was no chance she'd be given the benefit of that context in the episode. Maggie McKee Cracks Under Pressures of Housework. I could see the headline now, much more entertaining than Maggie McKee Exhausted After Long Red-Eye Flight.

Under any other circumstances, someone who spent more time at the house than Maggie—which these days meant pretty much any of us in the room—would tell her where to find the Pine-Sol. But Lauren kept her fingernails dug into my arm, preventing me. Maggie swallowed, and she grabbed some paper towels from the counter to blot up the sauce. Finally, Jason stood up. He stretched his shoulder, looked right into Rahul's camera with a roll of his eyes. He took the entire trash can and carried it out to the garage.

Dan called cut so that I could get the proper equipment and mop up the spill. Maggie shut her eyes and pressed her lips together, then went back to cleaning out the fridge.

"I can finish that," I said. Normally the housekeeper would have taken care of both the trash and the refrigerator, but Lauren had given her a few paid days off, timed perfectly to Maggie's homecoming. Of course, this wasn't fair to Maggie, but as Lauren consistently reminded me, our job wasn't about fair. We were tasked with turning mundanity into a fairy tale. Every hero had to have their trials; otherwise, the happy ending wouldn't be earned. I listened to Lauren explain this, and it made sense, but I still didn't like it.

Jason came back into the kitchen with the emptied trash can while I was finishing up the floor.

"It's not that hard to change the liner," he muttered to Maggie. She looked at him pointedly, giving her head a little jerk over to me. "Oh come on, she doesn't care."

I forced a smile to show that I didn't.

"It isn't my job," Maggie hissed through her own smile, "to take out your trash."

Jason was smart—he started clapping out a random pattern with his hands so that, on the chance it was still being captured, Vinnie couldn't use any of this audio. "Well, if you'd been home, it would have been your trash too."

"I was working."

"That's my point." All of this whispered, under the guise of their forced cheerfulness. I bent to get a new garbage bag from under the sink.

"It is not my fault," said Maggie, now tapping her lavalier mic as she spoke, "that no one has hired you as a commentator."

"That's low." *Clap* clap clap. "Even for you."

Could I crawl into the space under the sink and hide, or better yet, come out through the cabinet around the corner? I wondered if it was smarter to remind them that I was here or be as still and silent as possible. I decided to brave it.

"All done!" I tucked the bag into the bin, aware that as I did so my face was contorting into an expression I hoped read *none of my business*. What was happening now between Jason and Maggie seemed like more than the cutesy back-and-forth they'd played on Season One. All signs pointed to trouble.

"Thank you, Cassidy," said Jason. He was no longer clapping his hands.

"And thank you for your discretion," said Maggie. "We know you'll keep this to yourself. Some things are better left off camera." She put a hand on my shoulder. "As in, say, making out in somebody's private pool." Her tone was totally mild, clean of the frustration she'd had a moment ago when snapping at Jason. It took me a moment to process what she'd said, and as I did, I felt the blood rise to my face.

"Of course," I said. "I'm not going to . . ." My heart was beating so loud I was sure they could hear it. "I mean, I don't know what you're talking about. What I would even keep quiet."

She was talking about me and Gabe. When they were in Mexico, I must have missed turning off one of the cameras. Was the footage just out there for anyone? It couldn't be—if Dan and Lauren had known, they wouldn't have hired me back on the show. It must just be Maggie and Jason. They'd had all holiday season to reveal me, and instead they'd held on to it. For leverage?

"We understand each other, then," Maggie said.

I left the kitchen in a daze, almost walking right into Rahul, who caught me before I could knock over his lights. "Awkward in there, huh?" I shrugged, then nodded. He scratched at the stubble on his jaw. "What's up? You're being weird."

I looked around the foyer. David, the new camera assistant, was doing something on the floor, maybe taping a wire. Lauren stood by the bathroom, nodding along to someone talking through her headset. I didn't care about David—if he went the way of the other assistants, he'd be gone in a few weeks—but I didn't want Lauren to know I was worried. Lauren was a hawk. She heard everything. And I didn't trust the *Honeymoon Stage* house, not anymore. Not after I would have sworn on my grandmother's grave that I'd turned off the breakers, and somehow Maggie still knew I'd been with Gabe.

"Just tired," I told Rahul. "Learning things I'd rather not, you know?" He raised his eyebrows, but I wouldn't say more.

"Whatever you say." He patted me on the shoulder, a wry smile on his face that made it clear he thought that what I'd said was bullshit. Lauren watched this interaction, face impassive, biding her time.

⚜

On the way home that night, I called Gabe from the car. He picked up a few rings in, voice groggy.

"Did I wake you?" It was only eleven. "I'm sorry."

"It's fine."

After our weird coffee date, I had been waiting for a real reason to call him. Cruising down the mostly empty 101, I was all set to dish on Maggie's implication, but something stopped me.

"Sorry," I said again.

"Is everything okay?"

"Yeah, I guess I just didn't realize how late it was." Suddenly, I didn't want to bring Gabe into my *Honeymoon Stage* drama. What use was burdening him with the knowledge of something he couldn't control? I wasn't Maggie—I could take out my own trash. All I had to do was keep quiet about Jason and Maggie's marital troubles, and the tape of me and Gabe doing whatever it was we did that night in their pool would never surface.

"It's cool."

I wasn't sure what to say now that I wasn't going to spill about work. I couldn't tell if his own reticence was just because he'd been asleep or something greater.

"I'm off next Tuesday if you have some time to get together," I said. Mine was the only car on the expressway, and this made me bold.

"Lemme check, but I think Tuesday might be booked," said Gabe. I sighed, and he heard me through the phone. "I swear I'm not blowing you off," he said, now sounding fully awake. "I want to keep this going. I want to see you. Let me see what I can do."

The next morning, I woke up to an email from Gabe: Tuesday won't work, I can't get out of my thing. I promise I am not blowing you off. What about that Monday night?

Maggie kept a grueling schedule, but she was contractually committed to film for us a certain number of hours per week. In mid-January, she had a gig in Kansas City performing at some company's corporate retreat, and for the first time in my tenure as a *Honeymoon Stage* PA, I got to go with her.

It was no great treat to leave Los Angeles for Missouri in winter. At the airport, other travelers gawked. I pushed the luggage cart—that same cream leather suitcase—while Maggie stopped to sign her name on people's plane tickets. Someone asked her to autograph the inside of a hardcover novel.

"Like she reads," Dan scoffed. He was annoyed by the fans' attention, rolling his eyes and all but saying *Let's get on with it,* but Lauren loved the crowds. She kept directing Rahul to get certain shots of people noticing Maggie and nudging their traveling companions, digging through bags for their digital cameras. One little girl even cried. "Next time we'll fly private," said Dan.

Except we were already flying private, or as private as I'd ever flown. Once we'd gotten through security, we went into an exclusive lounge for VIP airline patrons, and the guys were allowed to turn off their cameras. While the rest of the crew debated whether or not they had enough time to order and eat full burgers, I went and sat a few seats down from Maggie. This whole time at the airport, she'd had on a baseball cap and sunglasses, which only seemed to draw attention, given the cameras accompanying her every move. She kept the accessories, even in the mostly empty lounge.

I was still thinking about the argument she'd had with Jason. I wanted to reassure her she had nothing to worry about on my end. I just wanted to clear the air. But with those sunglasses on and her mouth the careful neutral of someone who'd just spent the past hour smiling at her fans, Maggie was unapproachable.

I tried again on the plane. There were enough of us tagging along that I was pretty sure we weren't having the full fancy private-jet experience, though the seats did all face one another, which was new. I'd ended up diagonal to Maggie, who sat next to Brent, her hairstylist. Sally Ann had called in sick, so someone else was meeting us there to do makeup. Maggie had, at first, been apoplectic at the news, then resigned. As someone who regularly did my own makeup and didn't see that much of a difference between the pink eyeshadow smeared onto Maggie and the stuff that I bought at the drugstore, I was glad she'd landed on the side of reason. Turbulence kept sliding her undressed salad around on her tray.

Brent whispered something that made Maggie laugh. When he got up to use the bathroom, I figured this was my chance. From across the aisle, Lauren shot me a look as I leaned forward.

"Hey," I said. "About the other day." Maggie slid her sunglasses down her nose. Her blue eyeliner was expertly applied. "I just want to make it clear, you know, that I'm not going to . . . I mean things that are none of my business—" One would think that with the time I'd had to consider what I'd say to Maggie, I'd have come up with something more eloquent, but I could barely make a coherent thought. She raised her perfectly plucked brows.

"Cassidy, come help me with this." Lauren sat empty-handed, not even pretending to have an excuse for calling me away.

"I mean, I'm really sorry if I—"

"Cassidy." I unbuckled my lap belt and went over to Lauren. "Stop bothering Maggie."

A few months ago, I would have taken this comment as an insult. After half a season on *Honeymoon Stage*, I knew that Lauren was keeping me from contaminating her sample. *Honeymoon Stage* was a science to Lauren, and the more we treated the cast like they were our friends, the less conclusive our experiment would be. Lauren patted the empty seat next to her, and I, a good assistant, sat down.

We were back in LA less than twenty-four hours later, after watching Maggie gargle salt water and glad-hand and sing a few power ballads on the convention center stage. Presumably, the money she got from one day of fawning over medical-equipment salespeople was more than my annual salary. I came home with a sinus headache that lasted into the weekend—Saturday, when we filmed Maggie and Jason at a roller rink, and Sunday, when Maggie hosted her parents for dinner. By Monday afternoon it had developed into a cold, and I knew I was too sick to go to Gabe's. I texted to let him know.

Bummer. He got back to me immediately. Want me to bring you anything? I was tempted to take him up on his offer, but I wasn't going to have him drive all the way out to Silver Lake to bring me some sympathy soup. I wanted the next time we got together to be perfect: my hair flat-ironed, my conversation sparkling, my outfit impeccable. I went home to lie down in the dark.

A few hours later, I awoke to someone knocking.

"Cassidy?" Jen cracked the door. I wiped drool from where it had pooled on my pillow. "Your . . . Gabe is here."

"I'm sorry, what?" I'd passed out on a knit blanket, and when I raised my hand to my cheek, I could feel the pattern pressed into my skin. My hair was an unwashed disaster. "Can you delay him or something?" Gabe had seen me grimy from running around all day on the *Honeymoon Stage* set; he'd seen me in sweats; he'd seen me tipsy and naked. But this, to see me not only unvarnished but at home in my tiny bedroom, with its old mugs of tea and dirty laundry and clean laundry that, instead of folding, I had piled onto a chair—this was a level of vulnerability I hadn't anticipated.

Jen mouthed an apology, then moved back from the door to reveal Gabe behind her.

"Hi." I tried to casually adjust my shirt to make it less obvious that I wasn't wearing a bra. "I didn't expect you."

"I know," Gabe said. "I'm sorry. I was just going to drop this off, but then I had to buzz the door, and your roommate said to come up, so . . ."

"No, it's good. I just . . . didn't . . . you know." My underwire bra sat at the top of the clean-laundry pile, a conquering hero. Outside, a truck sang backup with an ear-shattering beep. Whatever cold I was dealing with hadn't moved into my chest, but my breathing was shallow. "Welcome, I guess."

"How are you feeling?" Gabe stood in the doorway holding a grocery bag. He hunched a bit, as if unsure he would fit through.

"Better," I said. "Now."

He came fully into the room. "They work you hard, huh?"

"It's very stupid."

"I brought you—this is going to seem weird, but—I brought grapes." Gabe came closer, and I scooted over so he could join me on my unmade bed. There was really nowhere else to sit down. His weight shifted the mattress, and I shivered.

"I guess that *is* kind of weird."

"I was going to freeze them, so we could do, like, a rain-checked Spanish New Year's Eve. Or put them in cocktails. I don't know. Some guy was selling them on the side of the road, and they looked good." Gabe was nervous. There went his jittering leg.

"That sort of makes it even weirder," I said. My hand inched out toward his. "But very sweet. I've never had a frozen-grape cocktail."

"As a garnish," he said, lacing our fingers. "They make a good garnish." Gabe moved closer. "I would kiss you," he said, "if . . . ?"

Then I knew that, despite my headache, despite Jen there on the other side of our paper-thin wall, we were going to have sex. I leaned over and brought my lips to his. The pleasure and relief of even this seemed almost unbearable.

I'd already learned the superficial terrain of Gabe's body: a birthmark on his upper thigh, the tattoos on his bicep and back shoulder. I knew the pleasure point at the small of his back, and how if I nuzzled his neck, he would tighten his grip on me. Each time there'd been the social lubricant of alcohol, if not already in play, then warming up off the bench. Earlier that evening I had taken three Advil, but that hardly counted. Here we were, sober, absolutely ourselves.

I lifted my arms, and Gabe helped me off with my T-shirt. I pressed my face into his chest. We had sex solemnly, careful and deep. Afterward he held me, the two of us squeezed into my twin bed.

"So," he said into my hair. "What's your deal?" I laughed and turned around to face him.

"You mean in general or with this?" I gestured to the two of us, together.

Gabe tilted his forehead toward mine. "I don't mean to be a fifteen-year-old girl about it—"

"Though that's a totally valid thing to be," I interrupted.

"True. You're right. But you know what I mean."

"I do. Go on."

He swallowed. "This was actually much easier when you weren't looking at me."

I laughed again. "Despite the fact you've built a whole career on being looked at?"

"Listened to. But still, touché." He pulled back a bit to see me, his fingers hovering by the hair that had fallen across my cheek. When he spoke, his voice was low, the growl of one of his love songs. "I really like you, Cassidy."

I froze completely. This was exactly what I'd wanted him to say, exactly what I'd planned to say to him.

He'd started to tuck my hair behind my ear when suddenly my stomach grumbled so loud Jen could probably hear it through the wall.

"Sorry," I said. "I passed out earlier without eating dinner." The apology was not just for my stomach, but also for making him wait. Gabe made a sound like he was trying not to laugh.

"You want a grape?"

⚜

We ordered a ten p.m. pizza and ate it out of the box while sitting on my bedroom floor.

"This is romantic," I said. Gabe guffawed. "No, I mean it."

"Good to know you're a cheap date."

"Oh, no," I said. "This only works once. You pull the same move next week and it's cliché."

"Noted." Gabe caught a falling pepperoni before it hit the rug.

"Can I ask you a question?" From my tone I knew he couldn't tell how serious I was being.

"Sure."

"Are you ever going to invite me to come hear your music? It seems like this whole other life you have. It makes me nervous." I was counting on him knowing me well enough to read between the words. *Am I enough for you? Who are you, really?*

"Cassidy." Oh no. I'd ruined things. I took an impulsive sip of Diet Coke that went down wrong and had me sputtering. "Cassidy." Gabe waited until I was done. He wiped his hands and reached them out to hold my face. "Of course you're invited to my shows, when they happen."

"If I can get off work," I joked.

"If you can get off work, you nutjob." Gabe kissed the top of my head. We sat in a mostly comfortable silence.

"I have a confession," I said.

"Oh?"

"I found a bootleg recording of you that I've listened to incessantly."

"I like this confession," said Gabe. "Solo stuff from the past few years?" I nodded. "Excellent."

"And I genuinely like it."

Gabe laughed. "Even better."

"And I have one more confession." I swallowed. Might as well. "Well, not a confession. Maybe a confession? Something that I haven't told you." I'd never opened up about my dad, not even to my ex when we'd officially dated in college. It felt so cliché, so predictable. Like I was someone's cheesy pop song. How many girls had damage from their shitty fathers? I wasn't special. Still, if we were going to make a real go of this, it seemed better Gabe should know from the start.

"Yeah?" He was waiting.

"I'm bad at relationships," I said. "But it's kind of not my fault? My dad ditched me and my brother and my mom when I was eight."

"I'm sorry," said Gabe. "That sucks."

"Yeah, it did and it didn't. Well, it did, but not as much as it sucked later, when I was fourteen, and he got back in touch with us and then decided he'd made the wrong call, and then bailed again."

"Woof." Gabe's hand inched toward mine. I closed my eyes against the memory of my mother sitting me down on the side of her bed to explain that while my dad had loved our time catching up, he wasn't in a place to make it a regular occurrence. Andrew had known how it would end from the start, declining the trips to Virginia, icing my dad out. I hadn't seen the reversal coming any more than I had that first time he left us.

"So, I might not be the best at this." I opened my eyes.

"Makes sense. That's pretty fucked." Gabe let us sit for a minute, in silence. Then he took my hand. "Thank you for telling me."

I felt less like a weight had been lifted than like a sandbag had been slit, its innards leaking slowly out. "You might be shocked to hear I'm not that great at trusting," I said. "I'm maybe scared that this is too good to be true." I waved my hands to signify all of it, the greasy pizza box and his mismatched socks and the way that our thighs pressed together.

"You think it's good?"

"Stop teasing me."

"I'm really asking. You're a hard woman to read, Cassidy Baum." But now he'd read me, and he knew it. I could tell by his grin.

"It's been good ever since that day at the studio when your band thought that I was a call girl."

"Not a call girl," Gabe corrected. "A groupie." He nudged the pizza box out of the way and moved to sit in front of me, his back to my overfull desk chair. "I raise you it's been good ever since you hit my car."

"Excuse me, *you* hit *my* car."

"A technicality. Anyway, I didn't care because I was like, 'Who is this sexy thing who has no time for me?'"

"Because you're used to girls just throwing themselves at you."

"False."

"You're this rock god who has his choice of any woman."

"Absolutely false."

"But you can see why I'd be nervous."

Gabe looked at me, considering for a moment before he spoke. "I told my mom about you."

"You didn't."

"I did. I told her I'd met someone special, and she told me not to screw it up." The teasing cadence was gone, Gabe giving me his own confessional. "The last time I was in love, it was with somebody who didn't want to be with me."

The last time implied there was another time. Meaning, right now, Gabe was in love. I resisted the urge to respond with a joke. Instead, I said, "That sucks."

"It does. It did." Gabe was still actively looking at me, and I could feel my heart beat faster. Here came the charisma, the celebrity wattage. Or was it just him, now that he knew me? Not something put on for a crowd, not a performance where the stage lights bleached the audience into a faceless mass. This was Gabe, unvarnished. He was simply a human being who shone. "Don't go breaking my heart," he said.

"I wouldn't if I tried." I'd fucked it up by misquoting the lyric, but Gabe didn't mind.

"Oh, you could. You absolutely could." He took a rascally bite of my leftover crust, then tossed it and scrambled toward me, a happy puppy, all long limbs and affection.

Part of me wanted to get so close to Gabe that I might smother him. Another part wanted to run before we ruined things, got bored with one another or sniped in front of the help about the right way to take out the trash.

"The only thing is—" Gabe began, but I held up a finger, sealing my own fate. I thought I knew this song. I kissed him.

"Let it be."

8.

In this episode, Jason sits down with a reporter on the patio of a restaurant in Encino. *Reporter* is perhaps too strong a word for this schlubby-looking white man, who might have dressed differently had he known, when he left the house, that he was going to be on television. Or maybe he would not have changed a thing—maybe he's the type to be smug about the difference between his uncombed hair and Jason's pomade, claims he would never waste his time on his appearance, despite working for a fairly trashy magazine. If he's so much more intellectual than Jason, why is that? They sit on adjacent corners of the outdoor table so that one camera can hold both of them in view.

"Those rumors of infidelity." Mr. Reporter lowers his voice, as if this whole thing won't be captured by our cameras. "How do you respond?"

"All couples in the public eye will have to deal with tabloid rumors." Jason's espresso cup is dwarfed by his large hands. "We don't let it bother us."

"It must be tough," says the reporter, "seeing stories about your wife. Her seeing stories about you."

"We're focused on each other," says Jason. His eyes dart up and away from the camera, seeking someone we assume should be responsible for shutting down this line of questioning.

"Do you regret opening your marriage to the public?" By the intensity of his cold blue gaze, you'd think the reporter was asking

Jason about whether he'd send troops into Iraq. Jason doesn't take the bait. He sips his coffee, leans back in his patio chair, smiles.

"Of course not," he says. "We're still giddy about it. *Honeymoon Stage* has opened so many doors for us. I love my wife."

⚜

"For the love of god, can we please screen these questions before Jason gets them?" Jason's publicist, a silver-haired woman named Simone, spoke to us without looking up from her BlackBerry. Lauren gave a toothy smile.

"Absolutely," she said. "We absolutely can."

"Didn't I already?" I asked Lauren once Simone was out of earshot. Together we shouldered the softbox lights and walked them toward the trunk of her car.

"Of course you did," Lauren said. "But you don't work for Jason." That was true. It wasn't the show's job to keep Jason comfortable, or even to tell him that his publicist was punting her responsibilities. If anything, it behooved us to have his team incompetent, because that gave us more interesting material. An interview in which Jason was caught off guard or forced to talk about the blind items that tied him to some dancer in Las Vegas was far more lucrative for Lauren and the network than some vanilla conversation about opportunity and gratitude.

Presumably, this was also true for me. My luck was Lauren's luck, and her golden staircase was mine to ascend behind her. As Lauren's direct report, I shared a common goal with her, and in theory, I should have been as gung ho as she was to catch Maggie and Jason in various foibles. In practice, I was still walking on eggshells trying to keep them from getting me fired for what I'd done with Gabe in their pool.

Without a union to protect Reality TV workers, people were fired all the time without cause. Honestly, we barely had HR, the network's cold corporate office constantly juggling any number of Hollywood creeps. I wasn't going to be punished by any external legal force were Maggie and Jason to pull up the footage I assumed they had of me having sex on their property. But I would lose my job, and thus my references, and thus my dream of a TV career. My financial safety net. Certainly my dignity. If the incident got wide, it would be massively embarrassing for Gabe.

And so, while I did not nominally work for Jason and Maggie, in practice, I found that I did. The day before, while hanging out in Video Village, I'd noticed a piece of spinach stuck between Maggie's teeth. While the rest of the crew filmed her like nothing was off, I'd sucked my own teeth and wiped at my mouth until she caught on and looked in a mirror.

My allegiance was mostly to Maggie. Even without the leverage she held, I suspect I would have tried to make things easier for her. Underneath whatever she'd become, I still saw glimmers of that gutsy little girl in Ohio. If I'd seen cheating rumors on a list of questions some sleazy magazine guy wanted to ask Maggie, of course I would have given her a heads-up. I would have told her if her publicist was overworked and overpaid and leaning on the production crew in place of an assistant. But my loyalty to Maggie over Lauren had to come at some cost, and that cost was often Jason.

After the interview, we all caravanned back to Calabasas, Rahul and Vinnie in the black car with Jason to catch any lingering emotional response or other screen-worthy moment, and Lauren driving me and the gear. Her hair was frizzy with humidity and bleach, and I could see the mental calculations she made as we pulled onto Ventura.

"You think we could have gotten more out of him?" I asked. After several months of good behavior, I had earned her conversation, so long as I framed it as wanting to learn from her. And I did want to learn from her. Lauren's mind could spin through every possibility before I'd even processed what was happening in front of me. I wasn't sure why she was doing this show instead of theoretical physics.

"We don't want to lose focus with Jason," Lauren said to me. "We need to get him doing something romantic. Start thinking about Valentine's Day." I couldn't be sure if that was a command—Lauren telling me personally to make plans for Jason on Valentine's Day—or just a general statement about our goals as a crew. "You know what we should do," Lauren continued, "is send him to a baby store. We get him holding little booties, America's collective heart melts." This was how talking to Lauren usually went—I would open her a bit, and she'd start spilling. Unlike some producers, she never seemed worried about me stealing her ideas, maybe because Dan already took so much credit. "Find out who of their friends is having a baby." Lauren glanced at me with that tight-lipped expression of self-appreciation that, for her, stood in for a smile.

"On it," I said. This would be a more exciting task than photocopying and maybe slightly less manipulative than filling the Calabasas house with rose petals and claiming Jason had come up with the idea on his own.

"And I'm sure I don't have to tell you this, but don't—"

"Tell Dan. I know." If this was Lauren's latest story pitch, she didn't want Dan finding out and pretending he'd come up with it. They were always playing politics, one trying to use the other one for power or clout.

"I knew I could count on you." Lauren looked at me with an expression I couldn't quite place, as if she was responding not to me but to my subconscious. "You remind me of myself. Very perceptive."

Lauren didn't give compliments—the closest she usually came was a quick jerk of the head to acknowledge that I'd done something smart. Something was up with her. She'd been especially snippy and looked wanner than usual—or was that just the change in hair color washing her out?

I didn't want to pull too hard at her praise and thus unravel it. Better to take this as a sign that the long hours and demeaning tasks on set were worth it. I was, in fact, making some progress toward my goal, which was not to be Lauren but to be the person above her. Surely, at some level, there was no intercrew competition, no one vying for your raise or your promotion. Just a room and the whole picture, the levers you could pull, the pieces you could move across the board.

The baby thing was a good move. People were always asking Maggie and Jason when they were going to have kids. Maggie would usually say that she still felt like one herself, and if he was in an uncharitable mood, Jason might agree with her. Many of the things Jason complained about in his wife might have been solved by marrying someone further above the legal drinking age. Supposedly Maggie wasn't great at keeping track of credit cards, though as the one who regularly brought in their mail, I had never seen any bills past due. She rarely cooked, and when she made the attempt, it did not taste like Jason's mother's food. She wasn't a very good driver.

During the first season, these complaints had been lovingly made. As we moved further into the second, I sensed that when Jason said he'd rather have a good three-bean chili than orchestra seats at the Hollywood Bowl, he actually meant it.

"Vinnie has a three-year-old," I said to Lauren.

"Too old. We need him looking at layettes, not potty training. We want people whispering about Maggie's baby bump."

"Maggie doesn't have a baby bump," I said.

"Cassidy."

"Oh." It dawned on me. "I got it. Find a newborn."

I broached the topic with Brent, the hair guy, while he was prepping Maggie's color. He touched her up every two weeks, using their private movie-theater bathroom as his personal chemistry lab.

"I'm flattered that you see me as the key to the chamber of secrets," he said. "But I've got nothing." Testing our ENG crew also left me nothing but a look from Eli that made it clear he didn't want to swap personal lives. Nobody at the network was pregnant, or at least willing to disclose. When I asked Sally Ann, she looked alarmed.

"I don't know why you'd ask me that." She repeatedly smoothed her hair behind her ears, a nervous tic.

"It's for production," I explained. Sally Ann sniffed. "Just, like, a segment they could film with Jason shopping. I'm not trying to get in your business."

"It's inappropriate." She blinked at me, then stretched her neck. Ever since the paparazzi had run her and Maggie off the road, she'd dealt with back pain. Vinnie and I both thought there was probably a lawsuit in there somewhere, but as that was not the type of content *Honeymoon Stage* needed, we'd stayed out of it. For all I knew, Maggie had brought a suit, or settled one. Sally Ann likely had her own doctors. She didn't need me.

Maybe it was because of the accident that Sally Ann was spending so much time at the house. She'd always been around for Maggie's primping, but these days I caught her by the pool when Maggie was out, hanging around waiting, when before she would have gone home. We all siphoned something off Maggie and Jason. Even I, the lowest on the ladder, was profiting from their notoriety. I, too, had used that pool. I didn't begrudge Sally Ann any of it.

"I mean, like, new babies. Not babies you've already had." I'd been inspired by Lauren to keep pushing but hadn't learned how to finesse. Sally Ann stared at me. Her hand rose to her locket. No one had said anything to me about the baby sister who might not actually be a sister since Rahul had told me his suspicions several months ago. That particular gossip had already been played out by the time I arrived.

"What are you talking about?" Sally Ann's fist clenched around the necklace. She must have realized she was acting weird, because she dropped her hand and put on a fake smile. "No babies here!" Her eyes screamed at me to go away and stop talking about this, and I was happy enough to leave the whole thing alone. It truly wasn't my business if she had some secret life.

When I returned to Lauren to let her know I'd come up short on new babies, she sighed and said we'd just have to wait a few months. At the time, I didn't read much into it. Jason was at an age when many of his cohort had children, so I assumed she must have meant one of his friends would announce and we could milk the baby shower for our show. It would be best to stir up the gossip, get the tabloids thinking Maggie was expecting, and then finally tease an episode that would reveal all, only to show that she was buying a gift for a friend. Disappointing, but not breaking our contract with the audience. There was an *all*—it just wasn't especially interesting.

Or we'd just lie. If we absolutely had to, we could just send them shopping. There didn't have to be a reason, or else it could be a bullshit reason. Sure, some viewers would complain that we were staging what we called a Reality show. But there were no rules.

It's funny now to think that I considered lying about a trip to the baby store to be the show's ethical breach. I was trying so hard to help make the sitcom, never noticing my real life had become a daytime soap. When I consider all the questions I didn't ask, all the rugs I walked across with no thought as to what people swept under them, I can't help but laugh. If the facade of Maggie's gullibility was the heart of *Honeymoon Stage*'s situational comedy, my own was its skeleton. Someone had to provide structure for the blood and the muscle. Someone had to be the unconscious perpetrator, the puppet for the many puppeteers.

I had forgotten that playing oneself is still playing. I had forgotten that playing is what spiders do with their prey. I'd been living in a California dream of open-plan kitchens and five-car garages and boyfriends who'd once been on TV. I was about to wake up.

October 2007

"Right." Here comes Lauren with her clipboard, turning my wedding day into network entertainment. "Now that you're here, we can start shooting." I can tell she's trying to keep her irritation in check. I may be late, but after all, I am the bride.

Jen raises a brow at me, but I've locked up entirely. I can't let Lauren know I'm having cold feet. Even if I'm hypothermic, I need Lauren to think that I'm fine.

"It's all right," I mumble. "We'll talk later." Celia practices her camera-ready smile.

"You don't mind being in your"—Lauren waves a hand at our various states of undress—"do you." It's not a question. I'm sure we've all signed something that waives our right to clothing.

While Lauren mumbles into her walkie-talkie, I scan the breakfast buffet, anxious to fill myself up before anyone starts filming me. Icing-piped Danishes that no one expects me to eat, a bowl of fruit with all the raspberries conspicuously picked out of it. I can't remember ever having less of an appetite, but I grab a cluster of grapes. They are still cold and hurt my teeth.

"Makeup's due in ten minutes." A random young guy in a headset sticks his neck into the suite. I picture the heavy door closing on him and wonder if he realizes that Lauren would guillotine him gladly if she thought it would get her in good with the network. That is, after all, why she's here. The network; her *Honeymoon Stage* tie-in that will prove once and for all she is more competent than Dan. Dan, who could show up in gym shorts and still get the promotion. "Dan the Man," Vinnie had called him. Today, Dan has not been invited.

I try Gabe's phone again, but it rings through. I could call one of the groomsmen, but I don't want to make more of a scene.

"Have you made up your mind?" Lauren sidles up to me as I eke the final drops of coffee from the generic white carafe. She's back in her usual uniform of slacks and a plain blouse, yesterday's glamour abandoned. My hand jolts, splashing coffee on the cuff of my robe. *How does she know?* A good producer knows everything.

But Lauren isn't asking about whether or not I'm going to get married. She wants to know about the show, *Real-Life Lovers*, that she's working on with Dan, the show she wants this wedding special to get eyes on. *Everyday people falling in love* had been her pitch to me, as if I, an everyday person, would immediately understand. I, the most everyday of everyday people, the perfect coproducer to come in and have her back against Dan. I'm pretty sure I've made up my mind there. I'll get Lauren to give me a reference, but no way am I returning to their obvious toxicity. Working with Lauren and Dan is like being a child of a messy divorce. No amount of money or career revitalization is worth being their go-between.

Or so I'd thought yesterday, when my future seemed laid out for me.

You can't tell anyone. I remember Gabe's words, and all at once, I am back on that bench, reconceiving the man I thought I knew. I can feel my heart hardening, my body steeling itself for devastation. I can also feel that small flutter of hope.

I need to know what actually happened four and a half years ago. I need to talk to Maggie. She should be down soon to get ready with us, and then the crew will film her talking head pieces soon after. I'll have to find a way to get her alone.

"Cass, what is with you?" Celia approaches under the guise of helping me clean up my spilled coffee. "You don't seem happy. Aren't you happy? What were you about to say?" She seems not to remember our time out in the garden last night.

Before I can answer her, the crew bustles in. As expected, they did most of their setup before I came down, so it's only a few seconds before I'm pulled away from Celia without answering her. She follows me to the makeup chair. "If you don't want to do this, you do not have to do this."

The makeup girl begins to plaster on my foundation.

I remember Sally Ann and Maggie giggling in the living room of the Calabasas house, flicking a fake eyelash as if it were a bug. Jason watering the lawn, turning to point the hose right at them so it blasted the glass door. My back against the washing machine. The scuffs on my Keds.

The rain begins in earnest while I'm having my eyebrows filled in, and despite the popular song, I know immediately that irony is not rain on my wedding day. It's not the black fly in my wine, the good advice I ignored, all those spoons. Irony is me prepping to be on TV. Irony is being in love and still not knowing if I'll say yes at the altar.

Irony is that I have my eyes closed when the door opens and, for the first time in years, I'm face to face with Maggie McKee.

9.

February 2003

Video Village was humming. Dan hovered in front of the monitors, reviewing notes Ian had left him, while Vinnie told us about his older daughter's dance recital. Three hours long and only six minutes of his kid. He'd sat through the entire thing.

On the monitors, Maggie messed with her rowing machine while Jason watched SportsCenter on an adjacent screen. "Poor Vinnie," I said. "First that and now he has to sit through this."

"I'm sure that was more interesting," said Rahul. "When is lunch?" I checked my watch. Only eleven a.m. This was going to be one of those long days of Reality that translated to thirty seconds of television.

"There's crap on the couch cushions again." Lauren came in behind Dan, gesturing to the living room camera feed, where Jason was rising from his vigil. Two back cushions of the sunken couch displayed a splatter of what I assumed was tobacco spit. Gross.

"Tyler must have been here," I said. The network didn't mind piles of dirty laundry or an unmown lawn, but the aesthetics of a white couch cushion spackled with tobacco spit were a problem for the test groups. There was only so much "just like us" the television-viewing audience actually wanted. The uncanny valley between overripe and rancid, the visceral difference between elegant flowers that went dry in the vase and those that turned rotten and pulpy on the vine after a surprise autumn freeze. "I'll take care of it."

"Okay, then let's figure out lunch," said Dan. "Sandwiches? Burritos? Pick a place you want and then go out and get everyone's order."

The dirty couch ruined what appetite I had. I grabbed the cushions and took them to the first-floor laundry room, which was packed with clothes, mostly clean and strewn unfolded across the machines. A pile of Jason's sweaty workout things lay crumpled in a corner. I ignored them and grabbed the special spray bottle of heavily researched solution I stored under the sink.

"Cassidy." I turned mid-spray to see Maggie behind me, wearing running shorts, a sports bra, and a full face of makeup.

"Hey," I said. "Can I help you with something?"

"You're the one doing the lunch run, yeah?" I nodded. I was always the one doing the lunch run. "I'm really craving Chinese," Maggie said. "Can you put me down for kung pao chicken, mild spice?"

"Sure." I finished up with the stain and grabbed a legal pad and a pen before going to get everybody's order. Dan wanted egg rolls. Eli passed. Lauren asked for a large tea and some white rice.

"You're doing that place by the Kinko's, yeah?" Sally Ann was setting up her makeup brushes, laying them out in an orderly line. As always, she was outfitted for the occasion of being on television: a low-cut top held together by shoestrings, low-rise jeans, a pair of three-inch heels. "I want the number seven, with chicken. And—"

"The sauce on the side and no nuts." I'd taken this exact order before. What kind of person wanted sauce on the side of their stir-fry? Only in Los Angeles.

"Thanks," she said.

I placed the order. Filming continued. Maggie's publicist had a message from *Sports Illustrated* on which Jason's publicist then had to weigh in. The publicist for *Honeymoon Stage*, who worked at the network, stopped by with a line of scented soaps. Someone came in to fiddle with the internet connection, which had been disrupted by construction down the street. Maggie looked through three different handbags for her car keys. I got in my car to go pick up our lunch.

When I got back from the restaurant, the whole Dean–McKee entourage was gathered between living room and kitchen, trailed by Eli and Rahul and their cameras, as they drank Diet Coke and talked about royalties and tried to choose a spot for Maggie's birthday dinner.

"Is that couch cushion clean yet?" Dan asked me, even before I'd set down the bags of takeout. "We need it back on set." He spotted Eli making some camera choice he disagreed with and moved toward him with a frown.

"I'll hand this stuff out and then check," I said to Dan's back.

"I can help." Jason came up behind me and grabbed one of the bags. The more success Maggie had, the more Jason had been playing up his down-to-earthness, but he rarely stepped up in a way that actually helped me out. I frowned. "What? I'm hungry." To prove it, Jason popped open a paper container and took a bite of an egg roll I knew wasn't his. I shrugged, putting my list on the counter so he'd know who belonged to what, and went back to the laundry room.

The cushions were not clean. I sprayed again, wiped, left them to dry.

I came out and sat behind the camera line, my fork in my fried rice. The flock of publicists had gone, and the guy fixing the internet was off in search of a real electrician. Eli filmed Maggie and Sally Ann as they leaned against the kitchen island, picking at their respective containers of chicken. Maggie said something about renting a movie that evening. Off camera, Lauren reheated her tea.

Sally Ann took a bite and then frowned. Maggie was still going on about the video store, whether they should make the trip or stick with something they already had at home. Sally Ann appeared offended at the thought. Her nose wrinkled, and she shut her eyes in a cute little squint that made her look like an anime character. Then she scratched at her neck with a fake fingernail, and made a sound like a vacuum cleaner revving, air sucked through a clogged straw.

That was weird. I put down my lunch. Sally Ann's neck and chest bloomed pink, face flushing. The microwave hummed its final countdown, and Lauren turned to look at me. I couldn't read her eyes, but I assumed that her tacit instruction was the same as it always was—do nothing.

"Cassidy!" Eli stood up, gesturing. What did he want with me? Was I in his shot? Sally Ann was bent over now, still making that alien sound.

Maggie understood him right away. She sped to Sally Ann's purse, a navy leather hobo resting on the back of the chair next to me, and grabbed what I suddenly realized was an EpiPen. Eli had the wall phone, giving the address to the 911 dispatcher.

I felt dizzy. *Is this actually happening, or happening for the camera?* Maggie plunged the needle into Sally Ann's blue-jeaned thigh, and Sally Ann tried to gasp. She was wheezing; the microwave was beeping. I couldn't tell if the pen had made a difference. Her lips were growing into overstuffed pillows.

I'd thought of myself as someone competent in the face of disaster, the one who'd do the calling of the ambulance and the checking of the pulse. It was my job, after all, to assist the production. But I just stood there, watching as Maggie and Eli helped Sally Ann to the door, where we could already hear distant sirens.

Lauren pressed her lips together, looking right at me. "It'll be okay," she said.

I nodded. It would be fine. The epinephrine would kick in, and Sally Ann would come to, and pretty soon, we would all laugh about this near-disaster. Postproduction would cut this into an episode, and the EpiPen would become another icon—alongside the dry boxed pasta and the Boyz II Men knockoff—another fan-favorite moment to print onto a personalized mug. People had allergies. Modern medicine was a miracle. The EMTs rushed in and loaded Sally Ann onto a gurney, and the ambulance pulled out of the drive.

No one had tossed my crumpled order list from earlier—there it sat on the kitchen counter, next to the empty paper bag now sticky with duck sauce. While everyone was gathered in the foyer to watch the flashing lights, I inched over. There, in my loopy handwriting, was written *SA—#7 chicken, no nuts, sauce on the side.*

⚜

Maggie went with Sally Ann to the hospital. Jason made a series of phone calls, though I couldn't imagine whom he might need to inform. The publicists? Lauren was talking to the network. Until we knew Sally Ann's status, we were told to keep filming. The allergic reaction was content, right up until it wasn't.

I replaced the missing couch cushions. I dabbed club soda onto the fallen soy sauce staining the rug.

"Should we have sent a camera to the hospital?" asked Lauren. Rhetorical, because we would not send one now. Maggie texted Dan to let him know that Sally Ann was being taken into the ICU.

What had just happened? The entire past hour was a parallel reality, the same people and places of my usual life but out the other side of the looking glass.

"She'll be fine," Lauren kept mumbling. Eli's camera stayed with Jason, who was mostly on the phone. It felt gauche to turn on the TV before we knew if Sally Ann was okay, so he had the basketball game on the radio.

It was Dan who found me in the laundry room, where I'd been sorting Maggie's socks for lack of anything else tangible to do.

"Lauren says she'll be fine," I said, pairing a novelty set printed with half-peeled bananas.

"They don't put you in intensive care if you're fine." Dan wiped his forehead with the heel of his palm. "Epinephrine is supposed to kick in within twenty minutes."

"The food. The lunch orders . . . I didn't—" I half hated myself for being so focused on my own involvement when this was not about me. Yes, I hoped Sally Ann would be okay, but I also hoped this wouldn't screw me over. I'd delegated my one regular assignment, the passing of the lunch. Then I'd just stood there, watching Sally Ann's death scene play itself out. If I said nothing, it was possible my part in this whole thing would fly under the radar. But the words cascaded out of me, my moral compass stuck at north. "If I had double-checked to be sure they left the nuts out, she wouldn't have—"

"The production's not at fault here," Dan said. He was giving me that are-you-too-dumb-to-function stare. "Were the production at fault, we would have to figure out who dropped the ball. Any legal ramifications of today's events would then fall on that person." He paused. "Luckily, in this situation, production is not at fault."

Maybe I was too dumb to function. He was implying I should keep my mouth shut, right? Or was he asking me to take the fall?

"I don't think—"

"Good thing we don't pay you to think." Dan could be such an asshole. I usually had Lauren to buffer us, and I wasn't sure how she could stand him. That he sometimes brought in donuts for the crew didn't negate his condescension. Besides, they did pay me to think. Just not about this.

"If I had—"

"Let's wait and see what happens." Dan gave my hand a pat. He wrinkled his nose at the laundry room, then left me to my sock sorting.

I took a deep inhale of dryer sheet and slid my back down the laundry room wall. Breathe in. Breathe out. I'd always been so good about accommodating everyone's diets. No dairy, no sugar, sauce on the side. Jason hadn't known to be careful with Sally Ann's container. But wasn't it ultimately incumbent on the person with the allergy to check that they were eating the right food? It wasn't like I had tricked her.

I'd sat there. I'd sat there, wasting precious seconds, watching Sally Ann's throat swell while the antidote was next to me. I'd let her suffering be part of our show. Her purse was within arm's reach—I wouldn't even have had to stand up.

After digging my phone out of my pocket, I did what anyone would do and called my mother. As the house phone rang, I pictured my mother's kitchen: the kettle with the red plastic bird whistle that sang out when the water was boiling, the tiled backsplash that my stepfather despised but my mother said gave the house character, the used tea bag sitting on a spoon by the sink just in case someone needed more out of it. Afternoon in LA was early evening in Pennsylvania, but no one was home to pick up, which was probably for the best. Crying to my mother would only make her worry. She couldn't even give advice until we knew how Sally Ann would come through, and if she *had* given advice, I likely wouldn't have taken it.

The socks were all partnered.

"She'll be fine." Lauren filled the doorway. "Get off your ass and get back to work."

So, I sat on hold with the company that'd sent us the wrong lighting gels, then double-checked a set of permits. Lauren kept asking Jason questions, trying to get him to emote about the accident, and through it all she kept telling everyone that Sally Ann would be totally fine.

She continued to insist that Sally Ann was fine until she went to take a phone call and came back to tell us Sally Ann was dead.

I still had four hours left on my shift, but I immediately walked out the door.

10.

Instead of going home, I drove to Gabe's. I didn't trust myself to make it all the way back to Silver Lake. I existed outside my body. Had I eaten? I couldn't remember.

Gabe wasn't home, so I waited in my car, outside his building. Five minutes might have passed, or fifty—I'd lost all track of time. He eventually showed up with a trunk full of plastic-bagged groceries and noticed me while trying to balance a gallon of milk in the crook of his elbow. I couldn't help but wonder what a twenty-five-year-old man living alone was doing with a full gallon of milk. I got out of my car, grinning idiotically despite my panicked fugue. Maybe because of it.

"Cassidy?" I hadn't texted or called, just gone instinctively from my shuttered laptop to the driveway to the 405. Gabe put his bags down on the hood of his car.

"I've had the most terrible day," I said, smile crumbling. Something about my face or the tone of my voice clued Gabe in to just how terrible, and he gathered me in a massive hug. He didn't ask me why I wasn't at work, why I was parked on his street, why I was crying.

"It'll be okay," Gabe said. "Whatever it is, it'll be okay."

I wanted to believe him. I wanted to pour myself an entire bottle of wine and pass out in his bed and wake up to a repeat of this morning, when Sally Ann was still alive. This was, in fact, what I intended to do—minus the time travel—but first I had to tell him what had happened.

I don't remember much of that initial conversation. Gabe said something like *Oh fuck* and assured me the whole thing was a crazy freak accident. He made me a dinner that I barely ate and let me borrow a T-shirt to wear as pajamas. He was so tender. So sweet. I wish that I'd had less to drink, that I could clearly remember the exact planes of his face or how he held himself. I wish that those were the moments that had been stealthily captured on camera—that I had video footage of me and Gabe, holed up in his condo in Sun Valley, the evening I drove over and he held me while I cried. This was the hinge, for me and Gabe. This was the moment when we'd either crossed the border into actual intimacy or he'd officially pulled the wool over my eyes. Between my memory and the hard drives of raw footage, I have most of the story of that day, but this stretch of time with Gabe is lost to me. Gabe on the phone with his mother. A glare of light against the kitchen counter, an episode of *Frasier* playing muted on TV.

In the morning, I woke up to a voicemail from Lauren telling me that I should not have walked off set but she was willing to forgive me. Production was on pause for the rest of the week, but I should come in on Monday, as usual. Her tone was no different than it had been in the previous voicemail she'd left me about buying paper doilies. Death did not faze Lauren; she was immune to the weaknesses of human emotion in a way that I decidedly was not. Maybe because she hadn't been the one to fuck up. Maybe because she had hardened her heart to anyone who appeared in front of the camera line. Would this be part of Season Two's story? If legal would let Lauren use it, I sensed that it would. So much for romantic comedy—we were in dead-girl genre now.

Sally Ann was dead.

Was that little girl in her locket her sister or her child? I should have given her the lunch order myself. I should have known to get the EpiPen—it was sitting right next to me. Instead, I'd watched, done nothing. Maggie had had to walk clear across the kitchen, an extra thirty seconds that might have cost Sally Ann her life.

I put down my phone and pulled the curtains open, inviting the midmorning light.

Gabe's place had slightly more flair than your typical bachelor pad. He'd clearly paid someone to decorate—there was no way the Gabe I knew would go for chintz. But that overstuffed chair added a certain warmth to the otherwise austere bedroom, with its dark jersey sheets and off-white curtains. An acoustic guitar leaned against a hamper. A framed photo of his niece and nephew, aged one and five, sat on a mostly bare dresser. There was another photo of him with his parents at what I thought was maybe Niagara Falls. It all smelled like that piney soap he used—what had been like a drug to me last week was helping to ground me in the present.

"Hey." Here he was with coffee. "Do you want breakfast before you go?" I shook my head. Gabe was a good cook, but I couldn't stomach anything.

"They're stopping production for a while," I said. "I don't have anywhere to be."

"Except right here," said Gabe.

"Except right here." I closed my eyes tight, pulled my hair into a ponytail. Gabe sat on the side of the bed.

"We can hang around here today," he said. "If that's what you want." It was exactly what I wanted, though I knew he must have plans he'd be abandoning on my behalf.

"What a weird day," I said. "What a weird everything." Gabe shifted so he was next to me, our backs against his headboard. "Do you ever think about how every person you encounter could just drop dead at any second?"

Gabe pointed at himself. "Kool-Aid club, remember? Existential angst has always been my jam." I chuckled, then felt I shouldn't. How could I laugh when Sally Ann was lying in a morgue somewhere? "Hey," Gabe said. "It makes sense that you're shook up. It happened yesterday. It's traumatic."

"Did I just kill someone? I can't figure out if I just killed someone." I was going to start crying again; I could feel the pressure build behind my eyes.

"You didn't kill anyone." Gabe's voice was firm.

"But if I had just—"

"You could have dug through the order, and there still might have been oil in the sauce. She could have made a bigger deal about the allergy. She got the medicine. You can 'what if' yourself into anything."

"It feels like my fault." I pressed the heels of my hands against my eyes.

"It's not your fault." Gabe gathered me to him. How strange that life went on, that even in my well of guilt I could take pleasure in the nearness of his body, the feel of his fingers stroking my hair. "If you want to smoke weed and play video games, or do a marathon of bad TV, or get ice cream, or just sit here and feel it, whatever you want to do, I'm here."

"I love you," I said. It just came out of me. Were I in my right mind with any time to mull it over, I would certainly have talked myself out of telling Gabe that I loved him. But I felt it then, and I had bulldozed my defenses, so I said it. Gabe's face blossomed.

"I love you." He pulled me closer, resting his chin on my shoulder, his cheek next to mine.

"Fuck," I said. Gabe pulled away, concern wrinkling his forehead. "I'm not taking it back. It's just a shitty time to realize."

"Every time's a shitty time in some way or another," said Gabe. "But also a good one."

"What you are you, a songwriter?"

He kissed me. "It's going to be okay."

I stayed at Gabe's for six days, wearing his T-shirts and using a fresh toothbrush in shrink-wrap that he'd gotten from the dentist. I didn't want to go anywhere, so we hid from the world, curtains closed, bed unmade. I flipped channels and browsed Gabe's bookshelves. He cooked elaborate dishes he'd been wanting to show off to me: coquille Saint Jacques and chicken confit and some meat with a long braise. I didn't go to work on

Monday. I couldn't stomach it. I texted Lauren that I was sick, and I let my phone lose charge. Tuesday passed, then Wednesday. I was certain they would fire me. I only plugged my phone back in because my mother would probably be worried if she couldn't reach me after I'd called her mid-workday the week before. I did indeed have a voicemail checking in on me, as well as one from Lauren and another from Dan.

I called my mother back to assure her I was fine, had just been dealing with some weird stuff at work. I immediately felt bad about not letting her in. But I didn't usually give her the details of a day on the job, never asked her advice about handling Lauren's dry-cleaning or transporting equipment. This was just something that had happened; it hadn't even happened to me.

Sally Ann had died, and I was getting used to it. I no longer shuddered into recognition—the fact of it wasn't an avalanche that buried me anew each time I let my memory breach the past few days. Sally Ann hadn't gone to visit her family; she wasn't fired. She was nowhere; there was no more Sally Ann. I wasn't sure how I was ever going to be able to walk back on set. I felt pathetic and soft and—despite Gabe's continued insistence that I wasn't to blame, despite the lack of police banging down my door—extremely guilty.

I was inclined to let the work voicemails go.

"They're probably just firing me."

"But they might not be," Gabe said. "It's worth at least a listen." He was tuning a guitar. I was going to have to get back to work, if only to let him get back to work.

The first voicemail, from Lauren, was a quick heads-up that Dan was going to call. The second, from Dan, asked me to come into the main production office.

Production headquarters in Glendale was closer to Gabe's place than my own, but I opted to head home to get an outfit that wasn't the jeans and tee I had been wearing at the scene of the crime. Even if they were just going to fire me, I wanted to show up professional, smelling like my own shampoo, wearing mascara.

All the business and tech stuff happened in Glendale—the editing, the logging of footage, the phone calls where the network gave notes. Someone's intern led me into the lone conference room—a generic space with a large blond-wood table and swivel chairs and a sweating pitcher of ice water. Around the table sat Lauren and Dan and a guy introduced to me as EVP of programming, who messed around on his BlackBerry in the corner throughout the whole meeting. No one offered me a drink.

"Cassidy," said Lauren with what passed, for her, as warmth. "We've been worried about you." I didn't buy it, but whatever. There was no harm done in letting her play mother hen. "It's been quite a time for us all."

I'd been unable to cover the dark circles under my eyes with enough concealer to disguise my lack of sleep, but Lauren looked bright as a daisy. Her hair was pulled off her face, her pallor of the previous few weeks gone. You couldn't even tell she'd been in whatever chokehold with legal and the network had prompted this meeting right now. Funny that Rahul and Eli weren't here. Where was Vinnie? Shouldn't they be in on this? Or was I the scapegoat? We'd all been on that set, but they would foist the blame on me. There was a good chance I deserved it.

"What happened to Sally Ann was a tragic accident." Dan sounded like the voiceover on a history documentary. You'd think Sally Ann had been killed by someone's bayonet during the Civil War rather than by food paid for and distributed by production on his watch last week. "But we're going to carry on with the show. We know that's what Sally Ann would have wanted." Even he wasn't buying his own bullshit. He gave an awkward glance at the suit in the corner, who hadn't looked up. Yes, indeed, Sally Ann, a tangential member of the cast who'd hoped the show would be her own ticket to stardom, wanted nothing more than for us to keep on making money. They were going to put an *in memoriam* at the end of an episode and call it a day.

"The show must go on," I said.

"Yes!" Dan missed my sarcasm entirely. He looked relieved, flashing a doofy smile at Lauren. "That's the spirit." I'd never pictured Dan as someone who'd say *That's the spirit* in an unironic way.

"Cassidy, I know it seems callous." Lauren reached across the table for my hand. Her nails were short, green polish flaking. In the six months I had spent working beside her, she had never once touched me. The ceiling fan clicked above us. "But when you think about the money and time we've invested here, we can't just shut down indefinitely because of one accident."

"People have families to feed." Dan was not good at this. Lauren shot him a please-shut-up glare.

"Shouldn't there be more of an investigation?" I said.

"Into what, exactly?" Lauren's tone was sharp.

"I mean . . . she died." I wouldn't let them see me cry about this. They exchanged a glance that I couldn't quite read.

"Cassidy." Lauren seemed to think that if she said my name enough times she could tether me to her point of view. "People die." This was essentially what Gabe had said, and I couldn't help but see myself as naive. Everyone else understood that accidents happened and the world didn't end, but here I was, unable to function. Thinking it was all my fault because when Lauren had given me that do-nothing stare, I had obeyed.

Or was I acting like a human person, not a Reality TV sycophant who threw away whatever interactions didn't suit the plot?

"We understand that this whole thing has been upsetting, and we're making counseling available to you, if that's something you think that you need." Dan was back in History Channel mode, reciting a memorized script.

"We're also prepared to offer you a different role in the production process." Lauren glanced at the EVP, who had yet to acknowledge that we were having a conversation right across from him.

"I don't—" I began. Lauren interrupted me.

"The health of our employees is our number one priority. We would never want to put you back in a situation that made you feel unsafe." I was losing them now.

"Therefore Laur—*we*—think it best to move you into postproduction," said Dan. "You'll be in an extremely important role. We're going to have you log the footage. You'll be first on the line."

This was not a promotion. Logging footage was an awful job, as grueling as PAing but without the excitement of the change in routine. Loggers sat all day at a desk, wearing headphones, writing down the basics of what had been caught on film. *Maggie paces hallway, waiting for ambulance. Jason makes phone calls. Cassidy hyperventilates and hides in the laundry room.* It was important in that it saved the editors from having to watch every dull moment.

"I'm sorry," I said. "Is this because I didn't come in yesterday? Why don't you just fire me?"

"Legal." Now the guy in the corner spoke, though he still didn't look at us.

"Our legal department advises against that," said Dan. "They're worried you'll bring workplace safety complaints. And isn't your brother a lawyer?"

"A doctor," I said. "Almost."

"We think this is a great opportunity for you, Cassidy," said Lauren. A great opportunity for me not to go public about Sally Ann's death. Also an opportunity for me not to throw away my past few months of work. They were going to make me sign something, weren't they?

"We've got this paperwork here for you, and then you can go check out your new space."

The executive left first, then Dan. I wasn't dumb enough to sign the papers without reading them, nor was I dumb enough to turn down the new job. Lauren sat there while I skimmed. An NDA that would prohibit me from talking about anything I'd seen on set, a commitment to finish out the season, etc., etc.

"You're in this, Cassidy," said Lauren. She was different without the men present, less inclined to hide her hunger. The job was easier when she didn't have to finesse both her *Honeymoon Stage* duties *and* Dan. "Whether you want to be or not, you're in this, and we might as well work it to both of our advantages."

"What do you mean?"

"When legal said we couldn't fire you, Dan wanted to keep you on set and just roll back your responsibilities. But I think it would be better for me to have someone in post, so I suggested that we move you." She didn't pretend to have fought for me to stay on, only for me to stay on in a role that made sense for her once she knew I wasn't leaving. "Dan has what's his name, that editor—they have each other's backs. Dan flags stuff for him to watch for, and he tells Dan what he needs, and together they make neat little stories, and the network promotes them. That's how they got that thing with Brent's boyfriend."

"Okay . . ." Dan had invited Brent's boyfriend to film at the house a few weeks prior, where he and Maggie had gotten into it over some proposed state law about strip clubs. It was going to make a great scene in a forthcoming episode, and everyone knew it. From Lauren's phrasing, I could now assume some story editor had sussed out their opposing views on the issue and told Dan to get them talking. Very clever. "But I'm not in editing. What can I do?"

"You're smart. You notice things."

"I mean . . ."

"I know you've seen things." She was looking at me strangely. Did she think I had known about the nuts in Sally Ann's food? Or was this about Jason and Maggie? I was in no real position to press her. She continued. "Whatever you see while logging, you bring it to me first. You get any ideas for story, see anything we can use in a way that might hit, we brainstorm before you submit your log so I can pitch it up above before the guys do."

"So go behind their backs."

"Around them." Lauren sighed. "Nobody's looking out for Cassidy Baum here. They're all looking out for themselves. When we have the chance, we take it—with me out there and you in here, we'll have everything we need. We can go far together."

I thought of Dan telling me about the mouths to feed. Explaining how a computer worked like I was his child and not his colleague. Sending me back to the drive-through because I'd gotten him the unsweetened iced tea.

"Okay," I said. "Can do."

Poor Sally Ann, I thought as I pulled out of Glendale. When Celia talked about her auditions, she made it clear that she was always one of many in the folding chairs, lined up against the walls. All mumbling the same sides, wearing the same version of whatever outfit. In Hollywood, there was always someone else to take your place. Girls all over with the same dream—generally to be in the spotlight but also lots like me, who wanted to direct its gaze. Step out of line or voice a reasonable complaint, and the higher-ups would quickly replace you. Even Maggie McKee was expendable, prey to the next well-endowed triple threat wearing a newer spangly bra. Sally Ann wasn't a person to mourn but a job opening that now needed filling. I bit my lip so hard it bled.

For whatever reason, Lauren thought I was special. Could it be she saw in me what I wanted to see in myself? Or had I simply lucked into the right kind of screwup: one that could bring legal scrutiny where nobody wanted it, that wasn't unequivocally my fault but wasn't *not* my fault either. Whichever it was, I'd be stupid not to team up with Lauren, turn this all to my advantage to help my career. I might be racked with guilt, but I was certainly not stupid. Or so I thought.

In retrospect, I kept my job because the network was scared I'd find a way to bring charges against them, and Lauren was scared I'd dug up secrets that were still buried deep.

I don't think Maggie and Jason were scared. At least not yet.

11.

A silver lining was that my new role granted some stability. I was not going to have to fly off to Tallahassee at a moment's notice, or drive an hour for the right-color button, or get the oil changed in Dan's car. I didn't get stuck on the 101 midday, or wear down the heels of my shoes plastering posters that proclaimed the crew was filming in large public spaces. I showed up to the Glendale office at eight thirty, watched four hours of footage—noting who went where and at what point someone spoke—took a lunch break, and then clocked back in until five. On the bright side, my evenings were my own. I could go out with my friends for a drink, or go to see one of Gabe's shows. I could go to a movie, do my shopping. My pay didn't change.

Jason and Maggie remained in Calabasas, but in a way, I saw even more of them than I had when we were under the same roof. All day I watched one or the other or both of them, sitting in my swivel chair behind the fourth wall and tracking who they met and what they ate and whether they had interesting reactions. I'd write *Maggie pedicure—asks for warmer water 11:13,* or *Jason trips on rug 45:08. Maggie-ism about refrigerator 1:07:18. Bird flies into wall 1:10:06.* Always, I was searching for something that Lauren might use, hoping the perfect footage would rescue me from my new workplace purgatory. As much as I'd complained about the fast pace on set, it was infinitely preferable to sitting alone in a small room for hours on end, tracking Maggie McKee's movements.

Thank god for Gabe and the promise of meeting him for dinner. My butt would be numb and my foot asleep and my eyes about to burn out of my skull if I saw any more footage of Jason Dean watching SportsCenter, but then I'd imagine what Gabe was going to sear for me that night in his cast-iron skillet, what wine we'd have, how he'd hold my hips and put on jazz and make me giddy with the promise of adulthood. How he'd nuzzle my neck and make a dumb pun about something in the news. I'd think about how happy I was in my personal life, even as work broke down around me.

Even as Sally Ann had died, and we kept filming a TV show.

Sad pensive look—Maggie 2:00:16.

In one episode, Maggie's parents are coming to dinner. At four thirty p.m., she realizes they have nothing to eat. She sends Jason to go pick up something catered. She changes her clothes. When he returns, they pour each individual carton of salad into a large teak bowl, move the beautifully caramelized lasagna from the aluminum into a porcelain casserole dish, put the rolls in the oven. Maggie's mother compliments the cooking, and Maggie and Jason share a hidden smile before Maggie blows their cover and admits it's from Al Prato.

That's what aired. Now here's what I saw:

> CAM A 0:00–6:22. M comes in door, on phone talking about something that just happened at recording studio, seems stressed (somebody named Denny?)
> 6:25—Remembers dinner—*good face*
> 6:30—opens fridge, opens cabinets, rolls eyes and mutters something indecipherable, sits drinking a Coke (jib bounce)
> 9:00—calls for J, downstairs couch, watching TV

9:10–13:00—awkwardness about who was supposed to make plan . . . him, her, blah blah he'll get from Al Prato (mic taps: can't use sound)
13:12—J leaves (see CAM B)
13:20–23:15—M shower, no visual
25:00–40:00—M blow dry, robe
45:00—M makeup
54:11—M downstairs couch
1:13:18—M emptying dishwasher
1:26:00—M downstairs couch
1:37:09—J comes in with bags, empties things into containers
1:52:12—Both couch

So much couch. So much dishwasher. So much blow-dryer and closed bathroom door. The minutiae of a life might be interesting to Proust, but only because he wasn't watching from the outside. Imagine seven volumes of text where a guy very slowly sits and eats his cookie and you never know what's going through his head. That was my gig.

Two weeks into my sentence in postproduction, I showed up to a huge roll of tape at the top of my pile. *Old security cam by garage,* someone had scrawled—Ian maybe, who ran the crew opposite Dan's. I'd grabbed a croissant from Celia's coffee shop on the way to work and had buttery flakes all over my black pants. I was more focused on sweeping them under the swivel chair's carpet pad than on the slightly grainy footage on my monitor.

Between the pool house and Jason and Maggie's garage was an awkward strip of space I'd always thought to be completely camera-free. The tripods couldn't fit between it, and there'd been no reason to bring any handhelds back. I supposed someone could hang out in there if they wanted to, but it was mostly just runaway knapweed, so what would be the point? It was a non-place. Barely worth watching. My day would likely be a long one, tracking clouds making shadows and wind ruffling grass. I preferred couch.

I sighed and opened AOL Instant Messenger, keeping one eye on my buddy list, waiting for Gabe's name. A lizard darted across the dirt on my screen. I cracked my neck. Considered taking up knitting. Even if I did see something good here, what could the editors even do with it? The angle was awful, and the lighting changed so often there was no way to account for continuity. The sound was raw, not anything we could air.

Just as I was debating refilling my to-go cup with the break room's awful coffee, I heard a shuffling sound coming through the speakers and watched a figure slide into view. Vinnie. The camera was mounted on the pool house at an angle that showed me Vinnie from above as he dug into his pocket for a cigarette. He leaned against the garage, lighting up with obvious relief. I knew it. I'd never outright seen Vinnie smoking, but there were definitely times I caught a whiff of Camel Lights, despite the fact that I'd heard him swear to his wife he was quitting. This must be his hiding spot, the sneak. He stubbed the butt out on the siding and took it with him when he inched back off the screen.

I played the tape at triple the speed. More shadows. More wind. Vinnie, back again several hours later.

The footage was dated just after Thanksgiving, and I wondered if production actually wanted me to watch three whole months of it. Gabe wasn't on AIM. Since my multiday breakdown, we'd spent almost every night together. I had a drawer in his dresser, my preferred yogurt sitting in his fridge. But he must have been at work or running errands, so I was left with clouds and shadows. Vinnie again. I'd run these out at 10x speed and blast through them by the end of the week.

I was just about to majorly fast-forward when something caught my eye. A movement that was neither a lizard nor Vinnie. I rewound. Sally Ann.

This wasn't her ghost come to haunt me. It made sense that, like Vinnie, Sally Ann might find refuge in this seemingly camera-free part of the property. Didn't we all have moments we wanted to do something private like smoke a verboten cigarette or clear a stuffy nose? Moments we wanted to exist without the pressures of another person watching us. Working on the bustling set, I had occasionally locked myself in a bathroom just to breathe, and I wasn't even in front of the camera.

But Sally Ann wasn't looking for a rare moment of peace, because Sally Ann wasn't alone.

I recognized him immediately. He stalked like a big cat, sleek and muscular, with purpose. Jason Dean was always in control of his body. Therefore, Jason Dean was in control of his body as he pressed Sally Ann up against the taupe garage siding and kissed her.

My breath caught. This was a development.

On-screen, Jason unhooked Sally Ann's bra, and she batted his hands away, laughing.

"Not here!"

"Sorry." He helped her refasten it. She stuck her leg between his thighs, and he said "Baby" in a tone that made it clear that this was not their first time being intimate. Apparently Sally Ann wouldn't go topless, but she wasn't opposed to helping Jason get off. I grimaced. This felt dangerously close to amateur porn. How was I supposed to log this? *CAMJ: Jason makes out with Sally Ann*—I checked the date—*about three months before her fatal accident. Visuals blurry, bad sound. Good expressions.*

I sped through the nonspeaking portion of their rendezvous, then ran the feed again in real time when they started making themselves presentable. Jason left first, and Sally Ann messed with a fingernail while waiting for her own cue to exit. Nothing about her expressed any remorse that she'd just done stuff with her mouth to her friend's husband. She looked around, her eyes momentarily meeting the camera. I waited for her to wink, to grimace, to make some acknowledgment from the ether that told me she knew I was watching her, but she seemed as oblivious to the camera as the rest of them. She left the screen, and I was back to the shadows, the wind stirring dust.

Oh my god. Jason and Sally Ann.

It made so much sense—she was a slightly younger, less confident version of Maggie. Both bottle blond, both skinny, but when, in real life, Maggie rolled her eyes, Sally Ann would look at Jason as if he'd just hung the moon. She was always around. Well, she had been around. She wasn't any longer.

I felt the itch of something, a budding suspicion. A question I wasn't sure I could allow myself to ask.

Just off-screen, someone was using the hose, and the residual spray dampened my patch of grass and gravel. I sped the playback up again.

If Lauren wanted drama, here was drama. If I gave her this footage, we both would be gold. But did I want to hurt Jason, who had always been kind to me? I wasn't overly superstitious, but digging around for no good reason felt like inviting bad juju. Sally Ann had just died for her job; I might as well let her be. Maggie didn't need to see her husband's sex tape.

There were still weeks of tape to get through, so I went back to normal speed and left the roll running while I went to the break kitchen. A few unrinsed mugs sat piled up next to the sink, which told me the meeting I had not been invited to that morning was probably over. Muffled laughter came from down the hall, and despite my workplace loneliness, for once I felt no inclination to seek out camaraderie. The coffee vat was empty, and I thought about my options while the next pot brewed.

If this was the only time Jason and Sally Ann had canoodled between the pool house and the garage, I could pretend I hadn't seen them. No one was breathing down my neck about security footage, and no one else was going to painstakingly go through that tape. Letting it lie seemed like the respectful decision. But making the respectful choice would never help me helm the yacht that was Reality TV.

I could tell Lauren that I had an inkling something was going on between Sally Ann and Jason, say I got the feeling from something I'd seen on the other cameras. Part of me was tempted to pull out all the old tapes and reinterpret any look between Jason and Sally Ann, any brush of the hand or unusual tone. With the right editing, we could build out the whole story—they meet, they fall for each other, they agonize but then begin a hidden romance. Then what? She dies?

This was why I needed Lauren. She'd be able to weigh the consequences of torpedoing Jason and Maggie's perfect love story, the love story that had been the whole point of our show. What was *Honeymoon Stage* without the eternal devotion of its heroes? They were supposed to live happily ever after.

But maybe there was a reason all the fairy tales ended at the wedding. How long could we sustain a show where everything went Maggie and Jason's way? There were only so many carriage rides an audience would watch, only so many candlelit dinners.

The coffee maker beeped, and I poured myself a cup. I had to tell Lauren. That was the only rational thing to do. That was what she would say she was paying me for.

I made my way slowly back to my desk. Setting down my coffee, I pulled my email up on my second screen and started drafting my message to Lauren. Hi, I found a story. We should dig up any cheating or infidelity conversations, with reporters or otherwise. I don't know if you want to go in this direction, but I've found some tape that proves Jason's unfaithful. Should I not send this over work email? Are our communications supposed to be private?

I tapped on the delete button, getting rid of everything but my first sentence. Then I glanced at my video monitor and pressed down on the button until that opening salutation disappeared too.

Because there, on the video monitor, was Lauren sucking face with Dan.

I had been given the nuclear codes. I had the power to explode *Honeymoon Stage* in an instant, be it with allegations of inappropriate workplace conduct or proof that the whole premise of the show was a lie. With great power came great responsibility. No way was I going to relinquish any of this information until I had watched every scene. It seemed I was one of the few people who had not taken advantage of the strip between the garage and the pool house, its supposed lack of cameras. I watched as, every few days, one of the alternate-shift PAs sat down there to cry.

Vinnie smoked his Camels. Eli stashed a camera that he didn't want the other crew members messing with, and one of the camera assistants dry heaved until he'd gotten past the worst of his hangover. Dan and Lauren were engaged in an enemies-to-lovers situation, or maybe just got off on the fact that they hated each other and he was her boss.

"We're going to have to reshoot them in the kitchen," Dan said as he zipped up his fly. "If Maggie doesn't want to cook a full meal again, she can at least make peanut butter sandwiches. What we have now is ruined by her mother's yapping dog."

"Send the dog off with the makeup girl. Solves two problems at once." Lauren, of course, could reapply her lipstick without looking in the mirror.

"Yes, ma'am." Even through the fuzzy mic, I could pick up on the disdain in Dan's tone.

"Fuck off."

"This time tomorrow."

Jason and Sally Ann were also regularly fucking. That was the only way to phrase it, uncouth as it sounded and loathe as I was to speak ill of the dead. Every few days they would stumble into the outdoor crawl space. They'd tear at each other, hungry and giggling, trying positions I would never have imagined could work in a nook of about ten feet by four.

I was going to keep watching these tapes, even if they slowed down the rest of my log sheets. This was the good stuff and, when I figured out just how to use it, would virtually guarantee my promotion. More than savvy PAing or slipping ideas to Lauren, this footage could cement me in the industry.

I had a few days to focus before anyone would catch on, after which I'd pull an all-nighter and get caught up with the more current tapes. Maybe Gabe would want to join me, have takeout and a bottle of wine over footage of Jason Dean getting his car washed.

I'd been afraid to let Gabe see me vulnerable, eye-dropping dribbles of insecurity as slowly as I could over our first few months. With Sally Ann's death, I'd tipped the bucket, and rather than both of us drowning, things were better than I'd dreamed that they could be. We goofed off at the grocery store. I let Gabe take me hiking. I said hi into the phone when he talked to his mom. He had even suggested a double date with Celia and whoever she was seeing, a magnanimous offer that had her incredibly excited.

Usually when Gabe asked me what I'd done all day, my answer was "Not much." Today, I could tell him honestly that I'd watched two-time MLB All-Star Jason Dean take off someone's bra with his teeth.

By midafternoon I'd only gotten through early November. I'd gone and made some microwave popcorn, and the arrow keys were greasy from my sudden stops and starts. For most of the tape, the space was empty, and I'd gotten good at zoning out until something of notice flickered into view, at which point I'd rewind a few frames and settle in.

That night, Gabe had a show at nine. It was an important gig for him, the first I'd be at in an actual venue, and I was so pumped that I wasn't sure how I would get through the eight hours of work beforehand. I was supposed to meet Celia for dinner. On a normal day, I'd clock out at five on the dot, but I was so caught up in the new footage that it wasn't until Celia called me at five forty asking where we were eating that I remembered our plans and powered down my computer.

On the drive home, my thoughts kept racing. I had no natural instinct for cutting throats. But I knew that if I wasted this information, I might as well pack up and go back home to Philly. I'd been trying to balance PAing with protecting Jason and Maggie, and look where it had gotten me: stuck in Glendale with no foreseeable way out. Something had to give, and this was it.

Hadn't Lauren been trying to tell me all along that this was the job? If I had to pivot from helping Maggie and Jason build their images to burning those same images down, I resolved that I would do it. And it wouldn't even really hurt Maggie. She might be embarrassed to have her husband's affair public, but in a way, I'd be doing her a favor. She could find a better husband, one who wasn't sleeping with her friend. And if she couldn't? I'd still be back on set in Calabasas. All was fair in love and Reality TV.

I needed to figure out how to approach Lauren with the information about Dan in a way that positioned me for career success. I could threaten to report her to HR (what little we had of it), or casually let her know I was in on her secret (that seemed more promising), or I could just double down on our crusade against Dan (which, now that I knew their situation, took on a whole new, twisted light). Then it struck me that maybe Lauren thought I'd already known—that their affair may have been what she meant when she kept telling me I saw things.

"I've had the strangest day at work," I said to Celia once we were both dressed for the night and headed out to her car.

"Do tell." She had on a magenta going-out top with rhinestones sewn along the neckline that I knew were going to scratch up her collarbone all evening long.

"Hypothetically," I said, buckling into the passenger seat, "if you could prove that your boss was doing something they didn't want anyone else to know about, what would you do?"

"Doing something or someone?" Celia barely missed clipping the front bumper of the car behind us.

"What are you, psychic?"

"It's Hollywood. Everyone's sleeping around."

"Everyone? Harsh."

"I mean not, like, Gabe. Can you imagine?" Celia laughed. I wasn't sure whether I should be offended or flattered. Outside, the endless sunny day of Los Angeles began to turn into its endless balmy night.

"I'd rather not imagine," I said. "But why do you think it's so unlikely?"

"Well, first off he's dating you," said Celia, making a sudden left turn. "So why would he?"

"Good save," I said.

"But also, he's nice. He does jigsaw puzzles. He's taking us to Al Prato. He spends all weekend making soup."

"So?"

"I like him!" Celia parked the car. "He's great! Forget I said anything, and let's go back to talking about how you can blackmail your boss."

For dinner, we'd chosen a smoothie spot that also sold what they called "fusion" empanadas. I knew Celia would order a protein shake and swear that was enough for her, then end up eating half of whatever I got. We'd done this before—her aspirational Los Angeles diet no match for her urge to eat chewable food. I doubled up on barbecue-chicken empanadas.

Celia didn't have any good advice on the Lauren front, though in her defense, my reluctance to share details made it hard for her to help. By the time we pulled up to the Balladeer, we were back to our usual game of bemoaning the fact that Celia's rival, a girl of the exact same height and build, had beaten her out for a commercial they had both been called back for.

We got our hands stamped by the bouncer and wandered through the bar into the concert space, winding our way to the stage. I felt a sudden burst of pride for Gabe. I knew how hard he worked, how important this was to him. I'd seen him perform before, solo at bars, but since we'd started dating, he hadn't done anything big with the band. This was a part of his life that I would finally be let in on. An equipment guy was testing something on the drum kit, and when he saw me, he sent us backstage.

"You made it!" The band sat lounging on the greenroom couch. The other guys were drinking beers, but Gabe seemed sober. I could tell he was anxious, those fingers jittering a mile a minute. This was a big venue for him, not necessarily in size but in prestige.

"Of course," I said. "I wouldn't miss it."

"Opener's on in five," a frazzled stage manager yelled at us through the door.

"Go get a drink," Gabe said. "I'll find you after."

"Yes, sir." I kissed him, and he grinned at me, and I thought about how weird it was that my boyfriend was about to sing love songs to a room full of strangers.

The opening act was something of a downer, and Celia and I'd each made it through two vodka sodas by the time they announced their last song.

"Thank god," she said under her breath. "I was about to fall asleep." We were surrounded by people about our own age, likely early to mid-twenties, most of whom were dressed in jeans and bedazzled tops, wearing heels, sipping booze out of stirrer straws. The lights came up so the crew could change out instruments, and an avalanche descended on the bar. This was the scene I had been missing, all those long hours on set in Calabasas, when instead of mingling, I'd been spreadsheeting with Dan and replacing Maggie's light bulbs. Celia pulled me out of the crowd, and we found a relatively roomy spot on the balcony, where we could see the stage well and avoid the press of people.

When Gabe came out in his slouchy black tee and black jacket, his hair gelled up and rope bracelets artfully stacked on his wrist, it took a minute to square rock star Gabe with the guy who made me pancakes in pajama pants and glasses.

"He is so hot," Celia whispered.

"You take it back that he's not cool enough to cheat on me now, don't you?" I said. Because no matter how much of a dork he was in real life, when Gabe started to play, he was coolness personified. Confidence and vulnerability, his voice raspy but strong, no sign of the gawky kid he'd been on *The Tiger Crew*. When he leaned into the microphone, it felt like he was telling me a secret, and the grin he gave the crowd might have been for me alone. He'd occasionally look over to where Celia and I stood up top, meeting my eyes.

"Nah," said Celia. "He's so into you, it's gross."

Gabe and the band did their set, and by the end, I was too many drinks in to hold on to any dignity. I pulled Celia down through the crowd to try and intercept him when he went offstage.

"You can't be back here, ma'am." Of course there was security, the beefy respectful type who'd call me ma'am, though I was wearing an outfit that screamed broke and in my twenties.

"But I can be," I said. "I was earlier." Luckily Gabe appeared before we were dismissed.

"She's with me." He grabbed my hand and pulled me through. "They both are."

I didn't want to let go of him to let him back onstage to do the encore. What more did these people need? He'd already given them a full hour and a half. It was my turn to take him home and make him Easy Mac and share his shower and lie naked in his bed. But alas, this was the price I had to pay in agreeing to date him. Other people wanted my boyfriend, and that was why he made money—if this gig did, in fact, make money; I still didn't have a good handle on Gabe's finances.

Celia and I stood at the side of the stage and watched the band give their encore, and Gabe smiled that pleased, bashful smile and tossed his guitar pick out into the audience. I finished the beer I was holding. It was already almost midnight, and I realized that I was not going to pick Gabe's brain about the new security footage and Sally Ann and Lauren. I was going to wait for him to get through signing people's tickets and posing for their digital cameras, and then I was going to get in his car and try not to fall asleep on the drive back to his condo. The thought made me unequivocally happy.

We ate leftovers out of his fridge and also microwaved some pizza rolls, and I borrowed a T-shirt to sleep in. Around five in the morning, I woke up for a glass of water, and he woke up as I was getting back in bed. He kissed my neck, and I got on top of him, and we had sweet, silent sex and then fell back asleep. Gabe was still sleeping when I left for work at eight.

Because of my late night and our early-morning workout, I didn't bother to go home. I showered at Gabe's and put on yesterday's jeans and one of his smaller Gabriel Leighton shirts tucked artfully in, as if I wanted to be party on the bottom and merch slinger on top. If it was gauche to wear my boyfriend's face plastered across my chest—his blue eyes pensive and his name written graffiti-style in embarrassingly large purple letters—it was even worse to opt for last night's spangled halter. Luckily it didn't really matter, because the only person who saw me was Monica at the front desk, who gave a little wave before focusing back on whoever was on the phone.

After popping into the kitchen for sustenance, I readied myself for another day with the new footage. It was mentally exhausting and morally—even legally—questionable. Despite the waivers they'd signed before coming on set, these people didn't think that anyone could see them. Imagining someone watching me in my most intimate moments sent a shiver down my spine, and I felt every stiff mixed-cotton fiber of Gabe's T-shirt.

But then I remembered that someone *had* watched me. Maggie had watched me. Maggie had done exactly what I was doing now. I pictured her sitting down to the security camera footage, wondering, I supposed, what had been happening in Calabasas while she was in Mexico. What had she been looking for? Whatever the answer, Gabe and I were what she'd found.

On the monitor, the sun moved full force into the position that, for twenty minutes a day, cast the hidden area between the garage and pool in light.

Maggie hadn't gone public with what she'd seen of me and Gabe, and despite my conviction the night before, I wouldn't immediately go public with my new discoveries either. I would channel her and Lauren, the two poles of our show.

Be smart, Cassidy. Be patient. Be ruthless.

I played the footage at 10x. For three full days, not even a lizard or bird appeared on-screen. I was humming one of Gabe's songs and massacring my thumbnail when things finally got interesting.

Sally Ann and Jason again, but without their usual zippiness. She tugged him in front of the camera, standing with her back to me, and his whole face in view. They didn't touch one another, but from Jason's expression, I could tell Sally Ann was talking. With the computer volume all the way up, I could hear what she said.

"You know that it takes two of us to keep everything quiet." That desperation in her voice was so familiar, the same make-me-a-star longing she'd displayed every time she came on set, now stretched like Silly Putty until the holes were showing through.

Jason rolled his eyes. "She's not going to leave me over—" He gestured to the small space between them. "She's smarter than you think."

"Not her," Sally Ann whispered. I leaned into the screen, as if moving closer would give me a better read on Jason's blurred expression—a flash of, perhaps, panic, but I couldn't be sure. "I wouldn't tell Maggie."

"You wouldn't take this to the tabloids. That shit never ends well for the girl." He was right, of course. How many times had I seen the nanny or the personal assistant on the cover of the magazine, a hand up to hide her face, the headline something like Yes . . . He Was My Lover or Mistress

Tells All? Then two weeks later, the backlash; the nightly talk show hosts casting doubt, the paparazzi asking how it felt to break up a family, the watercooler conversations, the eternal relegation to the punchline of the joke. A decade ago, maybe Sally Ann would have thought to build a career on going public about sleeping with Jason, but that scenario had played out before, and he was right. It never ended well for the girl. She might have a moment selling belts on QVC or get a sit-down interview on a morning show, but aside from the initial payout, there were no real perks to that type of notoriety.

Sally Ann said something in response, her voice so quiet that I only knew she spoke because of the sudden change in Jason's face. Even with fuzzy image quality, I could see the shift come over him, a stillness that had not been there before. I rewound, scooted my swivel chair closer. Unplugged and replugged my headphones. It took me three tries before I figured out what she was whispering.

"I'd share what you told me that night in Reseda. Not just this."

I rewound to watch Jason's face fall three more times before I followed the tape further, to the moment when he punched the garage siding. My volume was still turned to the maximum level, and my eardrums rang with the strength of his "Fuck."

I checked the date. December 8. Season One had wrapped, and I had been at my mother's house in Pennsylvania.

Jason left the monitor first, clutching the hand that I assumed he had not broken. He'd been so irritable after the first-season press tour. He'd had that paparazzi altercation, the one that reinjured his shoulder. Everyone assumed it was because the photographers had done that wild chase with Maggie. But maybe everyone had been wrong.

Jason had been angry enough at Sally Ann to punch an outdoor wall. Angry enough to walk away mid-conversation. Angry enough, I wondered suddenly, to get rid of her?

Sally Ann's death was an accident. But what if it wasn't? What if it was somehow planned? My heart sped up. What were the chances that

Sally Ann would suddenly die before revealing whatever it was Jason seemed desperate to keep quiet? The coincidence was just too much.

Could Jason have taken the lunches from me knowing Sally Ann couldn't have peanuts? Had he switched Maggie's kung pao chicken with Sally Ann's nut-free stir fry? He'd been poking through the bag. He'd encouraged me to go back to the laundry room while he passed out the food.

Was Jason Dean—Philadelphia-hero, jovial, have-a-beer-with, Disney-prince, Ricky Ricardo 2.0 Jason Dean—a murderer?

The tape kept playing, but I slid my chair back to the opposite wall. My headphones yanked from the jack, their cord dangling.

I'd thought my jackpot was footage of my colleagues' private vices. A forbidden cigarette. A hidden hangover. A blow job for the boss.

But Sally Ann was dead. Jason had wanted her quiet. Lauren and Dan knew about her allergy, and they both had a secret to hide too.

In watching Maggie zone out on the couch, Jason hang photographs and water the lawn, I had assumed that I knew them. I'd spent up to twelve-hour shifts with Lauren, knew the moles on her arms and the bleached scent of her newly dyed hair. I'd thought I saw through Dan's facade of congeniality. But even Vinnie had flat out lied to my face about the cigarettes.

The remains of whatever I'd eaten last night—those empanadas, too much beer—churned in my stomach. The *Honeymoon Stage* set was a huge pit of snakes, and I was Indiana Jones down in the thick of them.

I had to call Gabe. He'd put this whole thing in perspective. Gabe was pragmatic. He was smart. He could help me. Jen would tell me to go to the cops, and Celia would catastrophize, and my mother would buy me a plane ticket east, but Gabe would keep a level head. Pulling the headphones down around my neck, I grabbed my cell phone and fumbled for his number.

Then my arms fell to my sides. The phone slipped from my hand.

Because there, on the monitor that I had been neglecting, stood a fuzzy Gabriel Leighton in an intimate embrace with none other than Maggie McKee.

October 2007

"Now blink," says the makeup artist.

It's my wedding day, and when I look in the mirror, I barely see myself as a bride. Instead, I'm haunted by the vision of Gabe in the garden last night, whispering, "You can't tell anyone. It'd be a disaster."

How well do you really know him, Cassidy?

I thought I knew Gabe. Thought I'd aired our dirty laundry, washed it clean. Instead, the lies and accusations all throughout the years have come barreling toward me with the force of interstellar travel.

I turn to get a better view of Maggie.

Here she is, in her own silk bridesmaid's robe, her face free of makeup and her blond hair held back with a claw clip.

"Hey, Cassidy." She's using her little-girl voice, I'm-in-front-of-camera voice. *Look at me—how could I do wrong?*

The makeup artist sprays something on my face to set the work she's already done.

The last time I saw Maggie in person, she was stretching her calf in front of a gaudy Calabasas fountain, face flushed. Her skin was paler then, pinker. She's clearly had a recent spray tan. Her teeth are impeccably straight and white. I should respond to her. I make a grunting sound that I hope can be explained by my current role as makeup model and try not to think about how it will play on TV.

Maggie goes over to Celia and Jen and introduces herself. Jen gives a polished smile and shakes her hand, but Celia's greeting is laced with an undisguised skepticism. I feel sick. I do not want her here, although I know so many reasons why I need her to be. I want to tell her to get out; I want to tell her to explain what really happened years ago with my fiancé.

"Now blot." The makeup artist hands me a tissue. I obey.

Jen is cordial, and Celia is not outwardly obnoxious. The cameras film the three of them, with their coffee and champagne, making small talk about the weather and the pastries—which mostly sit untouched. How was Maggie's flight? Does Jen live in the area? Maggie McKee seems almost like a normal human person. A new girl starts on my hair, which hisses when the flat iron hits it.

By the time the team is done with me—or at least my first pass, as I'm told they'll do touch-ups before the afternoon really gets going—I look enough like someone else, someone polished and camera ready, that I have psyched myself up to confront Maggie. Maybe the real Cassidy Baum couldn't do it—maybe the real Cassidy Baum is too afraid to go find Gabe and ask him outright to be straight with her; the real Cassidy Baum cowers in the face of celebrity and scandal—but whoever this is looking at me in the mirror has impeccable armor.

Somehow my lips seem twice their usual size.

The better to call you on your bullshit with, my dear.

12.

April 2003

Here came the sour dregs of beer, the milky coffee I'd been downing all morning. I beelined to the single-stall bathroom, headphones still around my neck, and emptied it all into the clean ceramic toilet. I felt a sudden chill and rubbed my arms as I remembered I was wearing Gabe's airbrushed face on my chest.

From the moment I first saw him, I'd sensed that his face would be my downfall. Gabriel Leighton, *The Tiger Crew* alumnus, working songwriter, aspiring pop-folk artist. The guy who stirred eggs so slowly that I actually liked eating them scrambled. Who rested his chin on the top of my head when he held me from behind. Gabe, who made me like hiking and hardware stores and really anything I was doing in his company, because I liked him so much it almost physically hurt. Gabe, who'd said he loved me. Gabe, who'd admitted to his childhood crush on Maggie.

The facts turned like a kaleidoscope, realigning in my brain to tell a new story. We had first met at the bottom of Maggie's driveway. He never wanted to come on set to say hi, despite the fact he had been friends with Maggie growing up. I'd told myself he was embarrassed that her career had taken off while his was slower to launch, or else embarrassed that she had rejected him when they were thirteen. I thought I might be sick again, but nothing came up.

The possibility of what I'd built with Gabe was a balloon we hadn't tied, and all the air was whooshing out. It made me dizzy. It made me feel like I'd been played for a fool. After my dad's second betrayal, I had sworn to myself that I would never again let another person make me feel like this.

All the time I'd thought Gabe wanted to talk to me—because of, what, my sparkling personality?—he'd actually been going after Maggie. He was still in love with Maggie. Who did I think I was?

Just remarkably stupid. Too dumb to realize that my bosses were sleeping together. Too dumb to know that the man I watched professionally 24/7 was cheating on his wife. Too dumb to see that the man I loved had always been in love with someone else.

My throat burned, and I figured I deserved it. I washed my hands with the bar soap, scrubbing far past the point of necessary hygiene. I willed myself not to cry.

The mirror hanging in the bathroom was a full-length with a bright-yellow frame, gifted by the wife of some guy on the production team. *It's an art piece,* the guy told everyone proudly. It didn't look like an art piece to me, not with my sorry self reflected on its surface, goose pimpled and haggard. My hair, which I'd washed but not blown out that morning, crimped in awkward tendrils around my tired face. I'd aged a decade in the past twenty-five minutes. Bags under my eyes like bruises, my eyeliner smeared. I looked like the morning after personified. I looked like an unhinged Gabriel Leighton fan.

Tucking my hair behind my ears, I headed back to my logging closet. Where else was I going to go? Work was suddenly all I had.

The tape was still playing, and since I'd dragged my headphones with me to the bathroom, the sound came through the monitors in a rustling of wind, the occasional creak of the siding, the rev of an engine in the driveway nearby. The space was empty again, innocuous, teasing me with its mundanity. Part of me wanted to rewind, to watch Gabe's hands on Maggie's waist, hers on his shoulders, to ascertain I hadn't imagined the whole thing. But I knew what I'd seen.

My phone lay face down where I'd dropped it, still flipped open. I nudged it with a shoe, like it might bite. Two missed calls from Gabe. How long had I been in the bathroom? It had felt like forever. The date on my screen showed me the footage had moved into the next day. Instinctually, I pressed the 10x replay.

All I could do was my job. All I wanted to do was my job. If I just sat there doing my job for the six hours until end of day, I would not have to acknowledge that things had irrevocably changed. Watching was the perfect buffer—I could sit in the safety of my voyeurism, avoiding my own foolish self. If I kept watching, I did not have to actually do anything.

"Cassidy!" I jumped.

It was Gabe, solid, in the flesh. Unshowered, his hair stiff with yesterday's gel, that pheromonal sweet-sweatiness that had drawn me to him from the moment we met. My chest clenched.

"How did you get in here?"

"The lady at the front told me where to go. You weren't answering your phone." He moved to touch my arm, and I gave an infinitesimal flinch. Gabe frowned. When he swallowed, his Adam's apple dipped. "You forgot your wallet," he continued, looking around at my empty popcorn bags, my coffee mugs and dented cans of Diet Coke. "I figured I'd drop it by on my way to that good breakfast-taco place . . ." Gabe's voice trailed off as he examined the footage on my monitor. I waited for him to realize what it was I had been looking at. He didn't. "Though maybe I should have done the taco place first, brought you some sustenance."

He waited for me to speak. Normally I would have made a joke or would have kissed him. Instead I stood awkwardly, arms wrapped around my torso, lips pressed tight.

I'd barely processed what I'd seen of him and Maggie. I didn't know what to do.

"Cassidy. Talk to me. Is everything okay?"

I closed the logging room door, an illusion of privacy. On the monitor, the sun came up in 10x speed.

Had he not shown up here, I could have dodged his calls and ignored him when he messaged me until he got the picture. We could have faded out, bittersweet but safe, rather than forcing a horrendous conversation. I fought the urge to turn my shirt inside out.

"I know about Maggie." My voice was raw. I clenched my teeth to hold back tears.

Gabe froze, and this reaction told me everything. I hadn't misread their gestures. I hadn't imagined the two of them there on the screen. Gabe and I stood in the fusty logging room, with its slight scent of Lemon Pledge and stale Doritos, each deathly still. This was it. Whatever this had been was over.

There was no more me and Gabe. There was me, and there was Gabe. A part of me had known that it was always going to end like this.

"Anyway, I'll get this shirt back to you," I said. "And whatever else you have at my place. Thanks for the wallet." I was an ice princess. I had to be, or else I would start bawling.

"Wait," Gabe said, still mentally catching up. "Cassidy, wait. Let me explain."

"No, it's okay," I said. "I get it. It's fine."

"Cassidy, let me—"

"I think you should go."

⚜

We both left the studio, though I waited to be sure he was totally gone before telling Monica at the desk that I felt sick. I went home and got straight into bed and lay there trying not to think about Gabe, trying not to replay that image of Maggie's hand moving from his shoulder to his cheek, trying not to hear his plea: *Let me explain.* His hands on her waist above her low-rise jeans. The easy way she leaned into him. *I had the most gigantic crush,* he'd said. Or was it *massive crush*? He'd been trying to tell me he was into her, that I was a stopgap. His chin on top of her head, the same position he held me.

My phone buzzed with texts, but I didn't look at them. What was there to say? I'd opened myself up, and look what it had gotten me. I hated that I cared.

I took a frowned-upon dosage of NyQuil and went to sleep.

Cassidy. Please call me back. Let's fix this.

The next morning I cleaned my Glendale workspace, saging Gabe out of my life via disposal of three-day-old Cup Noodles. I didn't call him back. We had a Dustbuster in a tiny hall closet, and I knelt to get every corner, suck up every crumb. Maybe the cleaning crew would thank me for lightening their load when they came through this weekend. At the very least, I thanked myself—I was saying goodbye to old, gullible Cassidy without having to cut myself bangs.

When all was vacuum striped and new, I went back to my monitor. I had a day or two of new stuff—Maggie taking a painting class, Jason playing poker—but I figured it could wait. Today was not a day for how people presented themselves, the polished laughs and faux embarrassment because the camera caught them exiting the bathroom; today was a day to uncover what it was that they actually hid.

Sex. Everyone was hiding sex. Basically I had a treasure trove of *Honeymoon Stage* pornos. Lauren and Dan: sex for business; Sally Ann and Jason: sex for pleasure, until she needed something else, and then they stopped the sex entirely, it seemed.

I might have missed the glaring red flags in my own personal life, but I wasn't going to miss clues about what had actually happened to Sally Ann. At least my own breakup hadn't yet led to a murder.

I spun my wheels a bit, literally sliding in my desk chair.

Sally Ann was allergic to nuts. Lauren and Dan knew that Sally Ann was allergic to nuts. Maggie knew—she'd gone right to the EpiPen. Who else knew?

I, oblivious idiot who could apparently spend months with someone and never know the truth of them, had not realized the nut allergy wasn't just another aspect of Sally Ann's skinny-girl fad diet. Everything said *Sally Ann, nut-free*, but it also said *Brent, no gluten*, and I'd seen him down three regular donuts in a row when under stress. Had she told me and I'd just forgotten? But it wasn't my fault. I'd written down to the leave the nuts off the order.

This had to be Jason's fault.

Jason ate nuts all the time, and kissing Sally Ann had never caused a reaction. He must have known the extent of the allergy. I imagined the camera in front of us while Jason took the lunch bags, offering to lighten my load. I'd thought it was genuine kindness, but Jason was a performer, used to keeping his head straight in the middle of a tight game. A pitcher always had to think a step ahead. He'd give that goofy grin while unpacking the containers, hiding his true intention behind the mask of *Honeymoon Stage*'s Jason Dean. How easy would it have been to switch Sally Ann's meal with Maggie's, fork a few bites from one container to the other? All we'd need would be a shot of his hands, stabbing the chicken and replacing it. Ominous music. Zoom in on his eyes; if we got close enough, we'd always catch the tell.

The thing to do, I realized, was go back to the footage from the day of the accident. What I had seen was not what the camera had seen. I dug around in the computer until I found everything labeled "2/13."

No one had ever opened these files. I guessed once they knew Sally Ann hadn't made it, production considered the day a sunk cost.

I started with camera A, which was Rahul. Some outside stuff—a dog peeing a mud hole in the garden, a flock of birds, a shot of Eli through the living room window as he set up his own shot. This seemed to capture *Honeymoon Stage* with the most authenticity: people watching other people as they readied themselves to make life into not exactly art.

And then:

Jason putters around in the kitchen, replacing disposable chopsticks with forks. He hands a bag to somebody off camera. Pops a lid and sneaks a bite of what seems to be Maggie's chicken. Maggie comes over to playfully complain about the fact that he's eating her food. Her body covers the view of his hands, the containers. We see them banter about hot pepper tolerance before she eventually turns around to call Sally Ann to come eat. This is the moment. The opportunity is here. Maggie's back is to Jason for enough time for something to happen, if that something is well executed and has been carefully planned. Unfortunately, Rahul didn't catch it on camera.

Jason steps out from behind her, in one hand Maggie's open lunch, in the other Sally Ann's closed one. Because the lid is on now doesn't mean it has always been on. Is that a grain of rice, escaping?

And then here are Maggie and Sally Ann at the kitchen island, elbows down, leaned into each other.

"Not *Maid in Manhattan* again," Maggie moans.

"Why not? It's more fun than *A Walk to Remember*."

"Don't you ever just want a good cry?" Maggie spears a piece of chicken from the black plastic container, licks her lips for any residual sauce.

"Not really." The camera's behind Sally Ann, so we watch Maggie over her shoulder. Those shoulders, the spaghetti straps, the youth and potential that radiate off her—not something you ever considered when you saw Sally Ann in person, but it glows like the aura of a cartoon angel when you know she's going to die in the next scene.

Maggie bites her lip in a coquettish way that can't have been intended for Sally Ann. The camera angle changes. Sally Ann shrugs, eats some plain rice.

"Okay fine," Maggie sighs. "We can do *Maid in Manhattan*, if they have it at the video place, and you want to go pick it up."

Sally Ann grins and takes a bite. She frowns while chewing, her eyes suddenly flitting with fear. The wheezing starts, and she raises her hands to her throat, her elbow knocking a takeout lid, which falls with a clatter. That awful sound. The camera tilts down to the wood floor, and Rahul says, "Oh my god."

Then you can hear me say "Fuck," and the crew's footfalls as they leave Video Village, and Maggie saying, "Where is her purse?"

"Keep shooting," Dan instructs. But somebody turns off the camera.

⚜

Cassidy—began Gabe's email—You've been ignoring my calls and I want to explain. I want to apologize. I should have been open about what's going on with Maggie, why I was even at her house that first day. I can explain it all, if you'll let me. I am not seeing Maggie, I am not romantically involved with Maggie. It's really all about doing the music. I know I messed up here, but I don't want to lose you. Can you please call me back? Love, Gabe.

Delete. Delete delete delete. From my inbox, from my memory.

I'd shared the barest of details of Gabe's betrayal with my roommates. I'd delusionally hoped to get it past them, but when I spent the second night in a row watching *Dumb and Dumber*, they both knew something was definitely up. In the spirit of girl-power-hood, they told me I was better off without Gabe, that they'd always sensed something was off about him. Jen got me a backpack full of drugstore chocolate and a dartboard that hung over the back of the door.

"For your rage," she explained. But I didn't have rage. Rage would have been better than what I had, which was immense self-doubt, deep sadness. The sense that the world was, in fact, the ruthless place I had always suspected it to be, and being a good person couldn't protect you. If anything, being a good person made you a sucker.

> I know your texting plan is expensive and I'm sorry to bombard you but please can you call me.

Honeymoon Stage continued to be a ratings smash. News had leaked of Sally Ann's death—if you could call several strategically placed calls to magazine editors "leaking"—and public response was mostly sympathetic. Maggie had lost a dear friend, and since the audience had come to feel that they were friends with Maggie, by the transitive property they, too, had experienced a loss. Who hadn't lost a friend, be it to death or drugs or sleeping with their husband? And how brave of Maggie and Jason and the *Honeymoon Stage* team to keep on filming! If you watched the show in a bubble, you'd never even know that Sally Ann had died but for the dedication they were going to run at the end of the episode where Jason invests in a T-shirt company.

Jason Dean was still handsome, and Maggie McKee was still ditzy and hot, and people just wanted to watch them be famous, goddammit. Maggie got a sponsorship deal with Sally Ann's favorite brand of lipstick. Jason played golf.

I kept plugging away at my growing mountain of new footage to log, none of which provided any insight into who had caused the accident. Maggie seductively licking a lollipop. Jason doing a photo shoot for some brand of athletic socks. Maggie complaining about Pilates. I dipped back into the old stuff when I could, trying to figure out who'd been acting suspicious in the days leading up to Sally Ann's death, trying to find a good angle of the food being set on the counter.

I kept ignoring Gabe's emails and calls.

"Cassidy, I miss you. Please call me. I don't know what Maggie said to you, but it isn't like that with her, I promise. Maybe this—us—wasn't the same thing for you. Maybe it didn't mean what I thought it did. What it meant to me. To you, I mean. Damn it, please just call me back."

Looking back, it seems insane that I thought I, a brokenhearted twentysomething whose knowledge of criminal investigation came mostly from *Law and Order: SVU*, could single-handedly implicate either a genuine celebrity or his handlers in a murder, then use it as leverage for my own career advancement. But I threw myself into finding so-called justice for Sally Ann as if the case I'd haphazardly put together was my rebound relationship. I didn't have a bulletin board covered in red string, but I wasn't far off. Though the facts pointed to Jason, everyone was a suspect. This suited my current state of mind. Trust no one. Read between the lines of every conversation. Eat Twix bars for dinner. Deny my own possible guilt.

Jason punching that wall when Sally Ann said she'd reveal, not their affair, but something else, was what had me convinced he was involved in her death. People didn't just coincidentally die before they could publicize a life-altering secret. Somebody had to be responsible. The difference between pulling a string that made Maggie McKee seem vapid and another that made Sally Ann dead really was no difference at all.

Did I like poking around in this wound as a distraction from thinking about Gabe being with Maggie? Absolutely. I wanted to press as hard as I could on the bruise of Sally Ann's death until I made myself sick with it. But I also thought that there was something I was missing. I didn't want to get caught, yet again, with my proverbial pants down. I didn't want to be played for a fool.

I cornered Ian in the conference room after an all-hands production meeting.

"Hey," I said. "I have a question about footage."

"Okay, shoot." Ian made finger guns at me, and despite Dan's many flaws, I found myself grateful I had been on the other ENG team when I'd worked on set.

"Were you the one who gave me that new stuff last week? From the garage? It looked like it might be your handwriting."

"Ah yes, Coyote Cam." Ian put his notebook and little neon stress ball back into his bag, making it clear that he had limited time for me.

"Coyote Cam?"

"One of the developers working on the house thought he saw signs of a den. Put up a camera to try to catch them. He never got anything, though, and it's a bad space for filming. But who knows? If that guy's right, it could be a story." Always, production was looking for stories. Scavengers themselves, sucking on the bones of people's lives. Ian continued. "Remembered it again last week or whenever, and dropped it by for you to look at. Sorry if it was a bust."

"Did anyone else talk to that guy? The developer? Why wasn't the camera officially listed?"

"I figured it was gonna be pretty poor quality. Not one of ours, but good enough to get those yellow coyote eyes or a pup or something to stir up some drama. Any luck?"

"No coyotes," I said.

"Sorry about that," Ian said again. He started to leave and then turned back to me. "Hey," he said. "You see anything good, you come to me first. I'll help you out, if you know what I mean."

I didn't quite know what he meant, and there was a long line ahead of him, but I nodded and thanked him. Coyotes. How banal.

I found out that Lauren was pregnant the old-fashioned way, by which I mean she told me. She'd come into the office for what she called girl talk, and when she sat down at the table in the conference room, she kicked off her shoes.

"My feet are so swollen they're practically balloons," she said. "Second trimester's supposed to be the easy one."

I was twenty-four—my birthday had passed with cake and champagne from Jen and Celia, and some crying in my bedroom when

I drunkenly thought about Gabe—but no wiser to the language of pregnancy than I'd been at twenty-three.

"What?" For someone acting as the sole investigator into a possible murder, I was remarkably dense. Lauren blinked at me, confirming that fact. "What's second trimester?" I guess I thought it was a class she was taking or something.

"What, do you live under a rock?" Lauren scoffed. "Cassidy. I'm pregnant."

I hadn't seen her day-to-day since my transfer to postproduction. I never wanted to assume about someone else's body—god forbid they assume something about mine. But now that she mentioned it, she was a little larger in the middle. Her boobs were massive.

"I didn't know." Was I allowed to ask my boss about the father of her baby? I knew it must be Dan. "Who's the . . . lucky dad?"

Were I Lauren, I might have given myself exactly the withering look of pity that she gave me in response. I, too, would want to keep my crew from knowing I was sleeping with my director. But I wasn't Lauren's crew anymore. I was pretty sure she knew that I knew about Dan. Had I thought that she would tell me because she saw me as a friend? This was not the case. We were every person for themselves, adrift alone, until some shared plunder briefly united us.

"Anyway, getting back on track," said Lauren. "Have you found anything good?"

"Ummm, not really."

"Ian's pitching something about coyotes on the property," said Lauren. "Making Maggie and Jason go looking for signs, working them all up. Apparently he's got a contractor who'll say he saw some damage."

"That sounds silly," I said. "I haven't seen any coyotes on the footage."

"No one has. We can do better. Talk to me about what you've got. Something juicy. Something we can use." Lauren took a long swig of an orange energy drink that couldn't have been good for the baby.

"Jason lies about his bench press numbers," I said. *Jason might have killed his mistress,* I did not say.

"Nah, what else?"

I was biting my tongue so hard it was about to fall off. Despite everything, I still wanted to impress Lauren. I wanted her to bring me with her when she rose to the head of production. She was so sure of herself, it was impossible to doubt her. And I wanted to win something, now that I'd lost Gabe.

"Maggie's, like, one unpaid parking ticket away from getting a boot on her car," I said.

"Boring."

"I think that Maggie might have slept with my ex-boyfriend."

There it was. I hadn't said it in so many words to anyone. All of a sudden, I'd blurted it out to my boss. What a gift Lauren had, to line us all up, little toy soldiers, and wind us until we marched to her drum. She might have gotten a leg up by sleeping with Dan, but it was her own talent that would catapult her to an executive suite.

And now I had betrayed Gabe. I'd betrayed Maggie. In keeping other people's secrets, I had told on myself.

13.

Two weeks after I told Lauren about Maggie and Gabe, a photo appeared in *Us Weekly*. The two were seen at a lunch spot, shot candidly from the long lens of a paparazzo's camera. She wore a massive sun hat and oversize sunglasses, but it was still clearly Maggie, sitting so close to Gabe she might have been on his lap. The editors had circled their legs under the table and added the caption "Getting close," and I wanted to rip up the entire magazine and throw it into the fire.

On *Honeymoon Stage*, Maggie and Jason were still living out their perfect marriage, not just in the Season One episodes we'd filmed six months ago that aired every week, but also in the new footage that I logged and transcribed. No rocky waters here—just a couple adorably fumbling their way through that first year of marriage. Trouble in Paradise? read one grocery store headline. Not according to this hour of Maggie giggling while Jason rubbed her feet. Jason Dean Dethroned? Only if you meant that he had trouble installing a new toilet in the pool-house bathroom. At least that's how they were playing it. I didn't know how much Jason actually knew about Maggie's infidelity. I didn't know how much she knew about his. What did it matter, if they were still raking in cash for *Honeymoon Stage*? As long as the viewers saw them as happily married, who cared what was actually happening?

Well, I did. My contempt for Jason knew no bounds, but after the first few days of feeling totally betrayed, I returned to my eternal fascination with Maggie McKee. She was the one married to a monster.

She might have stolen my boyfriend, but she was a victim in this too. I was consumed with the idea that Jason had done something to Sally Ann. I wasn't sure how long I could comfortably keep that information from Maggie. Cheating was one thing; murder was another.

Although I fell to pieces every time they mentioned Gabe, I kept buying the tabloids. Tequila salt rims in my wound. My own disillusionment ruining my objectivity, making it impossible to go out to the bars without slurring some crap about how love wasn't true. Sherlock Holmes wasn't sidetracked by ex-lovers. Or was he? Detective Olivia Benson would never.

Luckily, I was often drunk enough that no one took my ranting about hidden cameras and switched chicken seriously. I still only had suspicions, no actual proof.

About a month into my lackluster detective work, Celia decided she'd had it with my moping around.

"So, the plan is to delete Gabe's messages and silently pine after him forever?"

She'd caught me flipping through a gossip magazine, slowly eating a Slim Jim, in rolled Soffe shorts and a polka-dotted bathrobe at three p.m. on a gorgeous LA Saturday. I felt I was taking a perfectly respectable amount of time to grieve my relationship, but I also understood the point she was making. Wallowing was a bad look. By this point, it didn't even feel good in the self-indulgent way that justified buying expensive bubble bath and gorging myself on chocolate.

"I'm not sure how he thinks he's going to explain this," said Celia, gesturing toward the tabloid I had spread open on our coffee table. "But if you're going to keep buying these, you could at least hear him out."

What could Gabe possibly tell me that would change anything? He was obviously still seeing Maggie, even as he sent me messages claiming to be groveling at my feet. A fire rose within me. Those messages were bullshit. Why should he get to keep acting like he was the good guy and I was the one who had done something wrong?

"You know what," I said to Celia. "You're right. I'm going to call him right now."

"Yes, girl!"

"I'm going to tell him to stop bothering me."

"Yeah, you are."

"I'm going to tell him that I do not forgive him and I'm totally over him."

I pulled out my phone, and Celia gave me an encouraging nod. I dialed, and as the phone rang, all my righteousness drained out of me.

"Cassidy." Gabe answered with an undisguised eagerness. I didn't know what to say in response. Celia was mouthing something I couldn't interpret, and I turned my back to her so that she'd stop distracting me.

"Hi." My stomach jumped into my throat. "I got your messages."

"I wasn't—" I imagined him blinking, telling himself to start over. "I know there were a lot. I just want to explain—"

"Okay," I said. "You can explain it."

"Like . . . right now? Is now a good time?" I had to ready myself. We had to meet over something totally harmless, like coffee. Coffee in a very public place, with a pressing engagement immediately afterward. No houses. No drinks. Absolutely no touching.

"Tomorrow morning?" I asked. Morning seemed like a safe time, until I thought about his hair, mussed and gold with morning light. Nothing was safe. No time, nowhere.

"Tomorrow morning works," Gabe said. "How about that trailhead at Angeles Forest?"

"Why not?" I said. "Sure."

I pulled into the lot by the trailhead twenty minutes early, and Gabe was already sitting on the hood of his car, waiting for me. He looked as wonderful as he always looked, as wonderful as he did before I'd seen his face plastered across the tabloids as Maggie McKee's side piece. This didn't mean he was the person that I wanted him to be. The whole time I'd thought of him as this Gabe, he'd been lying to me. There was no "this Gabe." I got out of my car.

"Hi." He hopped off and approached me like he would a wild animal, unsure if I would bolt.

"Hi." I swallowed the urge to cry. "How have you been?" It had been more than a month since I'd last seen him, and not much had outwardly changed. No new tattoos in fresh Saran Wrap, no wild haircuts or bold statement jewelry. Just Gabe.

"Not great, to be honest." He clenched the hand nearest me into a fist, and then released it.

"Oh," I said. *Oh,* the lamest syllable in the entire English language, signifying, I supposed, that I had heard him and had no other response. Together we started toward the trail.

With Gabe next to me, whatever was left of my resolve fizzled out. He kept rubbing his thumb and his forefinger together, and I wanted to reach out and hold them still. Another car turned into the lot. We both paused and turned to look at it, meeting each other's eyes in the process. His lips twitched. I looked away.

Ahead of us, the yellow scrub gave way to a single patch of green.

"I'm sorry," Gabe said suddenly. Goddammit. I wanted him to be smug and unapologetic. I wanted him laughing at me for being such a chump.

I didn't want to want Gabe, but I did.

"I have to tell you—"

"It seems like you—" We spoke at the same time, both stopped ourselves. I waited.

"Okay," Gabe said. Into the wilderness we went. This was a real trail, for actual hikers. A minute in we saw a guy who likely hadn't bathed in days hauling a backpack tent and an empty plastic liter of water.

"We're not going to do the whole hike," Gabe assured me.

"Yeah, I figured," I said.

We established a rhythm, slow enough for conversation but not so slow we didn't have to keep an eye on our feet. It seemed incumbent on him to raise the topic of our breakup, begin the explanation he'd been trying to give me for weeks.

"I'm going to tell you all of it," he said finally. And then he told me the story of Gabriel Leighton and Maggie McKee.

There is no episode to back this up. No footage. No one sees this part, not even me. I have only Gabe's word. Gabe is talking in a quiet voice while I trudge next to him. Eventually we come out of the woods to the view.

Gabriel Leighton loved Maggie McKee from the moment he laid eyes on her on a soundstage in Kissimmee, Florida, at callbacks for *The Tiger Crew*. She stood stone faced in a corner, getting made up by her mom, and when he saw her, Gabe thought, *That girl.* The casting directors did too. Gabe and Maggie were two of fifteen kids cast on the show, so they didn't always have sketches and scenes together, but Gabe would finagle a way to be next to her at craft services or when they did on-set school, which meant workbooks and essays. None of the kids were really learning anything academic, not in the way that I'd been pop-quizzed and called up to the chalkboard, but the network tutor did enough to satisfy the lax laws set in place by the state for nontraditional schooling. How could anyone expect Maggie to know the difference between a syllable and syllabub when she'd been given a word search as her only ninth-grade grammar lesson? Of course she would become who she became.

Still, despite what traditional education they lacked, *The Tiger Crew* was getting a masterclass in image control. They learned how to find their good angles, which colors were slimming, what hairstyles played best on TV. They also took voice lessons and tap. Maggie was apparently a savant at looking at a sheet of sides and memorizing the whole thing immediately, and Gabe could shuffle off to Buffalo like nobody's business.

So, Gabe had a crush on Maggie, and in turn, Maggie saw him as a very good friend—that lopsided relationship from all romantic comedies where one day the girl was going to wake up and realize the right guy had been next to her all along, listening to her complain about her meathead boyfriend and rubbing her back when she cried. In their downtime on set, when they weren't hitting educational requirements, young Gabe and Maggie goofed off in their trailers. They had a book club. They started writing their own songs. This was where Gabe's time pining for Maggie began to pay off. There was a musical tension between them—when he described it, I imagined it was like tantric sex, where you come so close to consummation that something's born out of the longing, a raw nerve in the form of a sound wave, a silence between notes on a guitar.

Gabe and Maggie messed around together with music—only music! (the lady doth protest too much)—and when *The Tiger Crew* ended, she sang harmonies on some of his solo stuff before her record label chewed her into bubble gum. Gabe moved to Nashville to work on other artists' tracks for cash, and Maggie came to visit him. They spent a week in his apartment, playing guitar on the kitchen floor. Listening to old LPs. Losing track of what meal should come next. Writing.

Apparently, they wrote something wonderful. They wrote the song of all songs, the one that could make their careers. A song that would show Gabe's parents they'd done right to uproot their lives so their son could perform, would show the record label that Maggie was more than just an underage sexpot.

He didn't say if they'd slept together, but I had trouble believing that they hadn't. Gabe didn't kiss and tell.

Immediately after that writing session, Maggie met Jason.

⚜

"Okay," I said. "Got it. You two wrote the best song in the world." We were ascending, still. I'd worn canvas sneakers, which were not the right choice. Gabe hadn't mentioned that this trail would be so steep.

"We had this song, and I thought I would record it with Maggie, since she was the one with the record deal. It was better than the stuff her label was giving her. You know they have her do that . . . gyrating shit, with the really thin vocals and all? This is the opposite. It's good."

"Tell me what you really think."

"But she didn't want it," said Gabe. "Or I guess the label didn't. It wasn't the image they were going for."

"Too good a song," I said. "Noted. So, instead, you recorded it yourself? Which one is it?" I knew most of Gabe's songs by this point, from listening to his bootlegs and listening to his concerts and listening to him play at the foot of his bed while I lounged in nothing but a borrowed T-shirt. His songs were thoughtful, poetic, occasionally angry in a cutting way you wouldn't expect if you knew him only casually. None of them screamed top of the charts.

"That's the thing. We never recorded it. We decided to sit on it, to wait. She'd make what the label wanted her to make and get a real foot in the door, and I'd keep doing my own stuff, and when we both had fan bases, we'd do it together and give it a chance to get huge."

"This was your idea?" I frowned at Gabe.

"No, Maggie's." Gabe pressed his lips together.

"So are you guys big enough yet? Are you about to take the music-listening world by storm?"

"Well, no. I want to record it alone, but she still won't give me permission."

"So instead of just asking her like a normal human person, you used me to get to her," I said, voice cold. Gabe winced.

According to Gabe, that was not the case. Also according to Gabe, he couldn't just call Maggie up and ask her, because of Jason.

When Maggie McKee met Jason Dean, he was at the top of his game. He had a chiseled jawline and white teeth and an arm that could strike out the most formidable opponents. He had a $200 million deal with the Braves and a tripped-out condo in Atlanta and a boat. From the start, Gabe did not like him. Gabe was a former child star living in Nashville with a roommate, pining for the girl who'd never seen him as more than a friend. He did not have ripped abs. He did not have endorsements. He did not have Maggie McKee.

He held his tongue for a while—by this point Maggie had realized that Gabe wanted more from her, and was giving him some distance. Her career was miles ahead of his and moving in a different direction. She was outgrowing him.

"I'm not in love with Maggie," Gabe said.

"But you care about her." Funny how urgent it seemed to look down at my feet.

"I do."

"Enough to mess around with what we had," I said. "Enough to lie to me."

Gabe didn't deny it. He stopped, but I kept going, the same steady rhythm. Up and over. One foot in front of the next.

"Cassidy." With his long legs it was easy to catch up to me. "Let me tell you the rest."

With Jason on the scene, Gabe talked less and less to Maggie, which made sense to him. She had another man in her life, and she had a career. They lived in different cities. Gabe was ready to let go. He had his own life; he was making decent money. He dated other people. He honkey-tonked in Nashville. He recorded an indie EP. Occasionally, he caught up with Maggie on the phone, but it was shallow old-buddies stuff. Then Jason got hurt.

Along with everyone else, Gabe sent them a note of condolence. *This sucks, how can I help, I'm here for you guys*—something along those lines. She must have known that Gabe was still in love with her.

"Anyway," said Gabe. "It was fine, and he did surgery and rehab and all that stuff you already know. And Maggie kept doing her thing, and I kept doing mine."

"But then the surgery didn't work." I wasn't sure where this was going. If I hadn't known this part already, I might have guessed that Maggie had left Jason once his luck began to change. Instead, when the money dried up and Jason's career was trash, they'd gotten engaged. "How is this relevant?"

Gabe looked around, making sure no one was watching us. He pulled me to the side of the trail, as if this next part required total privacy. I took back my arm.

"Jason wasn't okay after the surgery," said Gabe.

"Well, yeah. Everyone knows that. That's why he is where he is. That's why he's doing *Honeymoon Stage*."

"No. I mean like . . . mentally he wasn't okay. He was in a very bad place."

Maggie called Gabe one night at four in the morning East Coast time. Jason had been out; he was driving; someone sideswiped his car. He had called the police to report it as a hit-and-run, which in most circumstances would have been the totally appropriate thing to do, but in this case was idiotic because Jason was blasted out of his mind on vodka, Xanax, and cocaine. They'd have to book him. After calling the cops, he'd called Maggie, who told him to get out of there before anyone showed up. Just come straight home and pretend he'd been with her all night, had no idea what they were talking about. Jason was lucid enough to agree. One million thousand percent, he should not have been driving.

When Jason got home, Maggie came out to see the damage. The passenger side door was scraped, which tracked with his story about getting swiped in a parking lot. But the front bumper of the car was also totally crushed, as if Jason had hit something big. It was dark, and Maggie didn't see any obvious residue. She was scared to look closer.

Jason had no explanation. Adrenaline spent, he passed out in bed, and Maggie sat in the living room, the telltale heart of the wrecked car beating at her from inside the garage. She called Gabe.

"I told her she should call the cops, and obviously, she didn't. She'd had situations before—Jason drunk and locking her out of the house; Jason's teeth chattering because he was all hopped up on Adderall. I'd told her to get him help. She really should have called someone else, someone close by, who could help her. I think she called me because she knew I was too far away to do much more than listen. And because she knew I wouldn't go public."

We still stood in our little off-road area, and I was itching to get back on the trail. I could handle being close to Gabe as long as we were moving. When we were standing here, his eyes seemed so sad.

"Why didn't you go public?" I asked him.

"No one wants their lowest moments broadcast all over the tabloids," said Gabe. "Even though this did seem like the tipping point. The other stuff sucked, but this? To not know what Jason had hit? Fucking terrifying."

An internet search the next morning showed two hit-and-run accidents, at least one person dead in the general vicinity of Jason's midnight bender. Maggie had to call it in, no matter that it would totally ruin his good guy public image. Gabe tried to convince her, but the more time passed, the more she was adamant that she shouldn't. Maggie thought Jason should just go to rehab, and if he could stay sober, it would all be okay. Gabe told her it was not okay. Gabe told her Jason was dragging her down with him, that she should leave him. Maggie told Gabe that of course Gabe would say that—Gabe had always been in love with her; did he think she hadn't noticed? Gabe told her to leave him alone forever, or something along those lines. Maggie told him not to call her again.

The news about Jason never broke. It was possible that no one else knew about that night except the three of them. Maybe whoever had handled fixing the car. Gabe wasn't sure what they'd done about that. It was no longer his concern.

Gabe told me he was happy not to speak to Maggie or ever see her again. He'd live his life and she would live hers, and never the two would intertwine. Except that Nashville wasn't cutting it. The longer Gabe stayed, the more obvious it became that Tennessee wasn't the place for him. The people he worked with kept giving all his songs to guys with bass voices and strong Southern accents. He had some friends making music in Los Angeles who kept egging him on to join them, and the opportunity was more inviting by the hour. His family was all back in Sacramento. His sister, Janine, was pregnant with her second. Nashville was lonely.

When he moved out to LA, Gabe wanted to make a real go of recording his own music, saving his best stuff for himself. This meant he wanted that song. He was obsessed with it, fixated. He believed the song would get his band a major deal, would finally be the song that would hit.

"Must be some song," I said.

"The best one I've ever written," said Gabe. I felt my stomach drop. I zipped my track jacket farther up my neck.

"So you used me to get it. You were waiting there that first day when I crashed into your car."

"No," Gabe said. He put both hands on my shoulders and turned me so we were looking each other in the eye. "That's not what happened. That day I was there dropping off some flowers. I should have told you what was going on, that I was trying to get Maggie to answer my calls. I should have told you we had history. But I was never using you."

"Hard to believe it," I said. Gabe twisted his mouth. "And if you were going for blackmail, getting involved with me only messed things up for you."

"What do you mean?" Gabe asked.

"Well, now Maggie's got stuff on you too. From when you came by the house when they were in Mexico. Maggie has footage of us in the pool together." As I spoke, I realized that Gabe might interpret this as something I'd kept from him; how in truth it *was* something I'd kept from him, just as he had kept Maggie from me. But it wasn't the same. I had been trying to protect him, or at least save him from the stress of a situation he couldn't control. He had flat out used me and lied to me.

"I don't think so," Gabe said.

"What?"

"I'm pretty sure that there's no footage. Didn't you turn off all the cameras?"

"She knows, though. She knows you were there."

"Yeah," Gabe said. "Because I told her."

Once I'd given Gabe the house codes, he knew how to get to Maggie. She could ignore his emails and his calls, the flowers, even the letters from his lawyer, but she couldn't ignore his physical presence in her house. She'd have to talk to him, settle the matter of the song once and for all. While I left for Thanksgiving in Philadelphia, Gabe stayed in Los Angeles. *Honeymoon Stage* filming was on pause, so it was easy to wait until the cars were all out of the driveway and the equipment was gone and he could get Maggie alone.

I pictured him approaching her. She'd be in a bathing suit by the pool, reading a magazine. The sun would hit just right, and she'd look up and see him walking toward her, tall and handsome, dimples carved into each cheek. She'd think, *What was I ever doing letting this guy go?* She'd look up at him, push her sunglasses down her nose, smile. It would be easy to forgive him. Gabe was easy to love.

"We're friends," Gabe said. "We're old friends, and she's struggling. I should have told you, and I'm sorry."

Maggie was struggling? Jason was struggling. He'd almost certainly killed Sally Ann—his pre–*Honeymoon Stage* exploits confirmed it for me—and the addiction issues he regularly denied were now more than just rumor. But Maggie seemed oblivious to all of it. She was sad, of course, that Sally Ann had died. Her record was selling. Her show was a hit.

"That doesn't excuse things," I said. Gabe had been with her multiple times without telling me. The footage from Coyote Cam was dated 12/8/02. The photos of them in the tabloids had come out this past month.

"I know," said Gabe. We'd reached the crest of the trail. Angeles National Forest stretched out in front of us, peaks and valleys, clouds thin streaks of cream across the dishwater-gray sky. Beautiful, I supposed, but treacherous. We were going to have to walk all the way back to the cars. "I know it sounds wrong," Gabe said. "I know you probably won't believe me. But there's nothing romantic between me and Maggie. If you want to hate me because there's intimacy, yes, it's there, I can't deny that. But there's nothing romantic."

I didn't want to hate Gabe. In what world would I want to hate Gabe? I wanted to take everything he'd said at face value, to go back to what we'd had before I'd seen the two of them embracing on camera. There was a song they'd written together, probably a love song—I could deal with that. They had a history. But he had lied to me about it, and I hadn't, for even an instant, sensed that something was wrong.

How could I ever trust him again or trust myself when I was with him? Gabe had ruined us completely. I started to cry.

"I love you, Cassidy." He took my hand, squeezing it desperately. "I want this."

I couldn't do it.

"I still need space," I said. Then I removed my hand from his and started walking as fast as I could back the way we had come, making it clear that I didn't want Gabe to come with me. And Gabe didn't follow.

14.

The next day I sat back down in the logging room, protein bar in hand, and watched Jason Dean prepare for a charity golf tournament. An hour of him poking around in the garage, looking for a missing club. The laces on his shoe broke, so he had to stomp around and pout about it. An hour twenty of the drive to the mall, and the subsequent purchase of new shoes. Twenty minutes on the phone with Maggie, who was somewhere—Massachusetts?—for a concert. Kissy faces and *I miss you, baby,* and what were these two doing, seeing other people and then coming together to be America's sweethearts on TV?

Making money. That's what they were doing. Making money and celebrity.

Maybe it wasn't fair to lump Maggie in with Jason. She hadn't likely hit a person with her car. She hadn't poisoned Sally Ann. The woman of the pair always did take the brunt of the blame.

"I love you, baby. I'll see you tomorrow." On-screen, Jason hung up his phone and went off to stretch his shoulder.

I couldn't do it. I couldn't just sit and watch this footage knowing Jason Dean had almost certainly killed Sally Ann. He had a criminal history that by some act of god hadn't blown up in the press, and when she'd said, *What you told me that night in Reseda,* she'd meant that she was going to expose him. This would torpedo his TV career, and so he had killed her.

Jason's whole life and sense of self had been destroyed because his elbow tendon didn't quite click in right. Maybe it made sense that he'd done some drugs. He had some leeway to be stupid and reckless. I tried to imagine myself as his wife—or had Maggie been his fiancée then?—watching him implode and then not knowing what to do about it. It made sense that Maggie had turned to Gabe. He was a good person to call in a crisis. If only my own current crisis didn't feature him as its lead.

I sent postproduction an email saying I was feeling sick, said goodbye to front desk Monica, and headed home.

By the time I got through traffic, both Jen and Celia were already back at the apartment. I hadn't seen them for more than a quick second since my heart-to-heart with Gabe, and both immediately accosted me, Celia literally pulling me by the arm onto the couch, Jen plying me with a prepoured glass of wine.

"Tell us everything," Jen said. It was permission. Other than my drunken rambles, I'd been holding my suspicions about Sally Ann's death close to the chest—I was enough of a wreck about Gabe that I didn't need my friends adding "conspiracy theorist" to my list of undesirables. But I couldn't really hack it at the murder board all on my own. I needed Jen and Celia. I'd been waiting for a reason to include them, and Gabe's story had provided it in spades.

I began with the facts of the case: Gabe had a history with Maggie; Jason Dean had a history with drug abuse. I mixed up the stories until they became the same story: Maggie and Jason and Gabe and me and Sally Ann.

"But, Cassidy, how are you feeling?" Jen wanted to focus on Gabe. She wanted me to talk about how hard it had been not to grab his hand each time my foot hit a root in Angeles Forest, not to give in and take him back and pretend none of this was happening. Absolutely not. I wanted to talk about Sally Ann and Jason.

"I'm feeling like, if Jason really killed her, I should tell somebody." A package of Celia's silly diet cookies sat open on the table, and I grabbed one and ate it.

"Well yeah, okay, but did he?" Despite her concerted attempts to come off as bohemian and unique, it was already clear that Celia was going to be one of those women who thrived on true crime when the genre exploded. "He's a celebrity. You can't bring something against him without actual proof. You'd be totally steamrolled."

"He had motive! She was going to tell the press about his accident," I said.

"We assume he had motive," Celia corrected me. "You don't have actual proof."

Jen stood over us, landline in hand, about to order the takeout we so desperately needed. "You're deflecting," she said.

"Jason Dean knew she had an allergy and grabbed the bag of lunches, and Jason Dean's the one with reason to get rid of her." I palmed another SnackWell.

"What about all the people working on the show who would be screwed if she went public about screwing him? If they already had the next few episodes in the bag, wouldn't it ruin the show to have some exposé come out saying the marriage was a sham?" In her excitement, Celia knocked over a bottle of nail polish, Mango Magic dripping onto the magazine she'd been using as a placemat.

"When you hear hoofbeats, don't assume that it's zebras," I said.

"Excuse me, what?"

"It's something my mom says. When it's probably horses, you shouldn't guess zebras."

"If the simplest solution is the right one, this whole thing is just an accident." Jen came back to the couch. "I got us Thai."

"I still don't know what horses have to do with the fact that you can't go to the cops about something that looks like an accident and claim that Jason frickin' Dean masterminded it all." Celia righted the nail polish, trying to wipe up the spill.

"But, Cassidy." Jen sat down on the couch next to me. "What about Gabe?"

"What about him?" I said, sniffing.

"I know as your friend I'm supposed to be all, 'Girl power,' 'He's an asshole,' 'You'll be better off without him,'" Jen said. "But isn't there a way to forgive him and make this work out? You've been so happy together. He seems like he really wants to try."

"Does he?" Celia held up a wrinkled magazine page. "Sorry to be the bubble burster, but I don't know if he does."

A touch of Mango Magic remained streaked across Maggie's cheek, but there she was on the page, walking with Gabe through some parking lot. They both had on sweatpants and baseball caps, the kind of celebrity incognito that's basically a magnet for paparazzi. Maggie McKee's New Meat? The headline sat at the center of a series of photos, Gabe kneeling to pick something up, giving it to Maggie, receiving a hug. The picture from the magazine last week, their legs twined together under the outdoor table. A photo from *The Tiger Crew*, Maggie in ringlets and Gabe four foot ten. Underneath, the article claimed that Maggie and Gabe had been in a relationship for years, flaunting their love affair behind Jason Dean's back. It did nothing to endear Gabe to me, but the thing stank of some conniving publicist.

"'Maggie McKee plays the blissful newlywed on-screen, but in real life, things are heating up with former costar—'" Celia stopped herself from saying Gabe's name. She skimmed a bit, then resumed. "'Sources say that Jason is devastated. "She's not the girl I thought I married."'"

"Key word *girl*," Jen snorted.

"'Does this spell trouble in Calabasas? We'll be on the lookout for more signs that "Reality" isn't all it appears to be.'" Celia handed me the magazine, but I didn't want to look at it.

The buzzer rang. I went down to pay the driver for our dinner and avoid the looks of pity across my friends' faces.

I felt sorry for myself, yes, but I also felt sorry for Maggie. We were a generation of Spice Girl power, but that didn't mean that, below the surface, we weren't all just as misogynistic as our parents. We didn't paint everything pink and glittery because we ran the world, but because we were run by it. Maggie might have thought she was in charge of her story, but she was just as susceptible as Jason to the metaphorical elbow tweak that would throw her off course. Could you really take back power by leaning into the role you got stuck in? Maggie was trying to make "dumb blonde" a battle cry, but I thought that all it ever really could be was a scar.

I felt an immense sadness as I carried our pad thai and drunken noodles up the stairs to our unit, where Jen and Celia were waiting to coddle me.

"They might not actually be together," Jen said. "Didn't he tell you that they weren't together?" We doled out chopsticks and sat on the couch, eating straight from the containers.

"At this point it doesn't matter," I said. "I still can't trust him." Jen sighed.

"Who do you think the mysterious sources are?" Celia asked. "Who got the photos?"

"Probably Jason and his team," I said. "Trying to get ahead of things. Making Maggie's infidelity a major deal just in case something gets out about his thing with Sally Ann." Dopey old Simone, Jason's publicist, who'd counter rumors of him cheating with some of her own. Plant a story, get a photo spread. What a way to live.

"Well, you have to tell Maggie that you think he might have killed her," said Celia. To my surprise, Jen nodded.

"You might not have evidence to take to the cops, but if you know he has a history of violence, you can't just let her sit there, not knowing." Jen slurped a noodle. They were talking about Maggie and Jason as if they weren't people, just the characters they played on TV. I felt slightly sick.

"If it's going to be an all-out war and a messy divorce, and Maggie's getting thrown in the dirt, you don't want her to be totally blindsided," Celia said.

"I thought you guys were on my side."

"We're on the side of sisterhood." Celia seemed genuine. Jen scoffed.

"What about the side of preventing domestic violence?"

"Jason's not going to hurt Maggie," I said.

"You can't be sure." Jen poured us all more wine.

With Sally Ann, I had been ignorant. I didn't know she was with Jason; I didn't know she knew his secrets; I didn't know what he could do. But now I knew, and so I had an obligation. Telling Maggie would be awful. It would be picking the scab of a surgical wound, squeezing a lemon on top, and then deciding to just cut off the whole limb sans anesthesia. But then the information would be hers, to do with as she would. I wouldn't wake up in the night, sweaty with guilt, wondering if I was to blame. The onus would be on Maggie to involve the police, to start divorce paperwork, to do whatever had to happen next. I certainly didn't know what had to happen next.

"This is going to suck," I said.

"Majorly," said Jen.

"Absolutely," said Celia. "How are you going to do it?"

Around this time, an episode aired with Jason and Maggie experiencing Romance. This means they have a production-purchased bottle of champagne, and a production-purchased pound of rose petals strewn across the entryway. A professional violinist stands awkwardly to the side while they eat filet mignon prepared by a professional chef. She chews. He chews. The violinist looks pained for a split second before resuming the mask of his performance.

"It's so good," Jason says, swallowing.

"So good," Maggie agrees.

"Really just so, so good." Jason wipes his mouth with the production-selected cloth napkin.

Have you heard someone chew steak? When the meat is served rare, the mastication makes an unmistakable fleshy sound. Gulps of red wine. Nothing else is quite so sensual, or carnivorous. Instead of watching Jason and Maggie devour each other, we see them eating a different animal, and it tastes so, so, so good.

Getting Maggie McKee alone wasn't as easy as it might have been six weeks before. I wasn't some detective on a stakeout; I still had to do my job. I didn't have a good reason to show up on set. I had her private number, but now that I wasn't part of the crew, I worried about calling her and being caught on camera, raising everyone's suspicions.

Some mornings, Maggie went jogging. A camera usually followed for the first few minutes, but the logistics of keeping pace while holding a twenty-pound camera made sticking to her something of a challenge. It was possible she took up jogging simply for the solitude—early in the show, she'd done mostly aerobics, sweating in the home gym while the film crew looked on. If I wanted to get Maggie solo, I could intercept her on her route around the neighborhood, but this would require precise timing. I didn't know when she'd be leaving the house or how far she would go. I couldn't have Lauren getting involved, didn't want Rahul or Eli popping in and preventing me from being honest. I absolutely couldn't be in front of some hidden camera. It had to be while she was running.

I waited a full week and a half before pretending I had some urgent errand in her neighborhood and skipping work to drive to Calabasas one morning when I knew Maggie was in town. I had a whole thing in my head for what I would say if someone caught me—that I'd taken my own dry-cleaning to the place by the house, that I was waiting for it to be ready. The story had no legs, but in the end, nobody cared what I was doing.

I found Maggie rounding a path that skirted the man-made pond at the edge of the neighborhood, before the land turned from boutique suburbia to dusty hills and bleached grass. She had on gray sweats and an unembellished sports bra, hair in a ponytail, sweatband on, makeup impeccable. I didn't want to startle her, so I waited until she turned the corner and then held up a hand.

"Cassidy?" She slowed. "What are you doing here? They said I could have forty-five minutes." Did she know I'd been moved into postproduction and no longer worked on set? She must have known. Someone else had been rolling her suitcase for the past eight weeks.

"Hi, yeah, no," I said. "This isn't for the show." I wasn't sure what to do with my hands, so I shoved them deep into my jeans' front pockets.

"Okay?" Maggie raised an eyebrow. *We are not friends* emanated from her like the remnants of a nuclear blast zone. She was famous. She was seeing my boyfriend. Well, my ex-boyfriend now, but even before the change in status she'd been seeing him. She was right. We might have known each other as children, but we were not friends. What was I doing here?

"Um, this is awkward," I said. If I just left, I could pretend this conversation hadn't happened. I could let her keep jogging her way into domestic disturbance. This didn't have to be my business. She might tell me it was none of my business.

"Listen," Maggie said, surprising me. "I'm sorry about Gabe. That should never have been happening."

"Um," I said. "Oh, thanks." We were two different species, Maggie and I. She leaned down to stretch her left calf. "So I have—" I began, and then I stopped myself, unsure where I was going. "There's no real easy way to say this." Maggie looked up at me, brows raised. A bench faced the fountain a few meters away, and she gestured for us to move toward it. I sat down while she stretched her other leg. Maggie smelled like the Chanel perfume she wore everywhere, but also like salt and sweat and clear cherry lip gloss. Her back cracked when she lengthened her arms. "I think that Jason was cheating on you."

To my surprise, she laughed.

"Well, yeah," she said. "With Sally Ann. Do they think I didn't notice?"

"Who's they?" I asked.

Maggie waved a hand, implicating everyone. "I'm not as dumb as I play on TV," she said.

"I know." We were quiet. She used her hand to wipe sweat from the back of her neck.

"You're thinking, if I know already, why haven't I left him," Maggie said. "You're thinking why do I let his team sell stories about me to *Star* when he's the one with the real story."

"Sort of," I said.

"Haven't you ever been in love?" From the way Maggie looked at me, I could tell she knew that I'd been in love with Gabe. That I still was in love with Gabe. "You'll do anything for someone. You'll put up with a lot from them, especially when they're hurting. Jason's a good guy. He's been through it, and I've been through it with him. I can't just walk away. I don't want to walk away. We're building something, and it's not worth throwing out because he made a mistake."

I supposed this could be true. Who was I to tell Maggie to leave Jason? There were aspects of a marriage that even the film crew trailing ten hours a day was not privy to. Staying married was a choice. Maybe it wasn't what I would have wanted for myself, but that didn't mean that Maggie couldn't have it. But she should have access to all the information. She should know what she was choosing.

"I don't know if he is a good guy, though," I said. This was the moment I'd been dreading. Not that Maggie had Jason pegged as some Disney prince, but admitting to someone's major flaws was still different from admitting that they might be a murderer. Marriage was reversible; death wasn't. "I think he killed Sally Ann." Barely a whisper, but I'd said it. "I think Sally Ann knew about some of his past . . . indiscretions, and was going to go public. Ruin the show, ruin his image. Maybe even get him arrested, depending on statutes of limitations and all that. So I think that he killed her."

Maggie blinked at me. "Sally Ann's death was an accident."

I leaned closer, speaking quickly. "He passed out the food that day. He'd never taken it from me before, never offered to help. But he took the lunches, and he knew there were peanuts in your dish, and he mixed your stuff in with hers, and then she ate it. It's basically all on camera. He did it on purpose." I was trying to keep my voice steady, to sound calm and self-assured, as opposed to like some stalkery fan.

"You think Jason Dean—my husband, Jason Dean—worked all that out and followed through and now is getting away with an actual murder? The man can't even hang a shelf."

"I thought you said you were in love with him," I said.

"I am. I love him. Still, the guy isn't a criminal mastermind."

"But when you called Gabe in the middle of the night that time about the car," I said. "When maybe he hit something. Somebody. He got away with it then."

Maggie froze. Over the hill someone was skateboarding, the thwack of wheels on pavement. The fountain beside us hiccuped into action, sending a light mist our way. "How do you know about that?" Maggie whispered.

"Gabe told me." I didn't even think to lie to her. Maggie hissed in a breath. We sat for what felt like a long time, totally quiet. Then she turned so she was looking me in the eye.

"It's hard to watch someone you love so much lose hold of themself. You can't make choices for someone who's spiraling. They have to make their choices on their own."

"I get it," I said. "I do."

"You don't, Cassidy. You really don't. Imagine the most embarrassing thing someone could do to you. The thing you'd hate yourself for, even if it wasn't your fault, because you still were a part of it. Think about the thing you would never want anyone to know had been done to you, and imagine it on every front page of every newspaper. Imagine the whole world laughing at you—not just the kids who bullied you in middle school or the one cousin you hate, but like, grown men on network news. Your parents' friends. Anyone who'd ever sacrificed anything to get you where you are. All thinking they knew it all along, that it was always going to be this way, and it was all your fault because either you're too stupid to be where you are professionally, or you're totally toxic, or you're spoiled and undeserving, or probably a mix of all the above."

"I don't think people would say that," I said. Maggie ignored me.

"Now put the fear of that on top of watching the person you love, the person you've built yourself up around publicly but also in private, go through the lowest point of his life. You don't get it. It isn't possible for you to get it."

"But you could leave—"

"If I leave Jason, let me tell you what happens. He gets depressed. He relapses. The press paints me as the villain. Things get bad."

"But that has to be better than—"

"Besides, Jason didn't hurt Sally Ann. Give me a break. Jason's not the one who messed with her food." Maggie paused. I remembered the footage, Maggie's back turned to the camera, her hands on the takeout containers, deliberately out of view. I'd been so sure she was unwittingly covering for Jason. But she knew about the affair. She had a reason to hate Sally Ann. Had she actually been covering for herself?

Maggie gave me a pointed look, as if watching me come to this realization. Then she leaned closer to me, lowering her voice. "But if Gabe's been spilling, surely you know that already."

"What?" Even as she swore I had no possible idea about her life, I'd understood what we were talking about. Now she was losing me. "Gabe?"

She gave a fake look of concern—Maggie might have been good at playing different versions of herself, but she was never a very good actress. "He didn't tell you?" She licked her lips. How expensive must that lip gloss be to hold up through her jog and now this awful conversation? I felt dizzy. "Of course he didn't tell you."

"Tell me what?"

"We were in it together." Maggie looked triumphant, eyes sparkling, sweat at her hairline.

"We . . . ? Like . . . you and . . . ?"

"Gabe. Me and Gabe. The whole thing was his idea." I thought she was making a terrible joke, but then she started to cry. Not in the six months we'd been working together had I seen Maggie McKee cry, not while filming through the stomach flu, not when Jason got snippy, not watching ASPCA ads on TV. Even as a kid, she'd been preternaturally poised, able to plaster on a smile and bury inconvenient feelings. Now, she bit the inside of her lip and squeezed her eyes shut. She took a few long, slow breaths that I knew were the suggestion of some culturally appropriated wellness retreat. Her spiritual guide was probably a white lady who'd once been to an all-expenses-paid resort in India, and now Maggie was calling on the spirits of colonial infantilization to absolve her of the consequences of doing whatever the hell she wanted, regardless of cost. Her eyes shot open.

"I don't want to fuck Gabe over," said Maggie. "But I will if I have to. If this comes out, I'll go public saying he did it. We're already linked in the press."

"Gabe isn't part of this," I said. "He can't be."

"Maybe," Maggie shrugged. "But maybe not."

"You're full of shit."

"Am I? Why didn't he tell you he was meeting me? Once you guys were dating." Maggie shrugged. "How well do you really know him, Cassidy? I've known him for years."

She was right. Gabe had lied to me. That was why we were no longer together. If what she was saying was true, I'd made the right choice in deflecting his attempts to make things up. If this was true, the foundation on which I'd built the past few months had always been rotten. But it didn't feel true. It felt like Maggie, cold and desperate, trying to deflect blame.

I couldn't see Gabe planning Sally Ann's death, but I could suddenly see Maggie doing it. She was cleverer than Jason, more calculated. I remembered the way she'd stood just out of the shot, her body blocking the food on the counter.

She hadn't yelled for someone closer to Sally Ann's purse to get the EpiPen and use it. And wasn't that the thing to do? I didn't know to look for the EpiPen—how could I have known? Maggie had known, and she had chosen to wait before acting. She was a master of timing; that's why everybody found her so funny on-screen. I pictured her whispering in Jason's ear, puppeteering as he passed out the food. Counting down the seconds until she could administer the medicine and know it was for show; she'd missed the window during which it would be working.

Maggie wasn't a dumb blonde. She was a monster.

"Anyway, we don't even know what Jason hit that night," she continued. "It might have been nothing."

"It might have been nothing." I was repeating Maggie's words, but not really understanding them. She'd come out on the wrong side of the looking glass. What was this public image she'd hold on to at all costs? More importantly, what would she be without it? "It might all be nothing," I said.

"Exactly," said Maggie. "I knew you'd understand." She patted below her eyes with her fingertips, trying to keep her makeup from smearing. She stood up.

My head was pounding. I'd been wrong. It wasn't Jason. It was Maggie. Maggie had killed Sally Ann. And for some reason, I still felt bad for her. I'd wanted to help her, even as she'd threatened Gabe, even as she'd made excuses that leaked water like a sieve. Now I understood why Gabe was worried about her. Maggie McKee was absolutely not okay. If only Gabe had been worried enough to keep her from killing someone.

"Does my face look funny?" Maggie asked. "I don't want my face to be all weird. They get the cameras going right when I'm coming back up the driveway, but you know that already."

"It's fine. It looks normal."

"Good." She took a long breath, and stretched out her back. "Good talk," she said. Off she went to continue her jog.

That was the last time I spoke to Maggie McKee until the morning of my wedding, four years later.

15.

I sat on the bench by the fountain for at least twenty-five minutes, watching it spew water California could not afford to waste for the sake of the neighborhood aesthetic. Maggie had killed Sally Ann. What was I going to do? It was time to get the hell out of Dodge.

I didn't believe the Gabe stuff. It made no sense. I might not have been the world's best judge of character, but I knew I wasn't dating Patrick Bateman. Gabe wasn't so obsessed with Maggie that he'd kill Jason's girlfriend, especially not after the guilt trip he'd sent Maggie on with Jason's hit-and-run.

I did, however, see Maggie as the type who'd point her finger at Gabe if I went public with any of this, regardless of his actual involvement. Maggie was ruthless.

She'd been a snotty kid, but not sociopathic. Blame Jason for making her this way. Blame the record label or the network. Blame the way our culture liked to tie a girl in knots until the struggle to undo them only locked her in tighter. Maggie was running low on options.

At summer camp, there'd been this legend of a kid who wrapped a hair tie really tight around her finger until all the blood separated and it made a truly gnarly white line. She fell asleep like that, and then in the morning, when she popped the hair tie off, that blood bubble went straight to her brain and she was dead. This was Maggie. Maggie couldn't take the hair tie off, or else it would kill her.

I hated them all. Jason and Maggie and the people who'd made them. Gabe, for letting himself get caught up in her, for forcing me in further. The people who'd put Maggie on a pedestal so that they could look up her skirt. The ones who'd granted immunity to famous people's terrible behavior because it served as entertainment for the rest of us.

I was out. I was finished. If this was what it meant to see the whole game board, I would rather be a pawn. I was ready to call time of death on Reality TV.

But first, I had to do something about Maggie.

For a second I thought about driving straight to a police station and dumping the whole thing on their doorstep. But Maggie was a white girl most famous for being famous; she had money and lawyers, and I still didn't have proof. Likely they'd laugh at me. Likely they'd dig up some unpaid parking ticket and turn the whole thing back around on me. And if they did take Maggie in, if for some reason they decided to believe me, mine would be the final heel stomping on the face of the little girl I'd known in Youngstown.

Also, there was Gabe. I wasn't going to get back together with him, but I didn't want to make his life harder. Maggie knew that, and that's why she had told me she'd blame him. Even if it was all bullshit, the accusation that he'd killed his girlfriend's husband's mistress wouldn't cast Gabe as a lovesick Romeo; it would ruin him for life. Certain things men could get away with, if they were famous and good looking and they had enough money. Domestic abuse. Throwing things at waitstaff. Walking out on their children. But premeditated murder was across the line, and Gabe wasn't that rich or that famous. I couldn't walk him into the middle of the street and let Maggie hit him with a bus. He didn't deserve to be caught up in Maggie's drama any more than he already was.

I could call him. Instead, I called Lauren. She picked up from set—I could hear Eli yelling at the new camera assistant in the background.

"Cassidy. What's going on? You got something for me?" Chipper, terse. Reliable old Lauren. She could take on this mess. She'd know how to spin things, get Gabe out of the equation. I'd leave it all at her feet, and then Gabe and I could freely go our separate ways.

"Can you meet me at the office? Or is there somewhere more private? Somewhere better?"

"Diner off Topanga and Burbank," Lauren said. "Twenty minutes." If I had been at the office, there's no way I could have made it in that time, but from where I was stalled on the freeway, I could do it.

"Okay," I said, and pulled off to turn my car back around, heading toward Calabasas for what I knew would be the very last time.

Lauren's diner was a dive, the kind of place where you'd be equally likely to eat the best burger of your life or find a sliver of glass in your french fries. Burnt-orange vinyl seating and patterned carpet from the '70s. Even midday, the overhead lighting made it feel like it was one in the morning.

I got there first and picked a booth toward the back.

"Pie," said Lauren when she sat down across from me. "Pie and very black coffee."

"Are you supposed to drink very black coffee?" I gestured toward her stomach, which was now clearly full of child. Lauren rolled her eyes and flagged the server, who came with a steaming pot.

"What do you have?" Lauren asked, adding Splenda. I held my tongue about the loose definition of black.

"It's juicy," I said. "But you have to be careful." Lauren's eyes lit up like those of the cartoon cat spotting the anthropomorphic mice. Maybe this was a bad idea. I might be pitching *Honeymoon Stage: Prison*. But I had to tell somebody. Besides, Lauren cared too much about the success of her show to do anything drastic. I knew she wouldn't call the law to punish Maggie, but there'd at least be some consequences. Maybe they'd renegotiate the terms of filming in the bedroom and bathroom;

maybe Lauren would plant a mole and get Maggie to confess. She would do something.

And it would be something that did not implicate Gabe. If I was out of the picture, Maggie had no reason to drag Gabe's name into this mess. I'd let her win; I'd let her have him. The space I'd asked for would go on indefinitely until we were far enough away to be completely different people.

I swallowed. "Maggie and Jason killed Sally Ann." Lauren's face stayed blank. "Sally Ann?" I said. "The dead makeup artist? Maggie McKee killed her."

Lauren didn't respond, just kept sipping her coffee. It was a clear producer tactic, the sort of thing they taught teachers and cops and anyone else trying to get answers out of unwilling subjects. Sit long enough in silence, and people get uncomfortable enough that they can't help but talk.

"Also," I said. "I quit."

My patty melt arrived, greasy and covered in Swiss. I removed the top piece of bread. I could wait Lauren out.

She was thinking, making calculations. I envied the way she sat so still, her body never betraying her mind. "Okay," she said finally. "You're quitting. Why?"

"You heard the part I said first, right? About Maggie?" My mouth was still partially full.

"You want me to help move you back on set? Is that it? You're sick of logging."

"No," I said, dabbing my lips with a napkin. "No, I mean it. I'm totally done. But I'm leaving you this present."

What I saw as a morally clear but personally complicated shit show, I thought Lauren would see as a beribboned package of Reality television gold.

"Yeah, that's a no go," she said.

"What?" The bite I'd swallowed rested heavy in my chest.

"That doesn't help me. Too dark. We're not making that kind of show." Lauren put a hand on her belly. "Oof, this baby is kicking."

I'd thought nothing could surprise me, not after Maggie, and now here came Lauren. Not that I'd considered her the pinnacle of ethics, but it had seemed to me that her goals with the network were aligned with the goal of getting *some* justice for poor Sally Ann. Even if she didn't care about Sally Ann, Lauren cared about being a top show on television. For my entire time working with her, Lauren had encouraged me to look for the drama. What could be more compelling than this? Besides, we compromised Maggie constantly, from filming her workouts to paying off her housekeeper.

"You said you wanted good story," I said. "This is as good as it gets." Hysteria quavered in my voice, but Lauren stayed calm.

"For one of those shows about good girls rebelling or a women's prison or something. Our show is about being in love. Once this series wraps, maybe there's something we could do with it, but right now, I don't see it. Where is that pie?"

It took everything in me not to stand up on the ripped vinyl booth cushion and scream.

"Okay, whatever," I said softly. "I'm out."

Lauren made eye contact with the server, who remembered her undelivered order and mouthed an apology. Then she looked back at me. "Can I ask why?"

Because this business was corrupt and stretched the bounds of my morality? Because none of these people cared about anything but ratings and story and professional success at the expense of all else?

"You know that weird space between the garage and the pool house?" I said. "That, like, strip of weeds and rocks? There's a camera there. Just thought you should know."

Lauren raised a single eyebrow, a skill I hadn't known she had but wasn't overly surprised to discover.

"Cassidy," she said. "Don't leave the show. I can promote you."

"I know it's Dan's," I said. "The baby."

True to form, Lauren remained outwardly unfazed. Her cherry pie arrived, and she thanked the guy dropping it off. Her fork cracked the latticed top, plunging straight to the gooey center. "Let me promote you," she said. "You see things. You're patient. You've got what it takes."

This was because I had caught her on camera. Or else because she needed an ally against Dan. Whatever her motive, I knew it was less about me than about what I could do for her.

"I don't want it." I shook my head. "I don't want a promotion. I'm actually out."

"You're throwing away a huge opportunity," said Lauren. "If you leave, Dan's going to be pissed. He'll give you all the blame for anything that comes in from legal about Sally Ann's accident. It'll be hard to get the next job, without references."

Fine with me. I wanted far away from all of it; even scripted TV suddenly felt tainted. I had to shed the parts of my life that did not serve me. Recuse myself from this job. Renounce *Honeymoon Stage* and all its baggage. Sally Ann's death was Lauren's problem now—it wasn't my fault that she didn't want to deal with it. It wasn't Gabe's.

"You'll regret this." Lauren took another bite.

"I really don't think I will." I put down cash for my coffee and patty melt, paying for my own lunch the final severance of my servitude.

The diner doorbell clanged on my way out, and I could see Lauren watching me through the window by our booth as I walked out to my car. On my drive over, I'd imagined this moment as the iconic scene of action-hero Cassidy walking away from the ground-shattering explosion. Instead, the fuse was sputtering out. I tried not to look back.

October 2007

I'm no longer thinking about the altar or my walk down the aisle. Instead, I'm fully focused on Maggie. She's perched on a table, talking to the hair stylist working on Jen's updo. Sweet and innocuous, her robe fastened tight. She compliments Jen's engagement ring. Coos at Celia's earrings. Makes some joke about high heels.

I get another cup of coffee, which absolutely negates all the teeth bleaching I've done leading up to the wedding. The camera guy tracks me from chair to table and back again. Am I a bride or a zoo exhibit? I smile at him painfully.

Eyes are everywhere, and once again I need Maggie alone. I'm going to have to approach her in the toilet stall or take her to some obscure corner of the kitchen. Maybe the honeymoon suite, which sits camera-less and empty, waiting for tonight. If this were a lower-budget production, I could suggest that camera A go and find Gabe, but alas, he has his own Big Brother. I remind myself that we want this. I want this. This televised wedding is good for us—that is, if there is still an *us* once I've had my conversation with Maggie.

It's now or never.

"Do we have some time?" I ask Lauren and her headset.

"Time for what?" She frowns.

I take a split second to decide if wanting quiet reflection or wanting some time to throw up makes more sense, then settle on a mix of the two.

"My stomach hurts," I say. "Just to lie down for a minute."

"Cassidy," says Lauren. "Your stomach does not hurt. You're fine."

Jen and Celia are both pinned down in their own makeup chairs, but I see them exchange a look. Jen has scooted forward, about to beg off, when Maggie stops her. She understands her role as a bridesmaid and will fulfill it, even if it's a charade.

"I can take care of Cassidy," Maggie says. "After our years on set together, it's my turn, after all."

"Be back for your turn in the chair," Lauren says. Through her teeth, she adds, "Please."

Maggie waves a manicured hand to say either *Of course* or *Of course not.* Lauren can't really stop her, though—she needs Maggie even more than she needs me, and as a general rule, Maggie is much less obliging.

Maggie takes my elbow and says, "Come. Where to?" Tightening the sash of my robe, I nod in the direction of the stairs.

The halls are empty, though we can hear the bustling of the caterers and PAs as they make last-minute plans against the rain. Red plush carpeting lines the second story, and I sneak a foot out of my slipper to touch it, wondering how the staff keeps it pristine.

I'm correct in my assumption that the honeymoon suite will be unoccupied. We go in, and I immediately lock the door.

16.

2003

Honeymoon Stage Season Three was only five episodes long, as opposed to the ten each of the first two seasons. To its bitter end, the show insisted that Maggie and Jason were as in love several years into their very public marriage as they had been on the day they first met. Never mind that they started to say *babe* like the word was a knife, that she spent weeks on the road and then went to Palm Springs for the weekend instead of coming home to Calabasas, that the tabloids continued their relentless speculation. On *Honeymoon Stage*, everything was beautiful and nothing hurt.

I didn't know what happened behind the scenes, what sort of cajoling came from Lauren and the other producers. Maggie had sworn to me that she couldn't exist without Jason, but immediately following the third-season finale, she filed for divorce.

Speculation was everywhere. She was cheating on him. He was jealous of her career. He'd found someone younger. She'd broken his heart. A paparazzi shot of Maggie trying not to be photographed was worth thousands of dollars. She'd walk with her head down, one hand up to cover her face, and the headline would read What's Maggie Hiding?

Jason gave an interview to *Esquire* not long after they officially separated, ostensibly to promote the new line of sports drinks he'd given his name to, but mostly to whine about how Maggie had ruined him.

"I was totally blindsided," he told the reporter. "I had no idea she was unhappy. I thought it was something we could work on, but she just went straight to divorce."

Maggie McKee, somehow both savvy Jezebel and idiot who still couldn't spell *Mississippi.*

I watched the whole thing happen from my childhood bedroom in Pennsylvania. I was still on the lease for our apartment in LA and had been planning to go back there once I was done licking my wounds, but the months passed, and Jen and Celia found a subletter, and I did copywriting for a neighbor and helped my stepdad do work around the house. I wasn't done with TV, not entirely. I wasn't going to be one of those girls who let the city chew me up and spit me out. I just needed some time.

On late-night TV, Maggie McKee became synonymous with *slutty ex-girlfriend.* She was the butt of every joke for at least the first two months after announcing the divorce, and a swell of fan support for Jason led to rumors he'd be the next star of a well-known Reality dating franchise. Nothing came out about his drug and alcohol abuse or the chaos immediately following his injury. If she'd wanted to, Maggie could have smeared him. But she didn't.

Every so often, Gabe would appear on the list of men she was supposedly running wild with around Hollywood. Each time I saw his name or photo, I felt a splinter in my heart. I hadn't told him I was back in Pennsylvania. There he was, carrying a guitar case through a parking lot, Maggie beside him. There he was, in the pictures of a restaurant opening, clinking glasses with a slew of B-list stars. A photo ran in *Star* of him snuggled up to Maggie, his head on her shoulder, their arms laced. The night after it showed up on the Wawa magazine rack, Gabe called me. I was still awake, but I let him go to voicemail.

"Cassidy." He'd clearly been drinking, my name long in his mouth. "I think about you constantly. There's nothing with Maggie but the music. I promise. If you care." A pause, a breath. "You should delete this. This is dumb. Is there a button to delete this?"

I didn't call back, but I kept the voicemail. I'd play it late at night, phone cradled by my pillow, as if I had him there with me.

June turned to September. My brother, Andrew, had matched at his top hospital residency, and my mom threw him a massive party, renting out a room at her favorite restaurant for all my relatives to come congratulate her on making a doctor.

"And what are you doing, Cassidy, dear?" my great-aunt asked me. I was between projects, I said, stuffing myself with breadsticks to avoid elaboration.

Gabe had a radio single that seemed to be following me everywhere. It was a song I'd heard him play when I'd been out in California. There wasn't much story to it—boy in love with girl—but it had a catchy chorus and some interesting riffs. Watch me / Want you / I'll wait / Stay true. Lyrically not one of his best, but that was likely why it made pop radio. When I asked Celia on the phone if she'd heard it, she didn't even know what I was talking about. But I heard it often enough to think that fate was laughing at me. Often enough that Gabe was never too far from my mind.

I wrote Mr. Pichietti's weekly newsletters. Babysat my mom's coworkers' kids. Watched seasons of old television with Ron, popping the Netflix envelopes in the mail when he forgot, so we could get the next few episodes. I became especially adept at pulling weeds from the cracks in the sidewalk. An expert in *Beverly Hills 90210* fan fiction.

"What are you going to do?" My mother came in one night when I'd been home more than half a year, and sat down unceremoniously on the edge of my bed. The room looked about the same as it had when I'd returned in the summers during college—I'd done nothing to rid it of the remnants of girlhood. A poster of a palomino horse on one wall. My high school desk, old textbooks peeling. The duvet still pale pink with patterned white flowers. "You're welcome here for as long as you need us," my mother said. "But I suppose I'm wondering if you really need us." She had spent ages trying to get me to move back to the East Coast;

the fact that she was now kicking me out, however passive-aggressively, was telling. "I don't think you're happy here, Cassidy."

I didn't think that I was happy either. That said, I wasn't unhappy. I had a job, sort of, and I exercised.

"I don't know," I said. "It's hard." I wasn't sure what "it" was. Early adulthood? Sitting on information about a murder? Knowing I was too soft for the life I'd thought I wanted. Losing the person who'd helped me feel more like myself than I ever had and not knowing if that was my own fault or his.

My mother held my hand in hers, running a thumb along my knuckles the way she did when I was small and I would cry to her because some girl at school had been mean to me. She had always been a good mother. She'd let me regrow my feathers for several long seasons, and now she was nudging me back out of the nest.

"I've always hoped you wouldn't take the things that happened with your dad as a barometer," she said. "Most people aren't selfish pricks." I laughed, but it hurt—the memory of my father forever the last vestige of a bad chest cold, the cough that lingers, the breath you can't quite catch.

Although my stepfather treated my mother like a queen, my most formative childhood moments involved my parents' disagreements. My mom murmuring sharply to my father as he massaged his temples and said "I don't know, Cheryl," while clenching his can of O'Doul's. My dad parading us around his law firm's family picnic—horseshoes and face painting and everybody grinning but my mother, her face drawn. Try as I might to mine a memory of them happy, nuzzling or holding hands, I never could come up with anything but the vein in my mother's forehead, how it pulsed the day she told us that he wasn't coming home.

Once he was gone, my mother didn't talk much about my dad. She said she didn't want to poison us against him, though he was already adept at that himself. She never badgered him to see us. She never forced me to confess how deeply his leaving had hurt me. We slapped

Band-Aids on a gaping wound, out of sight out of mind. It was always going to leave a hideous scar.

Now my mother sighed and rubbed at a little stain on the sleeve of her scrubs. She was only forty-eight. She'd been younger than I was now when she'd had me, younger still when Andrew was born. The thought was terrifying.

"I never wanted you to grow up thinking everybody had an angle," she continued. "Your dad was always for himself. He wasn't cut out for a family. I should have realized you kids would need more help processing than what's her name that first year."

"The lady with the orange couch," I said.

"Yeah, her." I remembered those few sessions with Dr. What's Her Name—me and Andrew on that nappy couch, my mom kneeling next to us. The doctor was a couples therapist, mostly, which my mom must have found at least a little bit funny. I think she'd also been a friend of Aunt Dede's.

"But we have Ron," I reminded my mother.

"Thank god for Ron." This was a common refrain throughout my late adolescence, when Ron offered me his IPAs and came to Andrew's hockey games and talked Mom down from her initial reactions to our teenage shenanigans. "I wish I'd met him when you were younger."

"He's here now," I said.

"He is." My mother sighed. "I don't know, maybe I shouldn't have let you go stay with Dad in Virginia. I should have known better. But I wanted to give you a chance. You have to think the best of people, kiddo. Even if it might be scary or make you feel silly for trying, you still have to try." I leaned into her, my head against her chest so I could feel her heartbeat, hear the breath move through her. She smelled like peppermint lotion.

"It is scary," I mumbled.

"Don't let what happened with your dad be the big story of your life," my mother said.

I didn't respond. If I made myself hard enough, I wouldn't need him. But if I didn't need him, he was absolved of having left me. He'd be the tragic hero in his own story, even if he was forever the villain in mine.

My mother held me and we listened to the birds in conversation just outside, twittering their song of manic happiness.

"Mr. Pichietti says you can keep doing his newsletter from Los Angeles," my mother said finally. "While you get back on your feet, look for a more fulfilling job."

She had been talking to Mr. Pichietti about my career trouble, probably also my love life. It was this as much as anything that told me it was time to return to LA.

17.

I'd been gone almost ten months when I went back to Jen and Celia. Jen's sister had been renting out my room, and they were happy to boot her. Apparently, she ate everyone's snacks and vacuumed loudly in the middle of the night. She had a cat, who also left when she did. I kept finding traces of its hair.

I worked from our uneven kitchen table, translating Mr. Pichietti's rambling thoughts about lawn care into packaged bits of content he could send to former customers at variable intervals. The job didn't pay much, but it also didn't take up too much of my time, so in my off hours I trawled for production gigs. Much as it grieved me to admit it, I liked working in television. The pace, the excitement, the fact that, if you weren't stuck logging, every day was something new. If I could get a gig somewhere niche, like *Antiques Roadshow*, I wouldn't have to be manipulating people or building up somebody's ego. I avoided anything that hinged its drama on making cast members look stupid. This cut me out of the majority of Reality TV.

Unfortunately, I didn't have any contacts in scripted production, and everyone I knew in Reality was game to talk to me until I said I'd worked on *Honeymoon Stage*. I could see it in their eyes, the moment they realized I was *that* PA. Lauren had been right: My big opportunity had come and gone. Dan had let me take the fall once I left the show, and I was now the PA who had brought legal scrutiny down on the network. It was easy to put all the blame for the accident on me, however untrue their claims that my negligence had led Sally Ann to eat the peanuts. They didn't really care that someone had died. As I'd been told, people died all the time! But production companies couldn't risk a lawsuit, and therefore, they couldn't hire me.

The announcement came in the trades that *Honeymoon Stage* was not being renewed, which anyone with a pulse could have figured out, given the public divorce its two romantic leads were facing. I took this as a reason to go visit Lauren, whose baby, I regret to say, looked exactly like Dan.

He was fourteen months old and just going down for a nap. Lauren let me admire him for a minute before putting him to bed. I didn't ask about the financial situation that allowed Lauren to keep on as an on-set producer while single-parenting a baby. *Honeymoon Stage* had done well, and I supposed some part of that had ended up in Lauren's pocket. It certainly had not graced mine.

Lauren lived in West Hollywood, in a 1920s-style bungalow with a gorgeous back patio and a remodeled kitchen that she likely never used. She thanked me for the little stuffed duck I had picked up for the baby on the way over.

We sat outside. A concrete wall covered in vines hid any noise from the freeway. "So," she said to me. "The drama."

"With the show, you mean?" I asked.

"I told you you'd regret walking out." She'd made us each a Nespresso, which was too strong for me.

"I don't regret it," I said quickly.

"You do—otherwise you wouldn't be here with me." Lauren took her coffee down in a single shot. Steam still rose from mine, and I imagined her throat burning. "It's been very juicy. You'd have loved it. Those two hated each other by the end. They'd say 'Stop rolling,' and

Dan would have to remind them that if we stopped rolling we wouldn't have a show."

She was wrong that I'd take pleasure in Jason and Maggie's collapse. Lauren was always so sure we were alike in our ruthlessness. Given my trajectory, I wasn't sure why. "It would have been such good TV if they had listened to me," she continued. "The network, I mean. Mark my words, we're going to start seeing more real-life soap operas. People yelling at each other. That's the next wave. That's what people want, if they can't have a love story. Crying, screaming, knocking over tables. An all-out brawl between Jason and Maggie would have been television magic."

"Why didn't the network listen?" I asked. "Why didn't it happen?"

"Too many people on Maggie's team are caught up in preserving her image. Clearly it's already shot to hell, but they put someone in to make sure we were editing her the way we'd promised. A lesson to keep the cast and their teams out of production, at least if you want something sensational. Though they were both totally polite and restrained while we were at the house. It's not like we caught them saying anything we couldn't use. I tried to get in the room during their couples therapy, but my hands were tied, you know." She frowned.

"Why'd she leave him?" I asked. "Do you think?"

"Sounds like a good friend finally talked some sense into her. Unfortunately for us. We couldn't keep business as usual once they so clearly couldn't stand each other, but at least we could have finished a full season."

"You really think they couldn't stand each other?" I asked.

"Cassidy." Lauren snorted. "The second she became a bigger deal than he was, that marriage was over. The man's ego bruised like a fruit."

"And the thing I told you, the day I quit. About Maggie . . . ?"

"Being a murderer?" Lauren rolled her eyes. "You want me to get laughed off the lot? Nothing good will come of stirring that old pot. Poking around in that accident. Especially not for you."

We sat quietly for a minute or two, Lauren's mind whirring, me building up the courage to ask her to help me find work.

"So what are you going to do now?" I asked finally.

"Oh, Dan and I have a development deal with the network. A few irons in the fire." It seemed to me she didn't need Dan, that Maggie breaking away might have been an inspiration for Lauren to do the same. But I supposed there were only so many men she was willing to sleep with. She had a kid. It didn't matter how good her ideas were or how much better she was than Dan at managing a set. Lauren out from under the protection of Dan's maleness would probably follow the same fate as Maggie. She'd be cast as a striver, a slut. What an awful industry I was trying to go back to.

"Do you know of anybody interesting hiring right now?" I asked. The industry was awful, but I still wanted in. I was addicted to the speed of it, the power.

Lauren laughed out loud. "I knew it," she said. "I knew that's why you were here. I see through you completely, Cassidy Baum." She said this as if she was simply delighted that, despite what might have happened with *Honeymoon Stage*, my urge to get on set was still alive and well. "We're not anywhere near green lit yet," she said. "But once we need PAs, I'll call you."

"Not with you and Dan, I mean." I tried to keep the disdain from my voice. "Maybe something less intense?"

Lauren laughed again. "It's dog eat dog out there," she said. "Me and Dan might be all you can get."

I should have known I would run into Gabe eventually. Every city is just a small town, once you've lived in it long enough. Lauren's baby woke up, and I left her house feeling like I'd prostrated myself for no reason. Going back to my car was like returning to the first square of a game board, getting stuck in Gumdrop Gulch, or whatever it was called, after thinking I had made it to the lollipops. Not too far from Lauren's was a coffee shop I liked, and to cheer myself up, I went to get myself a treat. It didn't occur to me until I saw him that the reason I knew and liked that coffee shop was that it was around the corner from Gabe's studio. There he was, waiting at the counter for his order. The world was dog eat dog but also fairly predictable.

Gabe turned around at the tinkle of the bell on top of the door. Our most recent interaction was the drunken voicemail he'd left me nine months ago, of which I had never acknowledged receipt. His hair was shorter. He had on a shirt that I knew well. My stomach dropped.

We looked at each other from across the coffee shop, unsure who should speak first. I gave him a weird little half wave, my arm barely leaving my side. He smiled. There were those dimples.

I could sense him there, the nearness of his body, as we both waited for the person in front of me to finish their order. When it was my turn, I panicked and ordered some expensive froufrou drink I didn't actually want.

"With whipped cream?" asked the barista.

"Sure, why not."

By the time I made it over to where Gabe was standing waiting for his coffee, all I could think about was the birthmark on his thigh, the arch of his back, the particular velvet softness of him.

"Hey, Cass," he said. I almost melted. Had his eyes always been so blue? It took everything in me not to reach out to run a finger across the stubble on his jaw.

"Hey," I said. "This is a good coffee shop, huh?"

"It is." He swallowed. I wondered if he also was fighting the attraction. What was it about his body that so perfectly attuned to mine? "How've you been?" He held a sugar packet, turning it over and over between his fingers.

"Oh, you know," I said. *Terrible. Why did we break up again? Because a desperate pop star told me you had orchestrated murder?* Ridiculous, standing here with Gabe, to remember Maggie claiming he had been involved in all that stuff with Sally Ann. "You?"

One side of Gabe's upper lip curled. He looked me directly in the eye. He was about to say something when the barista called out "Gabriel!" He blinked.

"Your coffee is ready," I said.

"Tea," he corrected. He took the cup from the counter and threw away the sugar packet unopened. Never had I wanted to kiss someone so badly.

"Tea," I said. *I miss you. Please don't go.*

"Well," said Gabe, "good seeing you."

He was the one who had lied, but I'd asked for space. He was giving me what he thought I wanted. He was a good man. What was wrong with me? I bit down hard on the knuckle of my index finger as he turned to leave. He was walking away, those broad, perfect shoulders, that slight hunch, as if when not onstage, he was afraid to take up space. If I were brave, I would abandon the drink I didn't even want and follow him. I took a step away from the counter just as he turned back.

"I—"

"If you—"

We spoke at once, both stopped. I laughed nervously.

"I'm going out of town tomorrow. Taking the bus around the Midwest for a few weeks. But maybe when I get back, we can do this again?" He was vulnerable, stripped totally bare. I could see the twelve-year-old he'd been on *The Tiger Crew*, the little kid obsessed with Elvis.

"I mean, I'm always down for awkward coffee run-ins," I said.

"No better kind, right?" Gabe smiled.

"But yeah," I said, despite my better judgment. "That sounds good."

That night, after putting in a few hours for Mr. Pichietti and bemoaning to Celia my bad luck with finding work I actually liked, I checked my email hoping to hear back from one of the line producers Lauren had sworn wouldn't hire me. Nothing on that front, but I did have something from Gabe. The subject line read, "I'm Sorry."

Cassidy,

I think I've probably already said this, but not enough or in the right way. I am so sorry about everything that happened last year. I can try to explain it, but when you get down to it I hurt you, and I'm sorry.

It was really good to see you today. Very weird and unexpected, but also very good. You ordered a rosehip ginger latte with whipped cream, which makes me think it was also maybe weird and unexpected for you. Hopefully also good.

It's a lot easier to write a song than it is to write this email. I know you aren't one for what you think is corny stuff. I'm not going to show up under your balcony and play you a song about how much I've missed you, or even hold up a boombox. It's harder but probably better to just say outright: I've missed you.

In the spirit of just saying things, I have been seeing Maggie occasionally. Not "seeing" her as a euphemism for dating—the tabloid stuff is all made up. Our stuff from years ago is over, coffin closed. But we've been working on new music together. I've been helping with her album. It seems like something you should know right up front, given everything. Maybe that makes this all even more awkward, but I'm taking you at your word that you are interested in meeting up again, and I just want it all out there this time. I have a lot of regrets about the way I handled that before.

Anyway, I'll be back in town on the 7th. I hope this note isn't too much.

Love (I've deleted this three times but fuck, I'm just going to say it),
Gabe

C.isthe.Baum@aol.com to
Gabriel.Leighton@hotmail.com
October 8, 2004, 8:08 PM

Dear Gabe,
Hi. Thank you. For the email, I mean. It's not too much. It's actually really good to hear from you, and it was also good to see you, although not so good to get stuck with that drink. When you go back there, I do not recommend.

I also probably should have emailed you sooner, and/or called you back. The whole thing was (is?) sort of confusing, but I wish I hadn't bailed. Thank you for not showing up under my window with a boombox. Where are you guys headed?

Gabriel.Leighton@hotmail.com to
C.isthe.Baum@aol.com
October 9, 2004, 10:23 AM

On the way to Des Moines now, then Milwaukee, Chicago, Kansas City. Honestly off the top of my head I don't know all of it. I'll send you the link for the tour. I get why you didn't call. I'm glad you're emailing now. Celia said that you were back in Pennsylvania. (I promise I only asked her once.) We put out a few singles, and one of them got okay traction. Hence the tour. We've had some changes in the band, though. Jimmy quit, Jody got married.

C.isthe.Baum@aol.com to
Gabriel.Leighton@hotmail.com
October 9, 2004, 7:08 PM

Pennsylvania was not exciting. My brother graduated medical school, which I know pales in comparison to leaving a production assistant gig mid-season, but weirdly my mom sees things differently and now wants me to "get an actual job." Slim pickings out here so far, but I persist. I'm back with Jen and Celia in Silver Lake, and have been for a few months.
About the band—you should have known you would never get far.

I've heard the single, and it's catchy. It's a good song, but I also creeped around to hear some of the other new stuff and I like that even better.

Is it weird to ask about whatever happened to that other song, the one you wrote with Maggie? It definitely feels weird, but in the spirit of ripping off Band-Aids I figured I'd just ask.

(PS: Bryan Adams? Ha! You've got to try harder to stump me.)

Gabriel.Leighton@hotmail.com to
C.isthe.Baum@aol.com
October 11, 2004, 1:13 AM

In the Spirit of Ripping Off Band-Aids could be its own song. Even better than The Other Song, which I'm beginning to think might be cursed. The devil's music: sounds real pretty but keeps screwing with my life. I don't want it anymore. I don't need it.
Anyway, the Band-Aid song would go something like: Maggie and me/easy to see/we write well together but there's an impenetrable level of something that's still keeping her from saying it's okay to record what she actually feels and it's very frustrating as a collaborator/dum dee dee. Sounds better with music behind it.

I'm glad you think the single's catchy, and glad you've been keeping tabs on the band.

I'm writing this from a bus that smells like Axe Body Spray and stale McDonalds' french fries, but I really do think there's something to going after what you love.

I'm sort of wondering what we're doing here. I don't want to go into things expecting something that I shouldn't, just because you replied to my email. It can be lonely on the road (they say it's no place to start a family, etc.), and I don't want to be here reading into things.

Sending, yet again, before I make myself delete this.

-G

⚜

In early November, I drove to Gabe's gig just outside Las Vegas. He didn't know I was coming, and I stood near the back, watching him play. This was the final stop on what they called their Midwest tour, and I sipped on a watery vodka tonic while Gabe sang about the one that got away. I watched the familiar way he pushed back his hair, the flush of his cheeks under the lights.

I'm not sure when he saw me, how he knew I was in the mass of people filling the small venue. Maybe it was the same way that I sensed him when he was in a room, a radar screaming out the fact of his body, drawing me near.

The consummate professional, Gabe didn't flinch while doing his audience banter. A tornado could hit, and Gabe would say *Well, thanks, folks* with a smile. He retuned the guitar, an apparent cue to the rest of the band that he was going off script.

"I'm going to go solo for you all for a minute," he said. "We've got somebody special here tonight." Gabe was comfortable riffing. I didn't recognize the tune. "I'm going to try out something new. Something for the lady in the back." At this everyone turned around, but he was mercifully vague enough that I could keep sipping my drink, pretending I was looking back too.

"Hello, lady." Gabe smiled and started to play.

⚜

"Hi," Gabe said. "I've missed you." We were in my car, outside a motel in Nevada. He smelled like someone else's cigarette smoke. He had sweat through the back of his shirt. I thought I had been waiting for this moment since I'd seen him at the coffee shop several weeks earlier, but I had actually been waiting since that day at the production office when I'd spotted him on camera with Maggie and first broken up with him. I'd been waiting since the day I first met him, that quick glance out my rearview mirror as he stood there and I pulled the car away. This same car, the bumper still scarred. We were still the same people.

I had never wanted anything the way that I wanted to brush his hair off his forehead, get rid of his T-shirt. I had left and returned so many times. I'd called him to me and sent him away. But I was here now. I had come.

"I've missed you too."

18.

Gabe made me gourmet dinners on the nights he wasn't playing a gig. We watched stupid movies and brought picnics to the park. We met his band for drinks, and he came out with Jen and Celia, listening to them complain about their own love lives, dancing with them, but never too close. He gave me foot rubs while I emailed Mr. Pichietti and the friends who had joined him in requesting freelance newsletters, refilled my coffee and did the crossword puzzle, asked me how I wanted the AC. I emptied his dishwasher. He wrote jokey songs with my name in them, being as ridiculous as possible until I came over and kissed him to make him shut up. In the rosy glow of my second-chance romance, I almost didn't mind that I hadn't found another job yet in TV.

Gabe was working on other people's music projects, sitting in on writing sessions and messing with soundboards or computers or I wasn't sure quite what. Maggie's album was one of those projects. He told me exactly when he was meeting her, where it would be, what they did, who else was with them. He invited me to all his gigs, which felt less like a request for my companionship than an assertion that he'd be where he had told me he would be.

We were two months back in, and he hadn't addressed the tabloids or the paparazzi, who accosted us in a parking lot at one point but then, seeing I was obviously not Maggie, gave up and backed off. He hadn't told me if he was the one who got Maggie to break up with Jason.

"The tabloids lie," Gabe said with no elaboration. I guess he knew that having worked in Reality TV, I was firmly aware that what you see isn't always what you get. But that went both ways. I had Gabe; I saw him. I was trying to take my mother's advice. I hadn't mentioned what Maggie had said to me that day at the fountain in Calabasas.

How well do you really know him?

I hated Maggie McKee for watering this seed of distrust, yet once it had sprouted, I couldn't force it back into its cracked little husk.

Maggie was also going through it. In an overplayed interview for ABC, she was asked if she worried about setting a bad example for her fans.

"I don't understand the question." In the video, Maggie pops her gum. Her hair has been braided into elaborate pigtails that make her look younger than twenty-five. The interviewer, a white woman in expensive pants and small gold hoop earrings, blinks as though Maggie has an IQ of six. Whereas Jason winked at the audience when Maggie played dumb, this lady patronizes to the point of sticky sweetness. Aspartame kindness, ready to dissolve your teeth and give you five kinds of cancer.

"How do you feel about becoming a dangerous kind of role model for American children?" the interviewer repeats. Maggie presses her lips together and answers in her calmest voice.

"Shouldn't 'role model' be a job for their teachers and parents?"

"But surely you realize that young people's eyes are on you. Does that make you regret certain choices in your personal life?"

Maggie gives a sad little half smile and, with impressive serenity, responds, "I'm a singer, not a nanny."

Then the interviewer moves on to how it feels to know she's broken Jason Dean's heart.

I watched this particular interview while Gabe was at a show, not wanting him to know how much I still thought about Maggie.

Is Maggie M on a Bender? ran across a photo of her getting into a car after a night at a club. Maggie McKee, Don't Phone Me over an image of her visibly upset while holding her cell phone. For months it would seem like, finally, the Maggie McKee smackdown cycle was through, and then a slow news week would prompt another round of speculation on who she'd been cheating with and how Jason was dealing with the heartbreak and shock. To listen to the media, Jason was waking up every day with zero short-term memory, experiencing the supposed surprise of his wife's infidelity anew.

"She knows I'll always love her," he said in his own prime-time interview. "I told her that whatever happens between us, I'm always a phone call away. I'm here whenever she needs me."

This earned him a reassuring pat on the hand from the same Tasteful Hoop Earrings who had torn apart his ex-wife a few weeks prior.

Gabe's EP had finally gotten him a deal for an album with a major label. This was all in the works when I drove out to Las Vegas, and within our first three months back together, he had dotted all the i's. The day the paperwork was filed, Maggie McKee offered to sing on a track. Gabe brought me her proposal, laying it out over brunch.

The facts were these: Maggie was finished being flighty. Gabe could have that special song they wrote together in Nashville, the one he'd asked after for literal years. Maggie would even sing harmonies or a verse, and make rounds for publicity when it released.

I knew immediately that Maggie was in love with Gabe. She was sending me a message. Why else would she be offering this now when we'd just gotten back together? Maggie had held Gabe on the back burner for ages, but now that he had me again, she'd realized her mistake. She wanted him. Or maybe she just really hated me.

"Of course, I said no." Gabe cut a sausage link and popped it casually into his mouth.

"What do you mean you said no?" I pushed my chair back from the table.

All publicity was good publicity—well, so long as he wasn't in the news for killing someone. Maggie might be napalm for herself, but she was an excellent lighter for Gabe's candle. If Maggie toured with him, did interviews, a magazine spread—that would introduce a new audience to his music. It was the best hook he could ask for, the most certain to succeed. Everything he wanted—the acclaim, the reassurance, the respect—was within arm's reach, if only he would grab it. Yet here he was, immediately pooh-poohing.

"I told you, I'm over that song. It doesn't fit," said Gabe. "With us. It doesn't make sense." He leaned back in his chair, calm and decisive. I frowned.

"Okay, but career-wise," I said. "It makes a ton of sense for your career. You have to say yes."

"I don't think I do," said Gabe.

"This is the break you've been waiting for," I said.

"Do you agree that things are good here?" He gestured between us with his fork.

"Things are very good here, but that has nothing to do with it," I said.

"That has everything to do with it," said Gabe, looking almost smug. "That *is* it. I don't need Maggie, or her song."

Gabe leaned across the table to kiss me. His lips pressed into mine, and he smelled like sugar, and I felt his heartbeat, and I tried not to think about what I knew I would say next.

I still thought about Sally Ann. The kid in her locket, who took care of it, what it was doing. I had a recurring nightmare that I was endlessly passing out lunch orders. Whenever I thought about Sally Ann, I also thought about Maggie. *How well do you really know him, Cassidy?*

"Gabe," I began.

"Cassidy, I've made up my mind," Gabe said. "It's not going to happen."

"I have to ask you something," I said. Gabe's face went serious. He sat up straighter, his eyes searching mine. "Maggie said something to me that seems kind of insane, but before you make the call here and give up all her stuff for me, I have to know if it's true."

Open the door, I told myself; *be totally real with him.* What was the worst that could happen?

"Fucking Maggie," Gabe said under his breath. Did he know what I was about to say? My heart dropped.

"Before I quit the show, before I left LA, we had a conversation," I continued. "Me and Maggie." Every word felt like walking through a swamp, and I spoke quickly to keep myself from getting sucked down. "I thought when Sally Ann died—I'd seen some stuff that made me think it wasn't actually an accident. I mentioned it to Maggie because I thought that maybe Jason had . . . you know. She told me it was you."

Gabe frowned, an endearing little crease of the forehead. "She said what?" He blinked hard, then shook his head. "She told you what?"

"She said you were the one who figured out how to cause . . . Sally Ann's accident." I took a breath.

In the moment it took Gabe to parse what I was saying, I realized how insane I sounded. I didn't think Gabe had been part of the murder, simply Maggie's collateral. But why had *he* been her collateral? Was he really who I thought he was? I couldn't stand the not knowing.

His hands tightened into fists. "Maggie told you that I plotted to kill her makeup artist?" He was definitely mad, but I wasn't yet sure if he was mad at me. His tone had that half-joking veneer of disbelief that accompanies the absurd, but underneath it was actual pain. "And you believed her?"

"Well, no. I didn't believe her," I said. "I'm not saying I think that you did it, but I wanted to know why she would say that. If there was more that you weren't telling me. It seemed like something we should probably address."

"Okay," Gabe said, tugging at his hair. "Okay. Sure, I guess I get it, kind of?"

I moved to touch his arm. "Just to be clear," I said, "you didn't—?"

"I didn't do it. I don't know what she's even talking about." Gabe stood, began pacing the room. His fists clenched and unclenched. He inhaled long, then exhaled slowly, and in this moment, he seemed to understand what I was *actually* asking him, all that I'd avoided saying these past several months. "Okay." He sat back down and took both my hands in his, ignoring my half-bitten nail. "Cassidy."

"Yes."

"I didn't help Maggie kill anyone. It's ridiculous that I have to say this. I didn't kill anyone or help anyone kill anyone. And more importantly, I'm not sleeping with Maggie. I wasn't with her when we were together, I didn't sleep with her after we broke up, and I haven't been seeing her now in anything other than a professional setting. I'm being totally honest with you. Years ago, I knew some stuff about Jason and didn't tell anybody about it when maybe I should have. But you know all that. I've told you all of it. You know everything there is to know between me and Maggie McKee, and there won't be anything else to know because that friendship is over." He squeezed my hands hard while we spoke, willing me to believe him. "It's an easy decision. I don't need her help. I'm choosing you."

I thought about the tabloid photos: Maggie's head on his shoulder, their knees touching under the table. I thought about Gabe sitting here in front of me. That old voicemail he'd sent, slurring my name. The gentle way he kissed my neck under the earlobe.

I believed him.

"You mean this doesn't change your mind and make you want to take her up on her offer?" I cracked. Gabe rolled his eyes. "I'm sorry," I said. "I just couldn't not say anything. I couldn't let you make this kind of decision about work without letting you know it had been eating at me."

"I know." His grip had eased, and he was now stroking my hand with his thumb. I shifted my chair closer to him and leaned against his side.

We moved in together four months later.

19.

While Gabe's entertainment career showed signs of life, mine was flatlining. I took a million meetings, but nothing stuck. The jobs were either low paying or low prestige, too morally gray or too boring. The gigs I really wanted never called me back.

When I complained to her, my mother suggested that I write out a more specific list of skills I'd learned in my time on the *Honeymoon Stage* set so I'd be ready to sell myself in interviews. I sat at the kitchen table, trying to make "replaced dead flowers" sound marketable, and found myself imagining an entire conversation between me and Rahul about spraying the trees on the property with paint so that they'd shimmer more romantically on camera. Without meaning to, I'd made us sound ridiculous—not me and Rahul, but the work we did, the fact we'd cared so deeply. In a way, it *was* ridiculous, all the facades and shellacking that had made our show "real." If I fleshed it out, here was my sitcom.

Each time I got passed over for a job, I'd open up the document and fiddle: a character detail here, a wacky situation there. The producers on my imaginary Reality show weren't Lauren and Dan, but they weren't *not* Lauren and Dan either. The rest of the crew sprang from my imagination, save for the show's host, who was always flaking. That character was based on my dad.

"This is funny," said Gabe one afternoon, looking over my shoulder. "This stuff is good."

"It's just to blow off steam, nothing serious."

"It's a great idea," Gabe repeated. "Why not make it serious?"

"Gabe." I turned to him, incredulous. "I'd never work in Reality again. Talk about blacklisting. I pitch this seriously, and everyone would hate me."

"You know Jake's dad is a big shot at Fox. Jake's been looking for a project to bring him." Jake was one of Gabe's Hollywood friends, the type who did half the work for twice the reward simply by accident of birth. He'd be a great contact to have were I to try and take TV writing seriously. "Let me mention it to him," Gabe said. "Just float it."

I said why not. It was easy to agree, as I was certain nothing would come of it. I'd never envisioned myself as a writer. Gabe was the writer. I was just messing around until I redeemed myself and got back on a set.

Three weeks after Gabe's suggestion, I had three more job rejections and forty pages of a pilot for *Reality June*, a workplace sitcom about a plucky PA and her ENG crew. I let Gabe read the full draft, and he gave me a book about screenwriting the next day after dinner.

"Thanks for letting me down easy," I said when I unwrapped the package.

"The opposite," Gabe said. "It's for making an already good thing great. And I floated the concept to Jake. He likes it. A lot."

"Well, Jake can have the concept," I said, clearing our dishes. "Just not my expertise."

Gabe scoffed. "It's your idea. He can*not* have it."

I scrubbed vigorously at the sticky-sweet marinade congealed on the side of a pan. "Jake will have to find somebody else that he can sell to his dad. I'm not ready to make myself even more toxic in Reality TV."

"Okay, but why are you still working on it?" Gabe came over to join me at the sink. "If it's really going nowhere, why are you writing it?"

"It's therapeutic," I said. "Or maybe masochistic?"

"That sounds exhausting."

It was. Still, life went on. We went on a weekend trip to Sacramento where I met Gabe's parents—his dad looking sweetly down his glasses at me, his mother immediately hooking her elbow through my arm. I took up CrossFit. We talked about getting a dog.

When Gabe's album came out, it did okay but not great. He wasn't salty about the numbers, although I knew they weren't what he'd hoped for.

Between us sat the specter of Maggie McKee's declined endorsement. As I watched Gabe spin the wheel of rock stardom yet again without winning, I couldn't help but think that, despite all her manipulation, despite what it might have meant for my relationship with Gabe, he should have taken Maggie up on her offer. He would for sure have gotten that *Rolling Stone* profile with Maggie McKee as a duet partner. He could have booked bigger venues, gotten their music video in regular rotation.

Instead, he played his bars and local clubs and sang for radio DJs in the hope they'd catch on to what he was trying to do with his music and bring it mainstream. He'd sigh and say *Not all hard work pays off,* and I would just about want to die, knowing the easiest road had been his for the taking, and if it hadn't been for me, he would have taken it.

"You don't know for sure it would have made any difference," said Rahul when I met him downtown for drinks. He was working on a show about a seven-foot-tall man dating a series of short women, and I'd reached out to see if he knew of anything good currently hiring for PAs. He'd responded that if he knew of anything good hiring, he wouldn't be filming *Seven's Heavens*, but we should meet up anyway, it had been too long. After several martinis, I'd told him the basics about Maggie and Gabe. She'd been sociopathic, yes, but she would have been good for him.

"He would have had more opportunity," I said. "If I wasn't so jealous." Rahul shook his head.

"Might. You've gotta learn to embrace the *might*. Not everything is preordained. Working on a Reality set messes with you, but sometimes shit just happens." I was sure we were both thinking about the days following Sally Ann's death, when I'd spun out and been demoted while he sucked it up and kept doing his job. "Also, she's the problem. Maggie's always been smarter than they give her credit for, and by that I mean she's always been a total bitch."

"Well, I mean . . ."

"You know it's true. Jesus, who hurt her? People out here are all kinds of messed up. It's better to get on a show where the weird is on the outside. Somebody weighs nine hundred pounds or has half a face or something else that, in circus times, would have put them in a freak show."

"That's mean," I said.

"Is it?" Rahul popped a handful of bar peanuts. "Is it mean if they make money for it? If it's gonna happen to them anyway, isn't it better that they get to be in charge?" He sounded like Maggie.

"I don't know," I said. "Aren't the producers in charge?"

Rahul shrugged. He squinted at me. "You did say you *want* to get back into TV, didn't you?"

I thought I did. Didn't I? I certainly wanted out of the apartment. A job where I could interact with people face-to-face, build something meaningful. I missed the buzz of being on set, the mental *Tetris* of production. I didn't want to live vicariously through Gabe's career; I needed something of my own.

Rahul offered to drive me home that night, but I declined and took a cab. "If I hear of anything good, you're my first call," he told me when we parted. "In the meantime, go easy on yourself."

Several months after the release of Gabe's album, Lauren called me in the middle of the workday. Work, for me, meant writing sitcom treatments destined for some drawer, and Mr. Pichietti's semilucrative newsletter copy, as well as a growing list of blog and marketing updates for the dog-walking service I'd rejoined as a part-time walker, a position I'd then parlayed into an editorial role. I was no longer some bright young thing who could chase golden retrievers willy-nilly. I was a professional, interviewing dog psychics and giving pet owners tips on how to balance animal chakras. Instead of building out a select version of an actual person that my audience would think was the real deal, I was building out select versions of dog breeds. This was clearly less exciting than Reality TV, but much firmer ethical ground.

Although we had a small second bedroom that I could use as an office, when Gabe was out of the house, I usually worked from the kitchen table. When I saw Lauren's name on my caller ID, I saved a scintillating few sentences I had been writing about canine color theory and closed my laptop.

"Hello?"

"Cassidy. Lauren." The greeting sounded like boot camp roll call, prompting me to straighten my shoulders. "I have an offer for you."

I hadn't heard from Lauren since that day in her backyard. I'd assumed her offer to hook me up with a job when things with her show were ready to go was just a gesture. Yet here she was, on the phone, as if ages had not passed, although her baby was a toddler already.

"Hi." Why bother with pleasantries if Lauren was diving right into things? "What's the offer?"

"I have the show. The one I was just telling you about." Apparently, time worked differently in television. It was true, though, that at one point she had been telling me. "We got the go-ahead, but there's a problem."

I stood, phone pressed between my cheek and shoulder, and started tidying the kitchen counter, wiping coffee mug rings and toaster crumbs. I said, "Tell me more."

Lauren's show was called *Real-Life Lovers*, and it would focus on the trials and tribulations of a group of normal couples as they all lived together in a mansion following their marriages. The totally normal everyday problems of normal everyday newlyweds, full of backstabbing and cheating and pool parties and booze. She was trying to get Jason Dean to host.

Lauren's problem was Dan.

"He's power hungry," Lauren told me. "Success has gone to his head. We went in as co-executive producers, and he wants to bump me down. He's pretending the whole thing was his idea."

"When really the whole thing was your idea?" I asked.

"Of course it was." Lauren sniffed. "Anyway, I need allies. I want to bring you in to produce with me. To know you'll have my back."

Here was the job offer I had been waiting for, coming in at a level I wouldn't get anywhere else. Theoretically it was, like Maggie's offer to Gabe, a no-brainer.

"Umm," I said. I might be desperate for TV work, but having escaped Lauren and Dan's web once, I was not especially eager to get myself tangled back up in it.

"I want to ruin him," said Lauren.

"Oh?"

"I want to grind him down. I want to make production companies talk about Dan Iaconetti the way they once talked about Cassidy Baum." Lauren had fire in her voice. "Sorry, but it's true. I want to end him."

I squeezed my eyes shut, opened them to the home that I had built with Gabe Leighton. Mr. Coffee dripped out in its pot. A basket of laundry sat on the couch, waiting to be folded. A poster from Gabe's recent tour leaned against a side table, framed and ready to be hung on a wall. My daily life, small and uncomplicated. Drama-free. Mostly happy.

There were cracks, though, in that happiness. My work wasn't fulfilling. Gabe was hard on himself about his career. I worried he would wake up and realize that I was the roadblock, the big reason for his failures. If I went back to Lauren, I'd have more influence in Hollywood. I'd have a job in TV. I could find a way to help him.

"Let me think about it," I said. "When do you need an answer?"

"Yesterday," said Lauren.

"Let me think about it," I said again. "And I'll get back to you."

I planned to bring Lauren's proposal to Gabe that night and talk it over, but he came home in a mood. All he wanted was to run a bath and put on some music. He told me nothing in particular had happened. I thought that was likely the problem.

At this point Gabe had amassed a loyal following. His shows sold well; he got invited on the road. He made enough money and had enough clout that he could keep on making music, which he'd always claimed was the only goal. But I'd hear him on the phone with his family saying, "I'm trying, Ma. Hopefully soon." He wanted to make his parents proud, to make their many sacrifices for his career worth it, and all that it would take was one big hit. An invitation to perform on *SNL* or a song played on a popular TV show. The kind of opportunity that—I still insisted on believing—working with Maggie might have given him.

Gabe had been working since childhood, reinvented himself twice. Surely soon he would reap the benefits of what he had sown. I wasn't sure that he knew what those were—he didn't want the media circus, he didn't want bottle service at the club. He wanted the people he loved to be proud of him. I was so proud of him. I told him every day. He just had to learn how to be proud of himself.

I didn't bother pointing out how many musicians never even got this far—how many people would love to be in his shoes with a major-label record and a fan base and steady writing work that paid. It wouldn't have helped.

That evening I sneaked into the bathroom, sat at the edge of the tub. He had moody Led Zeppelin playing on stereo.

"You know a big career's not about the actual quality of the music. It's the whole marketing machine. They're like the kingmakers. It's about who gets the golden ticket."

"True." Gabe nodded, but I could tell I wasn't reaching him. I trailed a finger in the water, then reached up to touch his arm.

"It's totally random, which person gets the opportunity. Or gets born with rich parents."

"Cassidy, I had the opportunity." Gabe looked solemn. "I had *The Tiger Crew*. And I wasted it."

I held his head, and it made wet marks on my T-shirt. "You didn't waste anything."

"Cassidy." Gabe nuzzled me. "Come here." He pulled back, and then leaned forward to kiss me, a wave of bathwater rushing my bare legs in my ratty pajama shorts. "I love you," Gabe said. "Marry me."

I froze. My heart ran laps in my chest, panicking. "What?"

"Marry me," Gabe said again, sitting up so that more water splashed over the lip of the tub. "Let's get married."

"Umm." For the second time that day, I was responding to a major proposition with unintelligible bleating. Unlike earlier, I knew my answer immediately. "I mean yes," I said. *Yes, of course. Yes, forever. Yes. Yes.* "Yes, I want to. It's just . . . it's a weird way to ask me."

"I figured you wouldn't want the traditional kneeling and flowers," said Gabe, lacing our fingers. His chest hair glistened with water. "It's not out of the blue. I've been planning this. I have the ring already. I could have found a better time, but right now I wanted to ask you. So I asked you." His mouth was serious, but his eyes sparkled.

"Yes," I said. "The answer is yes." Gabe pulled me closer until I was almost on top of him, my shirt hem sopping.

"Get in," he said. "The water's great."

And so, I did.

October 2007

Inside the honeymoon suite, the wedding night stage has already been set. It looks like television—pillar candles on all surfaces and a variety of newly purchased throw pillows scattered artfully throughout the suite of rooms. A Saran-Wrapped fruit basket, and bath towels folded into swans. A Post-it note on the bed reads *rose petals 9pm—freezer*, as if the PA can't be trusted to remember. I peek into the minibar fridge and confirm the paper bag there, full of flowers. Thinking about me and Gabe making our way up to this candlelit paradise built by some twenty-two-year-old production assistant makes me lightheaded, and I have to sit down.

Maggie looks around the room, unfazed by the production. I wonder if this is where she came with Jason on her wedding night, if the staff gave them a similar setup. She runs a hand along the wooden bed frame, a massive four-poster, more Gilded Age than modern California. There's a fireplace up here, although I can't imagine why. With the curtains open, we can see the Pacific, clouds rumbling, white foam against piers. Maggie shuts them, on instinct. There's always someone looking in. She blinks at me. "Why are you guys doing this?"

"Doing what?" I say. "Getting married?" The makeup and hair were supposed to make me feel powerful, brave. Instead, I feel like a clown while Maggie stands in front of me with her bare face and her perfect poreless skin and her naturally long eyelashes.

"This whole thing," Maggie says, gesturing. She means the country club, the cameras. "It isn't you."

"You don't know me," I say.

Maggie tilts her head, acknowledging the truth of this. Then she shakes it, recommitting herself to whatever she had been about to say. "But I know Gabe."

I freeze. Maggie walks over to me. She's wearing pedicure flip-flops, the flimsy kind you're supposed to toss once your toenails have dried, and they slap against the hardwood floor in a limp, depressing way.

She doesn't know Gabe. Not anymore. I'm the one he shares a bed with, the one who brews his coffee, the one who waits up for him when his shows run late. And yet, somehow, I'm the one on the defensive.

Some of this must register in my face. Maggie gives me a patronizing smile.

"Here." She uncaps a water bottle stolen from the minibar. *Stolen* is the wrong word—the world is a gift to Maggie, has always been a gift—even while they drag her down, the magazines keep sending her free samples.

Despite myself, I drink the water that she offers me. I don't want to take anything from her, to owe her anything at all.

I hate her so fiercely. For having Gabe's heart, making me question him. For making me feel like I have never been enough.

20.

2006

The ring was a thin white gold band with one cushion cut diamond. Anemic compared to Maggie's monstrosity but exactly what I wanted. When I went to show it to Celia and Jen, I realized why.

"Oh my god, that took forever." Celia speared a roll of sushi with a chopstick, and it promptly fell apart. "He asked us ages ago what kind of ring we thought you wanted."

"He's very thoughtful," Jen said. By this time, she was sporting her own engagement ring, her fiancé's mother's old emerald.

"He's the best," I said. "I feel like I should get him a present."

"I thought you were the present," said Celia. "But if not, give him a blow job." Blunt, as always, but it wasn't a bad idea.

"He's been so down about his album," I explained. I'd filled them in on the near misses of Gabe's past, the pressure he put on himself to hit the big time, what he thought he owed his family. "It just sucks that there's nothing I can do to help him out."

"Clearly you're helping," Jen said, flagging down the server for the low-sodium soy sauce. "You guys just got engaged."

"But I can't help with this," I said. "I feel so guilty. If it weren't for me, Maggie McKee would have made him a star."

"You don't know that," said Jen. But I did. I was obviously the reason Gabe had severed ties with Maggie. If I hadn't come back into his life, he wouldn't have declined her offer. He wouldn't know about her plan for Sally Ann, how she'd used him as collateral. Maybe by now, Maggie would be the one with a new diamond.

"Well then, you'll make him a star," said Celia with a confidence I wished I'd ever once in my life come close to possessing.

"Very funny. I can't even make myself night sky adjacent." I paused, thinking of Lauren. "Unless . . ."

I should have known I couldn't start a thought in front of Jen and Celia without following it through. I might have avoided this whole mess if I'd just understood when to shut my mouth.

"Unless what?" Jen said immediately.

"What what what?" Celia bounced on the seat of the booth.

"This is going to sound crazy. Certifiable," I said.

"Spill." Jen took a long sip of ice water.

"What if Gabe and I got married . . . on TV?"

In this before-the-altar promo, Lauren sits down with us to explain the situation to our viewers.

"I'm Lauren Lin," she says, "former producer for *Honeymoon Stage*, and the mind behind the new show *Real-Life Lovers*, coming spring 2008. You've seen how the celebrities do it—now let's shine a light on people like you as they experience the highs and lows of their first year of marriage."

Cut to montage of Jason and Maggie's more blissful moments on the show, which doesn't make much sense to me, but okay, whatever.

"We're so lucky to be here with our first couple, letting us in on the beginning of their happily ever after. Our very own Cassidy Baum, the behind-the-scenes muscle on the original series, and her Prince Charming, Gabriel Leighton."

The way Lauren phrases this makes it sound like I was more than just her peon. It also makes it sound like we've agreed to do the full television series, which we certainly have not. Wedding weekend, sit-down interviews, another sit-down in six months for a where-are-they-now. Where will we be? Savvy viewers might guess—we will ideally be basking in Gabe's musical success. He'll have his first of a lifetime of Grammys. I'll have gone from freelance copywriter with credit card debt to full-time TV producer, thanks to the reference Lauren promised in exchange for letting her executive produce my wedding.

"Hi." Gabe gives an awkward wave that translates as adorably humble. I'm an actual deer in headlights, making a terrified tight smile.

Cut to montage of me and Gabe throughout our relationship, which has thankfully never been filmed. Instead of Jason leaning in to wipe whipped cream on Maggie's nose, we get a still photo of me and Gabe at Jen's engagement party, his arms in a bear hug over my shoulders, both of us wearing unironic goofy smiles. A still photo of me and Gabe at the Getty Center, squinting into the sun with the iconic city views spread out behind us. And then the pièce de résistance, the live footage of Gabe. Of course they have him short and grinning while he tap dances on *The Tiger Crew*. This is paired with a photo of me in my youth soccer uniform, one shin guard hanging and sock bunched around my ankle. Next, he's onstage at some bar, sitting on a stool with his acoustic guitar. I'm in college, hair and earrings both overlarge, my arms flung around two friends who've had their faces blurred. Finally, he's an opener at a larger seated venue, looking like uncut sex, sounding gravelly and gorgeous. Clearly, they should have ordered this differently, because here I am as the finale, caught accidentally on camera on the *Honeymoon Stage* set, reflected in a window behind Jason and Maggie. I'm wearing jeans and a T-shirt, and my hair is held back with two strategically placed pens. A trademarked Real-Life Lover if you ever did see one.

I am the nerd who will take off her glasses and get a full face of makeup painted on and then transform into a hottie. Gabe is the already-hottie who will see me, now that I'm hot, and fall in love, never mind that we are already engaged and have been dating coming up on three years now. He's also the hottie who will sell his song as the theme song to our special. If all goes well, this will also be the theme for *Real-Life Lovers*, hitting as big as Maggie's theme song did for *Honeymoon Stage*. Gabe will have eyeballs on him, more than just those of the few devoted fans and tabloid hounds who think he broke up Maggie's marriage. Lauren will have full credit for *Real-Life Lovers*, and a built-in premiere audience. I'll have a TV job—either with her or from her reference—and the knowledge that I've pushed Gabe back onto the track I'm pretty sure I led him off.

"Cassidy and Gabe will tie the knot at Palisades Pines, where it all started for our original duo. Tune in November 4 as the *Honeymoon Stage* continues."

October 2007

Which brings me to this moment. My wedding day. My Real-Life existential crisis, wondering what it is that Gabe hasn't told me.

In the honeymoon suite, awash in capital-*P* Production, I finish my bottle of water. Maggie moves one of the embroidered throw pillows to join me on the divan. It smells like it's just out of the box. Chemically, wrong.

I brace myself to ask her all my burning questions about Gabe. Was their relationship always more complex than he let on? Was I wrong in assuming that Maggie had lied to me?

But before I can speak, she beats me to it.

"When we were ten, you were so mean to me," Maggie says. "You really messed me up there, for a while."

Excuse me? I blink, and then I tell her, "We were nine."

"No," Maggie shakes her head. "Ten. Don't you remember?"

"Yeah, I do, and it was third grade," I say. "That was a big year for me, unfortunately. A colossal, shitty year, and I was nine."

"That's not when I'm talking about." Maggie fiddles with the pillow's embroidery, which is already unraveling. "I don't mean when we were in third grade. I mean when you were back at your old school."

I don't know when, after that year, I would have seen her. We didn't go back to Youngstown once my mom finished her first year of nursing school. I have absolutely no clue what Maggie is talking about. Surely if she wanted to rehash some childhood angst, she could have picked a better time.

"I wanted you to like me so badly," Maggie continues. "I worked so hard to make you want to be my friend."

"What are you talking about?" This is not what I imagined when I told myself I had to talk to Maggie.

I suddenly want off this divan, out of this room. This is wrong. This is the wrong story.

"You didn't need anyone," she continues. "You were cool. You had no interest in making friends, joining clubs, doing dance class. I was so jealous. I wanted to be you. I mean, I basically didn't exist to even myself unless someone was watching me perform, and there you were, just . . . independent."

"Well, yeah." I swallow. "My dad had just walked out on me."

"And your mom was awesome." Maggie ignores me. "And, of course, you had Dede. And that cute brother. Anyway, I felt anointed that you chose me."

"Chose you?"

"To be friends." Maggie laughs a bit, remembering something about me that I'm not privy to. It's a bitter laugh, a lonely one. I have no recollection of being Maggie's friend. Not then, not now. Or do I?

This must be why I couldn't bring myself to ruin her. Some buried memory, squeezed tight into the box of my early-childhood trauma, seeping out to cement loyalty to Maggie. Had we really been friends?

"Anyway, I was devastated when you stopped writing me."

"Writing you?" I am a parrot; I can't help myself.

"Cassidy. We were pen pals for, like, a year." Maggie blinks at me, then blows away her bangs.

"You were mean about my T-shirt," I say, as if hauling out my one full recollection will somehow bring me up to speed.

"Your T-shirt?" Maggie shakes her head. "I don't think so."

"Yeah, I had that GIRLS CAN BE ANYTHING T-shirt, and you laughed at it and said it was dumb."

"Cassidy." Maggie raises her toothpick eyebrows. "That was my shirt."

"No," I say.

"I wore that shirt to my Tiger Crew audition. My mom has a picture of me in it that's been framed by her fireplace for years."

Could it have been Maggie's shirt? That day has always been so clear to me. Her parted pigtails, snub nose looking down at me from on top of the monkey bars. Am I wearing the shirt, or is she?

Why can't the world ever stay put within the boundaries I make for it?

"But I remember it," I say, my voice plaintive even to my own ears. "I was going to be a firefighter, and you told me that I couldn't."

"I don't know." Maggie shrugs. "Maybe I said that. You'd be a terrible firefighter. You're not very good under stress. But that was definitely my T-shirt."

I stand, running my fingers along the closed velvet curtain. Not looking at her. "We weren't friends." It's almost a whisper.

"Well, not after you sent me the world's nastiest friend-breakup letter." Maggie's tone remains unchanged, slightly sardonic, above it all. "'Never write to me again.'"

I suddenly remember the purple pen, the state-flower stationery my mother bought me as a present. I remember being angry in Philly, lonely in our new apartment, with only after-school TV as a companion.

Just because I don't remember it all happening the way Maggie remembers it happening doesn't mean that she's wrong.

If I close my eyes, I can picture myself—*Full House* or *A Different World* playing in the background, an open bag of off-brand cheese puffs, that tea-colored stain on the ceiling that looked like the Blob—writing the letter that would break my heart before Maggie McKee could do it for me.

Even if it wasn't exactly like this, it was like this. Even if this new memory isn't the truth, it is still true.

Because that's me. I'm realizing now that's who I play in this whole story: the quick trigger, the fool. Pushing the pieces so far and so quickly that they fall off the board.

I told myself I needed to know if Gabe had been with Maggie, but I've known it all along. The question was never how far he'd gone, but how far Maggie would go to protect herself. I dig my thumbnail into the pad of my finger, and I turn to her. I want her to admit what she's done to me. I might have been a bitchy ten-year-old, but she's no angel. She's a killer. A liar. "He didn't actually do it, did he?"

"What?" Maggie looks confused. "Oh," she says then, nodding slowly. "You mean Jason. I don't know for sure, but he probably did."

I blink at her. "I mean *Gabe*. Gabe wasn't dating you behind my back. He didn't help you kill Sally Ann."

Maggie laughs. It's not the evil cackle of the villain exposed, nor is it the disdain of your average high school mean girl. I feel unmoored, unsure of the series of events that have led to me standing here with Maggie McKee in a honeymoon suite on the morning of my televised wedding. "Oh my god," she says. "Oh my god, Cassidy. I totally forgot about that!"

I played out this conversation all night long, then again in the morning. In no imagined scenario was this Maggie's response. Is she messing with me for forgetting our childhood drama? "How could you possibly forget about a murder?"

"You actually think Gabe—the Gabe you're walking down the aisle with in, like, three hours—planned out a murder? And you're still going to marry him?" Maggie looks sorry for me, although she was the one who practically told me Gabe had been her accomplice.

Maggie sighs, settling back into seriousness. "Okay, I'm sorry. I shouldn't have lashed out. I shouldn't have let you keep thinking that."

"So you admit you made it up. Gabe didn't help you kill Sally Ann?" It seems ridiculous, but I have to yank the full root of the weed.

"You're officially telling me Gabe is innocent and this whole time it was just you."

"Cassidy." One corner of Maggie's unpainted mouth curls up in what plays out as disbelief, tinged with a touch of patronizing pity. "I didn't kill Sally Ann. Nobody killed her. Sally Ann's death was an accident."

An accident? Nothing is an accident in television. Everything is outlined and then acted, filmed and then edited. I've already cut the Sally Ann episode, and in it, Maggie is clearly at fault.

I shake my head, but she continues. "You were there, weren't you? You think I planned to kill my friend and then suddenly changed my mind and tried to save her? I'm going to be reliving those last minutes for the rest of my life, wondering what might have happened if I got the epinephrine in her thirty seconds sooner."

"But she was sleeping with your husband."

"That didn't mean she should *die*."

My fingers clench around the PA's sticky note. "But you said you were the one—"

"Well, yeah, I ran with what *you* said. I was pissed that Gabe told you about Jason's accident, worried you were going to blab it everywhere and that would be the end of my marriage. And I was mad at you in general, for barely remembering me. Sending me that letter. Not to mention I was pissed you were with Gabe, and trying to mess with things between you." Maggie bites her lip.

"But it *was* the end of—"

"My marriage, I know. It all imploded anyway. Turns out you can't protect your partner from failure. Even when you set it all up perfectly, your husband might not hit his beats. Real life isn't TV. It served me right."

I close my eyes before she's finished speaking. Maggie didn't kill Sally Ann. The knowledge settles like slow-falling snow.

I've been angry with Maggie, and that anger has absolved me. I could forgive my part in things if there was someone else to take the blame for Sally Ann's death. So much of what I thought was about Maggie has always only ever been about my own self-preservation.

It strikes me suddenly that Maggie McKee knows herself—the good and the bad. She owns it. Can I say the same?

I've spent years of my life agonizing over total bullshit. Maggie has played me, and played me well. But more than that, my training to look for the story, to find the fissures and intuit how someone edited the episode, has made me blind to the enduring fact that life is not Reality TV. Not everything is a conspiracy. Not everything is about building clout. Sometimes accidents happen. Sometimes people say *I love you* and they mean it.

There was a mailbox down the block from our old Philly apartment. I can remember spraying my mother's perfume samples on stationery, peeling off neon smiley face stickers. The loopy LYLAS—*love you like a sister.*

Sometimes the person you think that you are, the character you've made yourself out to be in your own head, is no realer than the mask of a TV celebrity.

Though I'm reeling, there's enough producer in me yet to realize I've got Maggie in the mood to spill her secrets. I want the whole story, or at least Maggie's version.

"What happened with Jason? Not all those years ago with the car—I know that stuff already. With Sally Ann."

"You saw it happen," Maggie says. "He needed—he still does need—everybody to adore him. That was why Sally Ann made so much sense for him. He turned to her while I was focused on work, and she thought he was her ticket to success."

"What do you mean?"

"You know she had a kid living back with her parents?" This is the first time the rumor has been directly confirmed. I nod, and Maggie continues. "Apparently Jason said he would adopt it, take it on financially and raise it as his own. That's why she first got involved with him. He was going to be her savior."

"Seriously?"

"Well, obviously *he* wasn't serious, but she thought he was, and that was enough for her. He did that kind of thing all the time. Made big promises after drinking too much and forgot all about them the next day. If she'd have asked me, I'd have told her right away not to believe him."

I blink. "If she'd have asked you if she should sleep with your husband?"

"It's an expression, Cassidy." Maggie rolls her eyes. "He told her all sorts of bullshit. That he had a job lined up to be a baseball commentator, that he'd take her to Italy. He ran his mouth off every time he had too many beers. But Sally Ann never knew as much as Jason thought she knew. She didn't know about his benders or that night with the smashed-up car. He was so paranoid, but the only thing she'd ever have spilled was that he said he'd be a father to her daughter."

I realize that I've been unconsciously crumpling the PA's note about the flowers. Somewhere in the house, a grandfather clock sounds two long clangs. We don't have forever. Soon Maggie will have to return to the staging area. I'll have to walk down the aisle.

"How do you know all this?" I ask Maggie.

"Sally Ann told me."

"She what?"

"She was my friend." Maggie presses her lips together. I have trouble believing this is not one of Maggie's delusions. Maggie McKee, thoroughly unlucky in love and in friendship. Or maybe not. Maybe friendship can survive illicit affairs, salacious love triangles, if both people give in to and believe it.

"Why didn't you leave Jason right away," I ask, "if you knew all along he was cheating?"

"I still loved him," Maggie says simply. "I was willing to forgive him. I wanted to try. I tried as hard as I could. But he was jealous I was working, bitter that I got to do my thing and he couldn't do his.

And ultimately, I resented everything I had to do to keep him safe from himself."

"An impressively coherent analysis."

"Yeah, well it's not like we didn't try therapy." Maggie smiles sadly. "Life doesn't go the way you think it's going to go. You can't make somebody else's choices for them. Kumbaya and all that."

"You guys did therapy, or some woo-woo retreat?"

"Both." Maggie removes her claw clip so her hair falls down around her face, and then sweeps it back up again. "We did all of it, and wow, what a waste. The second we split, it was all-out media warfare. He sent the tabloids years-old pictures of me hanging out with Gabe, told his sob story all over the morning shows."

"Wait," I said. "Those pictures of you and Gabe weren't real?"

"No, they were real. Just most of them were from ages ago—before the show even started, before he moved to LA. I'm surprised you, of all people, didn't realize."

I think back to the magazines, the shots of Gabe and Maggie in parking lots, at restaurants. I'd thought tabloids were vague about details for legal reasons. It never occurred to me that *this* was where I might have been conned.

"You should correct the record," I tell Maggie. "Or at least confront Jason about it."

"How?" Maggie laughs. "I don't even have his number anymore. Though it's a good thing he's contractually obligated to stay away from me today. There's only so much biting my tongue I can manage. If the world knew half of what I know about Jason Dean, he wouldn't be the hero, that's for sure."

"Well, why don't they? Why not tell them?" If I were Maggie, I'd be livid. Jason has been sandbagging Maggie for years, first as her husband, then as her poor, puppy dog ex. No one could begrudge her the instinct to pull him down with her, not after they realized what he'd done.

"Wait. So what you're saying," I say slowly. "What you're saying right now is that Gabe Leighton had nothing to do with any of it? Not Sally Ann and Jason. Not you and him . . . ?"

"Gabe's a good guy," says Maggie. "He's not a cheater. He's a catch, and he's disgustingly into you. You better treat him right, Baum."

That's the TV pitch. That's our special. Gabe is a good guy, and he'll tear up when he sees me in my dress; viewers will swoon. We'll say *I do*, and he'll kiss me and sweep me back down the aisle, dancing in the corniest way possible to Bryan Adams's "Summer of '69." He'll pull me out of view of the cameras, to a bathroom or somewhere equally unromantic, and we'll leave Lauren scrambling for footage, panning from Maggie's tight smile to Jason's fake slaphappiness while the crew waits for us to reemerge. After putting in our time at the reception, we'll have the rest of our lives to live off camera.

It's so easy. I just have to find Gabe and talk to him. Gabe makes things so easy, if only I let him.

I feel immensely sad for Maggie, to not have a Gabe. To have only a Jason, and *still* to be covering for him. Jason, who actually deserves the villain edit I've been giving Gabe all morning in my mind. I imagine Maggie giving it to him on-screen. Maybe she'd come off as vindictive, but she could just as easily play it as a secret she can no longer keep. Speak now, or forever hold her peace. She could redeem herself. The audience could see the real Maggie McKee, how she is loyal and clever. Sometimes ruthless, but only because she's had to be, only because that's what we made her.

Another edit is forming in my mind. I have three hours. I have friends on the crew. If Maggie's up for it, I have one last bit of producing to do.

The guys' staging room is normally a boardroom, and their untied ties and fresh-cut cigars do nothing to disabuse it of its usual role. In here, the vibe is men's grooming aisle at the local drugstore, strong smells of aftershave and shoe polish residue, an open pack of Q-tips, an open flask. The groomsmen have demolished their own tray of pastries, and crumbs sit scattered across the thickly varnished table. They're surprised to see me, including the cameraman, who uses his zoom the second I walk through the door.

"Is Gabe in here?" I ask.

"Aren't you not supposed to see him until the wedding?" My brother, Andrew, comes over, confused. The camera follows us, while Andrew tries to figure out how he should compose his face for public display, settling on a smile that bares his teeth like he's mugging for the dentist.

"It's important," I say. "But don't worry. Nothing's wrong." I raise my voice to be sure one of the boom mics catches me. A little snafu with some paperwork, maybe, or a lost earring back.

Gabe comes over in his dress shirt, sleeves rolled to his elbows, his suit vest unbuttoned. Impossibly suave, perfect as always. I'd marry him right here on the boardroom table. He takes my arm.

"What's up?" he says, head close to mine. He smells like toothpaste. I shake my head almost imperceptibly. Gabe's microphone is already on, pinned to the collar of his shirt. He follows my gaze, then raises his eyebrows. I nod.

"Have to go to the bathroom," Gabe explains to the producer.

"That's not a—" the producer is saying, but it doesn't matter because Gabe has ripped off the lavalier mic and dropped it on a chair by the door. We're out of the room and walking at a brisk pace down the hallway.

"What's going on?" he asks again, and again I shake my head and guide him away from the production. I've learned my lesson about Coyote Cams, rogue PAs hiding in dark corners. I want to be alone with Gabe, actually alone. I pull him out the door, across the muddy lawn, down the garden path to the lone gazebo that looks like it belongs in a WASPy New England town rather than a stone's throw from Palisades

Park. It's the sort of cultivated specificity that makes this place so generic—a simulacrum of what "wedding at the country club" should be. Rain flecks Gabe's white shirt. I can feel my makeup melting, my updo coming uncoiled. I absolutely don't care.

"Cass, what's happening?" Gabe and I take shelter on the gazebo bench, still open to the elements when wind blows them our way, and well in sight of the main house, but the best I can do. The rain will hold the cameras back, at least for the time being. If Lauren wants a long-distance shot of us cuddled up out here, so be it; we'll give her *Sound of Music* chic.

"Obviously this breaks tradition," I say. A single plump raindrop trickles down the side of my face, likely leaving streaks of foundation. Gabe puts out a finger to catch it.

"And you know how tradition is so important to us." His face doesn't break with the wisecrack. He wipes his hand on the side of his pants, which are already stained.

"Fuck tradition," I say.

"Indeed," says Gabe. "So what's up?"

My heart is racing, but Gabe seems totally calm. Maybe it's his years of stage experience, the fact he's used to so many people watching him. Maybe this even disposition is an act. He doesn't know I overheard him outside the restaurant last night, but he must be thinking about whatever it is he's tried to hide.

He's waiting, mouth pursed, a hand on my knee now, expectant. His searching eyes look especially blue against the dreary gray sky. It's not an act. It's Real Gabe, vulnerable. This is Gabe, and I know him, and he loves me. I love him, and I would kill someone before I'd see him hurt. I understand now how Maggie could spend so long covering for Jason, how strong the urge can be to orchestrate a version of life that lets everyone win. I want Gabe to have everything he wants, to overflow with success, to know I'm proud of him. I want him to be proud of himself, whether it's because he has the balls to say no to Maggie or has his own Top 40 song.

But I can't keep Gabe from failure—however he defines it—any more than he can protect me from whatever it is that he's been hiding. I can't make his choices; I can only support them and try to trust that what he tells me is the truth. I can be honest, with him and with myself.

"I heard you," I say finally. "Last night at the restaurant when you thought you were outside alone, I heard you say something about what you aren't telling me."

Gabe looks confused for a moment. Then he swallows as recognition hits.

"You mean when I was talking to Janine," he says. *His sister?*

Janine is the last person I'd have guessed Gabe was talking to out in the garden. Janine lives in Sacramento with two children and a rabbit that makes their whole house smell like a pet store. Janine is a sales rep for a company that sells middle school textbooks. She shops with coupons. She listens to Michael Bolton. She's as slice-of-normal-life as a woman can be, and I am thrilled that she is going to be my sister-in-law.

"Did I say something dumb?" Gabe asks. "I can't remember."

I blink. He can't even remember? I'm seeing betrayal around every corner, thinking some editor is splicing my life into something I need to prepare for when, in fact, it's just a life. People make choices. They don't share everything. That doesn't mean a hidden cabal pulls the strings.

"You said, and I quote, 'I should have come clean with her.'" This, at least, is a tangible secret. Something I can ask Gabe directly. "Come clean about what?" I swallow, preparing myself for his answer.

"Oof." Gabe presses a fist against his forehead. "You heard that stuff? And you've just been sitting on it since last night?" He sighs and reaches for my hand, rubbing his thumb below my knuckles.

"I tried to call you. I've been trying not to totally flip out."

"Okay," says Gabe. "I'm sorry. I didn't mean for you to hear any of that."

"Obviously." He's still massaging my hand. "What were you guys talking about?"

Gabe lets go of me. Inhales, exhales. His forelock would flutter like a horse's with the force of his breath if it weren't so slick with rain. "I feel like an ungrateful idiot admitting it," he says. He doesn't meet my eyes. "But this whole thing . . ." He gestures to the lawn, the audaciously tasteful main house, the black bug's eye we can see pointed at us from a downstairs window. "It isn't . . . how I envisioned things."

"You mean you're not happy with the way they've set it up?" I ask. "You wish we were filming things differently?"

"I wish we weren't filming at all," Gabe mumbles. I can tell he's embarrassed, and sure enough, there on the bench, his left hand has taken up its habitual tapping. He squeezes his eyes shut, then looks up at me.

"Gabe . . ." I'm not sure what to say.

"I know this is big for us, and I know how hard you worked to make it happen. I'm not complaining. I appreciate you so much for this, for what you're sacrificing. It just feels . . . not quite right. You know?" He stands up, pacing now as everything pours out of him. "I mean, obviously we've committed. There's your career, and everybody here is counting on us. Our families are all out here. All our friends. And there's the money. We'd owe the network a ridiculous amount of money if we called things off now. So, there's no use complaining about it. It's a nonquestion, really. I was just a few beers deep, and Janine asked me how I was doing with all the cameras and the interviews . . ." He tugs at his hair, which is wet with rain and styling product.

He doesn't want the TV wedding. He doesn't want the publicity. I truly have been an idiot. Luckily, I've also been a genius. Apparently, I really am built for Reality TV. The most innocuous, most dangerous entertainment. I've already set up the board for what we're going to do next.

"Gabe," I say. "It's not too late to bail." His facetiousness from yesterday as we rehearsed our ceremony, repeated this time in sincerity.

"You don't—" I watch his face drop with relief, then entertain a sudden terror. "You mean you don't actually want—"

"Vegas by sundown? The courthouse by four?"

"You do still want to get married."

"I still want to get married."

"She wants to get married," Gabe repeats, beaming wide now. Any second he'll get up and break into a tap dance out there in the storm.

"Just not married on TV."

"Just not married on TV—goddammit, Cassidy, what did you do?" He's still elated, laughter bubbling in his voice despite the words. "This whole time I thought you were set on doing the show, getting the job, getting the theme song—all that stuff."

"Only because I thought that it was what you needed," I say. "The big career, the hit song. I wanted it for you."

"I wanted it for *you*." Gabe's still laughing. "Money's just money. We'll figure it out."

"Oh, we'll more than figure it out," I say. "I think I can get us off the hook entirely. Give them something even better than what Lauren's got planned."

"The mastermind at work." Gabe grins. "And if we finally give Reality TV the middle finger, you can work on your pilot—Jake's still bugging me about it. He wants it. June gets to live!" Gabe's happier than I've seen him since I initially said yes to his proposal. He squeezes me into a massive hug, still laughing.

"And you really don't care about your career opportunities? You don't care that your song won't be on the show, that you'll be giving up publicity? That what you and the guys have right now might be the peak of . . . your success?"

This is what scares me most—that he'll give up the wedding special the way he gave up Maggie's collaboration, and then he'll regret it and resent me. He'll look back and think he made a horrible mistake. He'll watch Maggie's star float past him, all the other Tiger Crew alumni hitting their version of big, and wonder why he'd chosen me over the glory.

"I don't care about that," he says. "I don't want it."

"And you're sure?" I have to know. I have to be certain that this won't come back to bite us.

"I'm one thousand percent sure. One million gajillion. I just want you."

And now I have to believe that Gabe means it. I have to trust him.

But I guess isn't that what it means to love someone? Isn't that what we're all doing, every second of every day? Deciding to believe that what we show to each other is real.

"Okay," I say. "Let's blow this popsicle stand."

Even without a bride and groom, Maggie and I can get Lauren her must-see TV. Palisades Pines can recoup their publicity. Gabe and I can handle disappointed parents and avoid the worst of the legal and professional fallout of our last-minute decision to elope. Our honeymoon stage doesn't have to end yet.

I send Gabe to our rooms and head around to the back of the venue. The kitchen entrance is camera-free, though with the caterers and staff preparing for the reception, eyes are everywhere. I promise the PA at the door that I am fine, just off to dry my dress and reapply my makeup. Of course, this is a lie. Once I'm out of view, I take the stairs toward Video Village. I'm banking on the fact that Lauren will be rushing around set and will have delegated last-minute tech logistics. I don't want her to see me. If I tell her what I have in mind, she'll try to talk me out of it. Too much liability, too much uncertainty. She'll tell me to stick to the original plan.

But Vinnie, who has also been called out of semiretirement to reunite the *Honeymoon Stage* team, looks pleased to see me.

"Not exactly camera ready." He gestures to my still-dripping dress after giving me a hug hello.

"Just checking in on things," I say. Vinnie nods sagely, as if this is a normal thing for me to be doing in the hours before I walk down the aisle.

The call sheet is taped to a bare wall. The first names are me and Gabe, along with our getting-ready locations and our phone numbers. Then Maggie. Celia, as my maid of honor. And then I see it: Jason Dean.

Vinnie is looking at something on the soundboard, so he doesn't see me punch the number into my cell phone.

He wishes me luck, but the phone's already ringing.

"Jason?" I say. "Listen, it's Cassidy."

In this episode, Maggie McKee returns to the bridal staging area to get her bridesmaid makeup done. She's chewing Bubblicious, popping it between her teeth. She sits down in the tall chair, submitting to the sponges and palettes.

"Does anybody have eyes on the bride?" A walkie-talkie in the background, clear distress on the set or else we wouldn't see the crew cross behind Maggie, breaking the camera line and ruining the shot.

"Negative." The voices are rising, louder and more frantic. "We also seem to have lost Gabe."

Maggie sits stone faced. Blows a bubble while the makeup artist readies her next brush.

"Well, where the fuck are they?" Lauren barrels through the room, the lower half of her body visible behind the black folding chair where Maggie sits daintily crossing her legs. "Go find them. Look harder."

"Confirming a car pulling out of the driveway." Lauren's walkie-talkie crackles. "Their suitcases are gone. We think it's both of them, Cassidy and Gabe."

"Oh my god!" This is Celia's voice, pitch rising in excitement. "Oh my god, are they leaving? No way."

"They wouldn't." Jen's voice, skeptical. "Or would they?"

"They've left a note." The walkie-talkie voice breaks through. "It says, 'Don't worry, drama coming. Until next time . . .'"

"What does that mean?" Lauren asks.

Ideally, in this moment, Maggie McKee would stand up and howl. She'd rip off her false eyelashes. She'd knock the little rows of blush and bronzer and shimmer powder and whatever else from their carefully laid-out tray; she'd yank the dresses from their hangers and stomp on the strawberries and use her bare hands to rip into the cream cheese Danishes she's not supposed to eat. There goes the dispenser of room temperature lemon water. The pot of green tea. Dishes thrown against the wall, lipstick smeared on the window. The cameras would topple, power cords snapping and zoom lenses broken clean off. With superhuman strength, she'd lift the tripod and send it flying through the window, panes shattering. Birds would fly smack into the remaining glass, more birds than ever before, arrayed in some mystical, witchy pattern. Maybe the whole place could go up in flames.

Of course, none of this happens. Who do you think Maggie McKee is? She has her reputation to uphold. It's someone else's she'll burn down.

"Wait, now Jason is coming in." The radio crackles. "Read, Jason Dean is coming into the prep room. Says he's been invited to film a sit-down with Maggie? Reminisce about their marriage in the place where it all started. Was that you?"

"Of course it wasn't me," Lauren snaps into her headset. "Get Maggie out—her contract says we keep Jason away from her."

Someone is rapping on the door. Impatient, oblivious.

A PA tries to usher Maggie away before Jason makes his entrance, but she shakes her head. She isn't going anywhere. She sits in her chair while chaos unfolds all around her. She lets her bubble expand until it pops, sticky white-pink sugar plastering her newly glossed mouth. She uses a beautifully manicured finger to peel the gum from her lips.

Then she smiles.

Acknowledgments

Forever thank you to Stephanie Delman, who is secretly an Aries, as well as Elizabeth Pratt and the phenomenal team at Trellis. Knowing I have not just my own excellent agent but also the rest of the crew's editorial and business savvy to depend on makes me the luckiest writer out there. I appreciate you all more than you could possibly know. Special shout-out also to Khalid McCalla for reading early on and getting the jokes, and David Kelley for fact-checking. Also, obviously, thank you to Izzy.

To Laura Van der Veer, who has guided me and Cassidy toward the best versions of ourselves—thank you for seeing the potential in this book and providing such a strong editorial vision. I absolutely couldn't have taken this step without you, and I am so proud of the work we've done together.

Thanks to the team at Little A: Karah Nichols, Tree Abraham, Rachael Clark, Logan Matthews, Tristen Bakker, Annie Sloniker, and Rachel McClure.

Thank you to Jessica Simpson, Britney Spears, Mandy Moore, and the other early 2000s pop stars whose interviews and memoirs inspired Maggie. The roles you played in popular culture deserve to be unpacked with nuance and respect, and I hope you see this book as one admittedly soapy attempt. (If you are somehow actually reading this: I've made it. I love you, and I know you'd never ever pull a Maggie McKee.)

Thank you to Donald Ian Bull, Pete Tartaglia, and Troy Devolld for your written insight into the behind-the-scenes of Reality TV.

To those who worked on and have spoken about your experiences, particularly with the early MTV celebreality shows—your oral histories, podcast interviews, Reddit threads, and YouTube tutorials have all been invaluable.

Writing a book is a lot less lonely with devoted coworkers like Sara Sligar, Katie Gutierrez, and Amy Jo Burns. Thank you three for riding the roller coaster with me, from the first glimmer of this book to what you have in your hands. May everyone have such wise, loyal, wonderful friends. This one is for you and because of you.

Thank you always to Rick, for the best partnership. Who knew that your extensive knowledge of Tommy John surgery would be so vital in my work? And last, thanks to Margot and Elliott. Nothing makes me prouder than being your mom.

About the Author

Photo © 2025 Collin Quinn Rice

Margaux Eliot is excited to give early aughts pop culture its due. Writing as Julia Fine, she is also the author of speculative novels *The Upstairs House*, *What Should Be Wild*, and *Maddalena and the Dark*. She lives in Chicago with her family.